PENGUIN BOOKS

RAISE THE RED LANTERN

Su Tong was born in Suzhou in 1963 and graduated from Beijing Normal University with a degree in Chinese literature. He is the author of the novel *Rice*, also available from Penguin. The title novella in *Raise the Red Lantern* was made into an internationally acclaimed film that was nominated for an Academy Award. Su Tong now lives in Nanjing.

Michael S. Duke is professor of modern Chinese literature at the University of British Columbia in Vancouver. His books include *Worlds of Modern Chinese Fiction* and *The Iron House: A Memoir of the Chinese Democracy Movement and the Tiananmen Massacre*.

RAISE THE RED LANTERN
Three Novellas

SU TONG

TRANSLATED BY MICHAEL S. DUKE

PENGUIN BOOKS

PENGUIN BOOKS
Published by the Penguin Group
Penguin Books USA Inc., 375 Hudson Street,
New York, New York 10014, U.S.A.
Penguin Books Ltd, 27 Wrights Lane, London W8 5TZ, England
Penguin Books Australia Ltd, Ringwood, Victoria, Australia
Penguin Books Canada Ltd, 10 Alcorn Avenue,
Toronto, Ontario, Canada M4V 3B2
Penguin Books (N.Z.) Ltd, 182–190 Wairau Road, Auckland 10, New Zealand

Penguin Books Ltd, Registered Offices: Harmondsworth, Middlesex, England

First published in the United States of America
by William Morrow and Company, Inc. 1993
Reprinted by arrangement with William Morrow & Company, Inc.
Published in Penguin Books 1996

5   7   9   10   8   6   4

Originally published in Chinese by Yuan-Liou Publishing Co. © 1990

THE LIBRARY OF CONGRESS HAS CATALOGUED
THE WILLIAM MORROW EDITION AS FOLLOWS:
Su, T'ung, 1963–
Raise the red lantern: three novellas/
Su Tong; translated by Michael S. Duke.
p.   cm.
Contents: Raise the red lantern—Nineteen Thirty-four escapes—
Opium family.
ISBN 0-688-12217-5 (hc.)
ISBN 0 14 02.6030 7 (pbk.)
1. Su, T'ung, 1963– —Translations into English.   I. Su, T'ung, 1963– .
Ta hung ti teng lung kao kao kua. English. 1993.   II. Su, T'ung, 1963 .   1934 nien
ti t'ao wang. English. 1993.   III. Su, T'ung, 1963– .   Ying su chih chia.
English. 1993.   IV. Title.
PL2904.T86A24   1993
895.1´352—dc20   93–14896

Printed in the United States of America
Set in Walbaum
Designed by Dorothy Schmiderer Baker

TRANSLATOR'S NOTE

My primary goal in this translation has been to preserve all of the images and figurative language, all of the linguistic artistry, contained in the original. I have added some explanatory phrases to avoid footnotes, but I have never paraphrased.

A salient characteristic of Su Tong's style is the use of very long multiple sentences marked with commas only. This is not a standard characteristic of modern written Chinese in general, although Chinese punctuation is different from that of English. I have tried to preserve Su Tong's style in translation by a liberal use of semicolons. I have also tried to preserve all of the deliberate strangeness of Su Tong's narrative. These include such things as intentionally unclear temporal sequences, occasional orphic intrusions by a first-person narrator, and unusual diction. The first two elements are an integral part of Su's attempt to create an imaginative history. For the third, the reader should be aware that wherever the English seems strange it is because the Chinese was also purposefully so.

I have translated the women's names, while only transliterating the men's names. The women's names are often thematically important, but the men's names are usually not. For example, in "Raise the Red Lantern," except for the ironic name Joy, besides helping to delineate their characters, the women's names carry thematically important references to nature and the cycles of nature. Chinese names are given in the pinyin romanization system used in the People's Republic.

Some explanation of the general title of this trilogy seems in order. The novella "Raise the Red Lantern" was originally titled "Wives and Concubines," but in the Hong Kong and the second Taiwan editions of the trilogy it became, as here, the title story for the book *Raise the Red Lantern* or *Da hong denglong gaogao gua.* The title was also used for Zhang Yimou's 1992 Oscar-nominated film. The red lanterns were the invention of Zhang or his script writer and were just one of many changes introduced in the transformation of this complex narrative. The English reader can now savor the full flavor of Su Tong's original conception.

CONTENTS

RAISE THE
RED LANTERN

RAISE THE
RED LANTERN

When Fourth Mistress, Lotus, was carried into the Chen family garden, she was nineteen; she was carried into the garden through the back gate on the west side at dusk, by four rustic sedan bearers. The servants were washing some old yarn by the side of the well when they saw the sedan chair slip quietly in through the moon gate and a young college girl, dressed in a white blouse and black skirt, step down from it. The servants thought it was the eldest daughter returning from her studies in Beiping; when they rushed forward to welcome her, they realized their mistake: It was a female student, her face covered with dust and looking unbearably exhausted. That year Lotus's hair was cut short, level with her ears, and tied up with a sky-blue silk scarf. Her face was quite round; she wore no makeup; and she looked a little pale. Lotus climbed out of the sedan chair, stood on the grass, and looked blankly all around; a rattan suitcase was placed horizontally beneath her black skirt. In the autumn sunlight, Lotus's slender figure appeared tenuous and delicate; she looked as dull and lifeless as a paper doll. She raised her hand and wiped the sweat off her face; the servants noticed that she wiped the sweat not with a handkerchief but with her sleeve; this minor detail made a deep impression on them.

Lotus walked over to the edge of the well and spoke to Swallow, who was washing yarn. "Let me wash my face. I haven't washed my face in three days."

Swallow drew a pail of water for her and watched her plunge her face into the water; Lotus's arched-over body shook uncontrollably like a waist drum played by some unseen hands. Swallow asked, "Do you want some soap?" Lotus did not speak, and Swallow asked again, "The water's too cold, isn't it?" Lotus still did not speak. Swallow made a face in the direction of the other maidservants standing around the well, covered her mouth, and laughed. The maidservants thought this newly arrived guest was one of the Chen family's poor relations. They could tell the status of nearly all the Chen family's guests. Just then Lotus suddenly turned her head back toward them. Her expression was much more wide-awake after washing her face; her eyebrows were very fine and very black, and they gradually knit together. Lotus gave Swallow a sidelong glance and said, "Don't just stand there laughing like a fool; wipe the water off my face!"

Swallow kept on laughing. "Who do you think you are, acting so fierce?"

Lotus pushed Swallow away violently, picked up her rattan suitcase, and walked away from the well; she walked a few paces, turned to face them, and said, "Who am I? You'll all find out, sooner or later."

The following day everyone in the Chen household learned that Old Master Chen Zuoqian had taken Lotus as his Fourth Mistress. Lotus would live in the south wing off the back garden, right beside Third Mistress Coral's room. Chen Zuoqian gave Swallow, who had been living in the servants' quarters, to Fourth Mistress as her private bondmaid.

When Swallow went to see Lotus, she was afraid; she lowered her head as she called out, "Fourth Mistress." Lotus had already forgotten Swallow's rudeness, or perhaps she just did not remember who Swallow was. Lotus changed into a pink silk cheongsam and put on a pair of embroidered slippers; the color had returned overnight to her face, and she looked much more amiable. She pulled Swallow over in front of her, examined her carefully for a minute, and said to Chen Zuoqian, "At least she doesn't look too dreadful." Then she spoke to Swallow. "Squat down; let me look at your hair."

Swallow squatted down and felt Lotus's hands picking through her hair, carefully searching for something; then she heard Lotus say, "You don't have lice, do you? I'm terribly afraid of lice."

Swallow bit her lip and did not speak; she felt Lotus's hands, like the ice-cold blade of a knife, cutting into her hair, hurting her slightly. Lotus said, "What's in your hair? Smells terrible; take some perfumed soap and hurry over and wash your hair."

Swallow stood up; she stood there motionless, with her hands hanging down. Chen Zuoqian glared at her. "Didn't you hear what Fourth Mistress said?"

Swallow said, "I just washed my hair yesterday."

Chen Zuoqian yelled at her, "Don't argue about it; if she tells you to go wash, you go wash. Careful I don't beat you."

Swallow poured out a pan of water and washed her hair under the crab apple trees. She felt she'd been horribly wronged; hatred and anger pressed on her heart like an iron weight. The afternoon sun shone down on the two crab apple trees; a clothesline was strung between them, and Fourth Mistress's white blouse and black skirt were waving in the breeze. Swallow looked all around; the back garden was completely quiet, and no one was there. She walked over to the clothesline, spat right on Lotus's white blouse, then turned and spat again on her black skirt.

Chen Zuoqian was exactly fifty years old that year. When Chen Zuoqian took Lotus as his concubine at the age of fifty, the affair was carried out in a half-secretive manner. Right up until the day before Lotus came through the gate, the First Mistress, his first wife, Joy, still didn't know a thing about it. When Chen Zuoqian took Lotus to meet her, Joy was in the Buddhist chapel counting out her rosary and chanting the sutras. Chen Zuoqian said, "This is my First Mistress."

Just as Lotus was about to step forward and greet her, the string broke on Joy's Buddhist rosary, sending the beads rolling all over the floor; Joy pushed away her amboyna chair and knelt down on the floor to pick up the beads, mumbling all the while, "It's a sin, it's a sin." Lotus went over to help her pick up the beads and was pushed lightly away by Joy, who just repeated, "It's a sin, it's a sin," and never once raised her head to look at Lotus. As Lotus watched Joy's fat body crouching down on the damp floor to pick up the Buddhist beads, she covered her mouth and laughed silently. She looked at Chen Zuoqian, who said, "All right, we're going."

Lotus stepped over the raised threshold of the Buddhist chapel, took Chen Zuoqian's arm, and asked, "Is she really a Buddhist? Why's she chanting the sutras at home?"

Chen Zuoqian said, "A Buddhist! Ha! She's just too lazy, hasn't anything to do, so she plays at being a Buddhist, that's all."

Lotus was enthusiastically welcomed into the rooms of Second Mistress, Cloud. Cloud had her maid bring out watermelon, sunflower, and pumpkin seeds, and several kinds of candied fruits for Lotus. The first thing Cloud said after they sat down concerned the melon seeds. "There aren't any good melon seeds around here; I have someone buy all the melon seeds I eat in Suzhou."

Lotus spent some time cracking melon seeds at Cloud's, cracking and eating until she was quite bored; she didn't like snacks like that, but she could hardly show it. Lotus stole a sidelong glance at Chen Zuoqian, hinting she wanted to leave, but he seemed to be intent on staying a little longer at Cloud's and acted as though he didn't see Lotus's expression. Lotus inferred from this that Chen Zuoqian was particularly fond of Cloud; then her gaze couldn't help lingering on Cloud's face and figure. Cloud's facial features had a kind of warmth and delicate grace, even though she couldn't hide the tiny wrinkles and the somewhat noticeable slackness of her skin; in her movements she had even more the appearance of a cultured, young woman from a good family. Lotus thought a woman like Cloud could easily attract men, and women would not dislike her either. She very quickly addressed Cloud as Elder Sister.

Of the Chen household's three earlier wives, Coral's room was closest to Lotus's, but Coral was the last one Lotus met. Lotus had heard of Coral's extraordinary physical beauty, and she wanted very much to meet her; but Chen Zuoqian refused to take her there. He said, "It's so close, you go on over yourself."

Lotus said, "I've gone over there; the maid said she was sick, blocked the door, and wouldn't let me in."

Chen Zuoqian snorted through his nose. "Huh, whenever she's unhappy she says she's sick." He went on, "She wants to be more important than I am."

"Are you going to let her?"

Chen Zuoqian waved his hand and said, "Don't be ridiculous! Women can never be more important than men."

Lotus walked by the north wing and noticed that Coral's windows were hung with curtains of pink lace drawnwork; a sweet scent of flowers emanated from inside. Lotus stopped in front of the windows for a moment; suddenly unable to control her desire to peek in, she held her breath and gently pulled open the curtains. The shock she received then nearly frightened her to death: Coral was also watching her from behind the curtain. Their eyes met straight on for only a matter of seconds, then Lotus ran away in dismay.

When night came, Chen Zuoqian came to Lotus's room to spend the night. Lotus helped him take his clothes off and handed him some nightclothes, but Chen Zuoqian said, "I don't wear anything. I like to sleep naked."

Lotus just looked the other way and said, "Suit yourself,

but it's better to wear something, otherwise you'll catch a chill."

Chen Zuoqian started to laugh. "You're not afraid I'll catch a chill, you're afraid of seeing me naked."

Lotus said, "I am not afraid." But as she turned away, her cheeks were already crimson. This was the first time she had a clear look at Chen Zuoqian's body. Chen Zuoqian had a body like a red-crowned Manchurian crane, bony and skinny, and his penis was as taught as a well-drawn bow. Lotus felt a little out of breath, and she asked, "Why're you so skinny?"

Chen Zuoqian climbed onto the bed, crawled under the quilt, and answered, "They've worn me out."

When Lotus rolled over on her side to put out the lamp, Chen Zuoqian held her back. "Don't put it out. I want to see you. Put out the lamp and you can't see anything."

Lotus touched his cheek and said, "Suit yourself. I don't know anything about it anyway, so I'll follow you."

Lotus seemed to fall from a high place into a dark valley where pain and dizziness were accompanied by a feeling of lightness. The strangest thing was that Coral's face continually intruded into her consciousness; that most beautiful face was also hidden in the darkness. Lotus said, "She's really strange."

"Who?"

"Third Mistress. She was behind the curtain watching me."

Chen Zuoqian's hand moved from Lotus's breast to her mouth. "Don't talk. Don't talk now."

Just at that moment someone knocked lightly on the bedroom door. The two of them were startled; Chen Zuoqian looked at Lotus and shook his head, then put out the lamp. In a little while the knocking started again. Chen Zuoqian jumped up and shouted angrily, "Who's that knocking?"

A timid girlish voice came from outside the door. "Third Mistress is sick; she's calling for the Master."

Chen Zuoqian said, "She's lying, lying again. Go back and tell her I've already gone to bed."

The girl outside the door said, "Third Mistress is very sick; she says you have to come. She says she's about to die."

Chen Zuoqian sat on the bed and thought for a minute, mumbling to himself, "What's she up to this time?" Lotus watched his uneasiness, then pushed him. "You better go. It would be terrible if she really died."

Chen Zuoqian did not return that night. Lotus listened carefully to hear what transpired in the north wing, but nothing at all seemed to be happening. Only a robin in the pomegranate tree called out a few times, leaving a clear and mournful sound lingering in the distance. Lotus drifted between disappointment and sorrow, and could not sleep. Very early the next morning, when she got up to put on her makeup, she saw that her face had undergone some sort of profound transformation; the rims of her eyes were dark black. Lotus already knew what Coral was up to, but the next day, when she saw Chen Zuoqian emerge from her north wing room, she went up to him anyway and inquired about Coral's illness. "Did you call a doctor for Third Mistress?"

Chen Zuoqian shook his head in embarrassment. He looked completely exhausted and was too enervated to speak; he merely took hold of Lotus's hand and gave it a long, soft squeeze.

The reason Lotus was married to Chen Zuoqian after already spending one year in college was very simple: Her father's tea factory went broke, and he could not afford her tuition. The third day after Lotus had quit school and returned home, she heard members of her family shouting wildly in the kitchen; she ran in and saw her father propped against the side of the sink; the sink was full of fresh bubbling blood. Her father had slashed his wrists open and gone effortlessly down to the Yellow Springs of the Dead. Lotus remembered the feeling of despair she had at that time. When she held up her father's icy cold corpse, she felt even colder all over than his body did.

When this misfortune occurred, she couldn't even cry. No one else used that sink for many days after, but Lotus still washed her hair in it. She did not feel the nameless fear and trembling that most young women would. She was very practical. As soon as her father died, she had to be responsible for herself. Lotus stood beside that sink washing and combing her hair out over and over again; it was her way of calmly planning for her future. Thus when her stepmother came right to the point and asked her to choose between going to work and getting married, she answered dryly, "I'll get married, of course."

Her stepmother asked further, "You want to marry into an ordinary family or a rich family?"

Lotus answered, "A rich family, naturally; do you have to ask?"

Her stepmother said, "It's not the same. If you go to a rich family, you'll be small."

"What does it mean: 'be small'?" Lotus asked.

Her stepmother thought for a moment and said, "It means to be a concubine; your status will be a little lower."

Lotus laughed coldly. "What is status? Is status something

people like me can be concerned about? No matter what, I've been given to you to sell; if you have any consideration for my father's affections, then sell me to a good master."

The first time Chen Zuoqian went to call on her, Lotus barred the door and refused to see him; "Meet me at the Restaurant Occidental," she said from inside the door. Chen Zuoqian thought to himself that since she was a college student she would naturally be different from most vulgar young women. He reserved a table for two at the Restaurant Occidental and waited for Lotus to show up. It was raining that day, and as Chen Zuoqian waited and looked through the window at the street made misty by the rain, his emotions were unusually warm and sweet; feelings he had never experienced before in his first three marriages. Lotus came walking slowly along, carrying a delicate little flower-patterned silk umbrella. Chen Zuoqian smiled happily. Lotus was just as pure and pretty as he had imagined, and just as young. Chen Zuoqian remembered that Lotus sat down opposite him and pulled a big handful of little candles out of her purse. She whispered to Chen Zuoqian, "Order me a cake, all right?"

Chen Zuoqian had the waiter bring them a cake; then he watched Lotus stick the candles one by one into the cake until she had put in a total of nineteen candles; she put the remaining candles back into her bag. Chen Zuoqian said, "What's all this; is this your birthday?"

Lotus only smiled. She lit the candles and watched them burn with nineteen bright little flames. In the light of the candles Lotus's expression grew exquisitely beautiful; she said, "Look how lovely the flames are."

"They are lovely," Chen Zuoqian agreed.

After she finished talking, Lotus took a long deep breath

and blew out all of the candles at once. Chen Zuoqian heard her say, "Let's celebrate my birthday early; nineteen years have gone by."

Chen Zuoqian felt that there was something to think about in what Lotus said. Much later he still often recalled that scene of Lotus blowing out those candles; it made him feel that Lotus possessed a kind of elusive yet beguiling power. As a man with an abundance of sexual experience, Chen Zuoqian was even more obsessed with Lotus's skill and passion in bed. He seemed to envision many kinds of ecstasy the first time he met her, and later on they all came to be confirmed in practice. It is difficult to judge whether Lotus was like that by nature or was reshaping her own disposition in order to please him, but Chen Zuoqian was very satisfied; the way he doted on Lotus was noticed by everyone high and low in the Chen household.

In the corner of the back garden wall there was a wisteria vine; from summer to fall the wisteria flowers weighed heavily on the branches. From her window, day after day, Lotus saw only those fluffy clumps of purple flowers delicately swaying in the autumn breeze. She noticed there was a well beneath the wisteria vine and there was also a stone table and stone benches. It was a very quiet, comfortable place, but no one was ever there, and the path leading up to it was overgrown with weeds. Butterflies flew by and cicadas sang on the wisteria leaves; Lotus remembered that last year at that time she was sitting under the wisteria at school studying—it all seemed like suddenly waking from a dream. Lotus walked slowly over to the vine, carefully pulling up her skirt so as not to let the weeds and the insects rub against it; slowly she pulled back a few branches of wisteria, and saw that the stone tables and benches were covered with a thick layer of dust. The walls of the well were covered with moss. Lotus bent over and looked down into the well; the water was a bluish-black color, and there were some ancient dry leaves floating on the surface. Lotus saw the broken reflection of her face in the water and heard the sound of her breathing being sucked down into the well and amplified, weak yet oppressively deep and low. A gust of wind rushed up; Lotus's skirt billowed out like a bird taking flight, and at that instant she felt a coldness as hard as stone rubbing slowly up against her body. She started back, walking very quickly now, and when she reached the hallway of the south-side wing, she heaved a long sigh. Just as she looked back at the wisteria vine, two or three clumps of flowers suddenly dropped off; they tumbled down quite abruptly, and Lotus felt it was awfully strange.

Cloud was sitting in her room waiting for Lotus. She immediately noticed that Lotus looked very troubled; she stood up and patted her on the shoulder: "What's wrong with you?"

Lotus answered, "What's wrong with me? I was walking around outside."

Cloud said, "Your complexion looks awful."

Lotus laughed and said that she had just got her period. Cloud laughed too and said, "I wondered why in the world you came over to see me again." She opened a parcel and took out a roll of silk: "Real Suzhou silk; it's for you to make a dress with."

Lotus pushed back Cloud's hands. "No, no, no—how could I accept gifts from you? I should be giving you gifts."

"Shush," said Cloud. "What do you mean by that? When I saw how very likable you are, I immediately thought about this piece of silk; if it were that woman next door, I wouldn't give it to her if she tried to pay me; that's just the way I am."

Lotus took the silk, put it in her lap, and ran her hands over it. Then she said, "Third Mistress's a little strange. But she's very good looking."

"Good looking? If you scraped Coral's face, a pound of makeup would come off."

Lotus laughed again and changed the subject. "I was just walking around by the wisteria vine. I really like that place."

"You went to the Well of Death?" Cloud shrieked. "Don't go there, that place is bad luck."

"Why do you call it the Well of Death?" Lotus asked in alarm.

Cloud answered, "No wonder you looked so bad when you came in here. Three people have died in that well."

Lotus stood up, leaned against the window frame, and looked over at the wisteria vine. "What sort of people died in the well?"

Cloud said, "They were all family members from earlier generations, all women."

Lotus still wanted to ask more, but Cloud could not tell any more; she only knew that much. She said everybody high and low in the Chen family avoids the subject; everybody's lips are sealed tight as a jar. Lotus stood there puzzled for a moment, then said, "Things like that, I guess it's just as well not to know about them anyway."

The young masters and young ladies of the Chen family all lived in the central compound. Lotus once saw the two sisters Yirong and Yiyun digging for worms in the muddy ditch; from their radiantly cheerful faces, so natural and innocent, Lotus could tell at a glance that they were Cloud's children. She stood to one side, quietly observing them. The two sisters noticed Lotus, but went on stuffing the worms into a little bamboo container as if no one were there. Lotus asked, "What are you digging worms for?"

Yirong answered, "To go fishing," but Yiyun stared rudely at Lotus and said, "None of your business."

Lotus felt unpleasantly awkward; walking on a few steps, she heard the two girls whisper, "She's a concubine, too, just like mom." Lotus was suddenly stunned; she looked back and stared angrily at them. Yirong giggled out loud, but Yiyun stared back at her with unyielding contempt and whispered something else. Lotus thought, "It's terrible for them to be so young and already saying such nasty things. Heaven knows what sort of education Cloud is giving those girls."

The next time Lotus ran into Cloud, she could not help telling her what Yirong had said. Cloud said, "That child just can't hold her tongue. When I get home, I'll pinch her lips good." After Cloud apologized, she went on. "Actually those two girls of mine are still pretty easy to handle. You've never seen the Little Master from next door. He's just like a dog, biting and spitting on anyone he runs into. Hasn't he ever bitten you?"

Lotus shook her head. She recalled the little boy next door, Feilan, standing on the porch eating a piece of bread and peering over at her, his oily hair combed back and shiny, with a pair of little leather shoes on his feet. Sometimes Lotus could catch a glimpse of something like Chen Zuoqian's expression on Feilan's face. Probably she was more disposed to accept Feilan because she hoped to give Chen Zuoqian another son.

"A boy is better than a girl," thought Lotus. "Who cares if he bites people or not."

After a long time only Joy's son and daughter remained unseen by Lotus. From this it was easy to discern their high status in the Chen household. Lotus regularly heard discussions concerning the son Feipu and the daughter Yihui. Feipu was always out collecting rents and carrying on real estate transactions, while Yihui was studying at a women's college in Beiping. Lotus casually asked her maid Swallow about Feipu, and she said, "Our Eldest Young Master is very resourceful."

Lotus asked, "How is he resourceful?"

Swallow answered, "Well, anyway, he is resourceful; the whole Chen household depends on him now."

Lotus further asked Swallow, "What's the Eldest Young Mistress like?"

Swallow replied, "Our Eldest Young Mistress is pretty and demure; she's going to marry a rich man someday."

Lotus laughed to herself. The tone of Swallow's praise for those two implied a criticism of her, and Lotus found it quite irritating. Taking out her anger on the Persian cat curled up at her feet, she kicked it away and cursed, "Stop licking your ass over here, you little tramp!"

Lotus became increasingly annoyed with Swallow; mostly because, whenever she had nothing to do, she would run over to Coral's room. But also because every time Lotus gave her a chemise and underpants to be washed, her face would take on a sullen expression. Sometimes Lotus would scold her. "Who are you trying to impress frowning like that? If you don't like being with me, you can go back to the servants' quarters, or even go next door, it's all right."

Swallow would defend herself. "I'm not. I wouldn't dare frown; I was born with this face."

Lotus would grab a hair brush and throw it at her, and Swallow would shut up. Lotus guessed that Swallow slandered her quite a bit throughout the rest of the house. But she could not treat her too harshly because she had once seen Chen Zuoqian come into her room and take the opportunity to fondle Swallow's breasts. Although it was a fleeting and altogether natural thing, Lotus had to control herself somewhat; if it were not for her master's fondling, Swallow would not dare act so insolently toward her. Lotus reflected, "Even a common servant girl also understands how to rely on a little fondling to build up her courage. A woman is just that sort of creature."

On the eighth day of the ninth lunar month, one day before the Double Ninth Festival, the Eldest Young Master, Feipu, returned home.

Lotus was in the central courtyard admiring the chrysanthemums when she saw Joy and the servants crowding around a group of men; one in the middle, dressed in white, was very young and, viewed from behind and far away, looked quite tall. Lotus guessed that he must be Feipu. She watched as the servants carried a whole cartload of luggage to the back courtyard, running round and round like colorful carrousel animals. Gradually everyone went inside, but Lotus was still embarrassed to go in. She picked some chrysanthemums and walked slowly toward the back garden; on the way she spied Cloud and Coral coming her way with their children in tow. Cloud grabbed her arm and said, "Eldest Young Master has come home, aren't you going to go meet him?"

Lotus answered, "*I* go to meet *him*? He should come to meet me, shouldn't he?"

Cloud said, "That's right, he should be the one to come to meet you first."

Standing to one side, Coral impatiently pushed Feilan on the back of the head. "Hurry up, hurry up."

It was at the dinner table that Lotus actually met Feipu. That evening Chen Zuoqian had the cooks prepare a banquet to welcome Feipu back home. The table was covered with sumptuous and exquisitely prepared delicacies; Lotus looked at the food and could not help thinking that the welcoming banquet on the day she first entered the Chen household was not nearly as grand as this one. She felt a little hurt, but her attention very quickly shifted to Feipu himself. Feipu was sitting next to Joy; Joy said something to him, and then he leaned over toward Lotus, smiled, and nodded his head. Lotus smiled and nodded back at him. Her first impression of Feipu was that he was unexpectedly young and handsome; her second impression was that he was very thoughtful. Lotus always liked to evaluate people's character on meeting them.

The next day was the Double Ninth Festival. The gardeners brought all of the chrysanthemum pots in the garden together in one place and arranged them in various colors to form the characters for "good fortune, prosperity, longevity, and happiness." Lotus got up very early and walked all around, by herself, looking at the chrysanthemums. There was a chilly morning breeze, and she was wearing only a sleeveless woolen sweater; she just folded her arms across her chest, held her shoulders, and walked around, looking at the flowers. A long way off she saw Feipu coming out of the central courtyard and walking her way. Lotus was hesitating, trying to decide whether or not to greet him first, when Feipu called out, "Good morning, Lotus."

Lotus was rather startled at his direct use of her given name; she nodded and said, "According to our generational difference, you shouldn't call me by my name."

Feipu stood on the other side of the flower beds, smiled as he buttoned up his shirt collar, and said, "I should call you Fourth Mistress, but you must be a few years younger than I am. How old are you?"

Lotus turned to look at the flowers in an obvious display of displeasure. Feipu said, "You like chrysanthemums too? I thought I'd be the first one to enjoy the scene this early in the morning; didn't think you'd be up even earlier."

Lotus replied, "I've liked chrysanthemums ever since I was little; I certainly didn't just start liking them today."

Feipu asked, "What's your favorite kind?"

Lotus answered, "I like them all, but I just hate crab claws."

"Why's that?" asked Feipu.

"Crab claws bloom too impudently."

Feipu laughed again and said, "That's interesting; I just happen to like crab claws best."

Lotus glanced over at Feipu a moment. "I figured you would."

Feipu asked further, "Why is that?"

Lotus took a few steps forward and said, "Flowers are not flowers and people are not people; flowers are people and people are flowers; don't you understand such a simple principle?" Lotus suddenly raised her head and caught sight of a strange gleam drifting by briefly, like a leaf, on the surface of Feipu's moist eyes; she saw it and she understood it.

Feipu stood with his hands on his hips on the other side of the chrysanthemums and said suddenly, "I'll take all the crab claws away, then."

Lotus said nothing. She watched Feipu take all the crab claws away and put some black chrysanthemums in their place. After a short interval, Lotus spoke again. "The flowers are all fine, but the characters are no good; they're too vulgar."

Feipu wiped the mud off his hands and winked at Lotus. "Nothing can be done about that. Good fortune, prosperity, longevity, and happiness is what the Old Master told them to arrange. It's the same every year, a custom passed down from our ancestors."

Whenever Lotus thought of the time she spent enjoying the chrysanthemums on the Double Ninth Festival, she felt happy inside. It seemed as though from that day on she and Feipu had some sort of secret understanding between them. Sometimes, when she thought of how Feipu moved the crab claws away, she would laugh out loud. Only Lotus herself knew that she really didn't particularly dislike crab claw chrysanthemums.

"Who do you like best?" Lotus regularly asked Chen Zuoqian while he shared her pillow, "Of the four of us, who do you like best?"

Chen Zuoqian said, "Why you, of course."

"What about Joy?"

"She turned into an old hen long ago."

"And Cloud?"

"Cloud's still tolerable, but she's a little flabby."

"What about Coral, then?" Lotus could never control her

curiosity about Coral. "Where does Coral come from?"

Chen Zuoqian said, "I don't know where she comes from; she doesn't even know herself."

Lotus said, "You mean Coral is an orphan?"

Chen Zuoqian answered, "She was an actress. She sang the female lead in a traveling Peking opera troupe. I was an amateur performer myself. Sometimes I'd go backstage and invite her out for dinner; one thing led to another, and she just came along with me."

Lotus stroked Chen Zuoqian's face and said, "All the women want to go along with you."

Chen Zuoqian said, "You're half right there; all women want to go along with a rich man."

Lotus began to laugh. "You're only half right, too; you should've said, 'when a rich man gets rich he wants women, wants them so much he can never get enough.'"

Lotus had never heard Coral sing Peking opera, but that morning she was awakened from her dreams by a few crisp, clear, long, drawn-out words sung in opera style. She poked Chen Zuoqian lying next to her and asked if that was Coral singing. Chen Zuoqian responded groggily, "That bitch, when she's happy, she sings, and when she's unhappy, she cries." Lotus opened the window and saw that a layer of snow-white autumn frost had fallen during the night. A woman dressed all in black was singing and dancing under the wisteria vine. It *was* Coral after all.

Lotus draped a cloak over her shoulders and stood in the doorway watching Coral from afar. Coral was already totally absorbed in her song; Lotus felt that she sang in a delicately plaintive manner, and her own emotions were aroused. After a long time Coral stopped abruptly. She seemed to have noticed that Lotus's eyes were brimming with tears. Coral threw her long flowing sleeves back over her shoulders and walked toward the compound. Some crystalline specks of brightness danced on her face and clothing in the morning light; her round, tightly coiled chignon was moist with dew, and thus her entire appearance was damp and ladened with sorrow, like a blade of grass in the wind.

"Are you crying? You're living a very happy life, aren't you? Why are you crying?" Coral asked drily as she stood facing Lotus.

Lotus took out a handkerchief and wiped the corners of her eyes, then said, "I don't know what happened. What was that you were singing?"

"It's called *The Hanged Woman*," Coral answered. "Did you like it?"

"I don't know a thing about Peking opera; it's just that you sang so movingly that I felt sad, too, just listening." As Lotus spoke, she noticed Coral's face take on an amiable expression for the first time.

Coral lowered her head, looked at her opera costume, and said, "It's only acting; it's not worth feeling sad about. If you act very well, you can fool other people, but if you act badly, you only fool yourself."

In Lotus's room Chen Zuoqian started to cough, and Lotus looked at Coral with obvious embarrassment. Coral said, "Aren't you going to help him get dressed?"

Lotus shook her head and said, "He can dress himself. He's not a child."

Coral looked resentful. She laughed and said, "Why does he always want me to help him on with his shoes and clothes? Looks like people are divided into the worthy and the unworthy."

Just then Chen Zuoqian shouted from inside the room,

"Coral! Come in and sing something for me!"

Coral immediately raised her willow-thin eyebrows; she laughed coldly, ran to the window, and yelled inside, "This old lady doesn't care to!"

Lotus had experienced Coral's temper. When she talked about it in an indirect manner with Chen Zuoqian, he said, "It's all my fault for spoiling her years ago. When she feels defiant, she curses my ancestors for eight generations. That little bitch of a whore, sooner or later I'll really have to punish her."

Lotus said, "You shouldn't be too cruel to her; she's really quite pitiful; she has no other family, and she's afraid you don't care about her, so she's developed a bad temper."

After that Lotus and Coral had some lukewarm contact. Coral was crazy about mahjong. She regularly called a group together at her place to play; they played from right after dinner until very late into the night. From the other side of the wall, Lotus could hear the clicking sound of the tiles noisily shuffled all night, and it kept her awake. She complained to Chen Zuoqian, and he said, "I guess you'll just have to stand it; when she plays mahjong, she's a little more normal. Anyway, when she loses all of her money, I won't give her any more. Let her play. Let her play until she drops."

On one occasion Coral sent her maid over to invite Lotus to play mahjong, but Lotus sent her back with these words: "Invite me to play mahjong? It's a wonder you could even think of it." After her maid returned, Coral herself came over. She said, "There are only three of us—we need one more; do me a favor."

Lotus replied, "But I don't know how; won't I just lose my money?"

Coral took Lotus by the arm. "Let's go. If you lose, we won't take your money." Better yet, if you win, you can keep it, and if you lose, I'll pay for you."

Lotus said, "You don't have to go that far; it's just that I don't like to play."

She saw Coral's smile turn into a frown as she was speaking. Coral said, "Huh, what have you got here that's so great? You act like you're sitting on a big pot of gold and won't move an inch; it's only a dried-up old man, that's all."

Lotus was so irritated that her temper began to flare up; just as she'd decided to tell her off and the curses were already boiling up onto her tongue, she swallowed them back again, bit her lip, and thought for a few seconds. Then she said, "All right then, I'll go with you."

The other two players were already seated at the table waiting; one was the steward, Chen Zuowen, but she didn't know the other one. Coral introduced him as a doctor. The man wore gold-rimmed glasses; his complexion was quite swarthy, but his lips were moist, crimson, and softly expressive in a feminine manner. Lotus had seen him going in and out of Coral's room before and, for some unknown reason, could not believe he was a doctor.

Lotus was quite absentminded as she sat at the mahjong table; she really could not play very well and listened, bewildered, as they shouted out, "My game," and "Just the tile I needed." All she did was shell out money, and gradually she began to feel bad about it. Finally she said, "My head aches, I need a little rest."

Coral said, "Once you sit down, you have to play eight rounds—that's the rule. You're probably feeling bad about your losses." Chen Zuowen chimed in, "It doesn't matter, to lose a little money wards off many calamities." Coral retorted, "Just consider that tonight you're doing Cloud a favor; she's been terribly bored lately. Loan the old man to her for one night and let her give you back the money you lose."

The two men at the table began to laugh. Lotus laughed and said, "Coral, you really know how to amuse people." But in her heart she felt like she'd just swallowed a hornet.

Lotus coldly observed the flirtatious glances passing between Coral and the doctor; she felt that nothing could escape her intuitive understanding. A tile fell off the table while they were being shuffled, and when Lotus bent down to pick it up she discovered that their four legs were wrapped in a tight embrace; they separated quite quickly and naturally, but Lotus definitely saw what they were doing.

Her expression did not change, but she did not look directly at Coral and the doctor's faces any longer. At that moment her emotions were very complicated; she was a little apprehensive, a little nervous, and also a little exultant at finding them out. "Coral," she thought to herself, "you're living too freely, too brazenly."

In the autumn there were many times when the sky outside her window was dark and damp as a fine rain fell unceasingly onto the garden, splashing off the aspen and pomegranate leaves with a sound like shattering jade. At times like those Lotus would sit by the window, wearily staring at a handkerchief hanging on the clothesline being drenched by the rain; her feelings at the time were turbulent and complex, and some of her thoughts were so personal she could not reveal them to anyone.

She simply could not understand why every time it was dark and rainy her sexual desires were heightened. Chen Zuoqian was incapable of noticing how the weather affected her physiology; he could only feel embarrassed at his inability to keep up with her. He'd say, "Age is unforgiving, and I can't stand using aphrodisiacs like three-whip spirit ointment." He caressed Lotus's warm, pink flesh until countless little frissons of desire pulsated just under her skin. His hands gradually grew wild in their movements, and his tongue also began to caress her body. Lotus lay sideways on the sofa; with her eyes closed and her face flushed, she listened to the pearls of rain crashing onto the window, and spoke in a low moan, "It's all because of the cold rain."

Chen Zuoqian did not hear her clearly. "What did you say? Gold chain?"

"Yes," Lotus lied, "gold chain; I want a beautiful gold chain necklace."

Chen Zuoqian said, "There's nothing you want that I won't give you, but whatever you do, don't tell the others."

Lotus rolled over and sat up quickly. "The others? Who the hell are they? I don't give a damn about them."

Chen Zuoqian said, "Yes, of course, none of them can compare with you." He saw Lotus's expression change rapidly; she pushed him away, quickly slipped on her underclothes, and walked over to the window. Chen Zuoqian asked what was wrong. Lotus turned her head back and said with slightly veiled resentment, "I don't feel like it now. Why did you have to start talking about them?"

Chen Zuoqian stood sullenly beside Lotus and watched the rain falling outside the window. At times like those the entire world was unbearably damp. The garden was completely empty; the leaves on the trees were green and cold; in the far corner the wisteria vine swaying in the wind took on the appearance of a person. Lotus remembered the well and some of the stories she'd heard about it. She said, "This garden is a little spooky."

"What do you mean, 'spooky'?" Chen Zuoqian asked.

Lotus just pursed her lips and faced the wisteria vine. "You know, it's that well."

Chen Zuoqian said, "A couple of people died in that well, that's all; jumped in and committed suicide."

Lotus asked, "Who was it who died?"

Chen Zuoqian answered, "You don't know them, anyway; a couple of family members from earlier generations."

Lotus said, "I suppose they were concubines."

Chen Zuoqian's expression immediately grew severe. "Who told you that?"

Lotus laughed and said, "No one told me. I saw for myself. I walked over to the side of that well and immediately saw two women floating on the bottom; one of them looked like me, and the other one also looked like me."

Chen Zuoqian said, "Don't talk nonsense, and don't go there any more."

Lotus clapped her hands and said, "That's no good; I still haven't asked those two ghosts why they threw themselves into the well."

"Why would you have to ask?" said Chen Zuoqian. "It could only be because of some filthy affair."

Lotus was silent for a long time and then suddenly burst out, "No wonder there are so many wells in this garden. They were dug for people to throw themselves into to commit suicide."

Chen Zuoqian put his arm around Lotus. "You're talking crazier all the time. Don't go on imagining things like that." As he spoke, he took hold of Lotus's hand and made her rub him down there. "He's ready again now, come on; if I die in your bed, I'll be perfectly happy."

In the garden the autumn rain was bleak and dreary, and for that reason their lovemaking had an aura of death about it. Everything that came before Lotus's eyes was black; only a few daisies on her dressing table emitted a faint red glow. When she heard a noise outside the door, she grabbed a perfume bottle close at hand and threw it in that direction. Chen Zuoqian said, "What's the matter now?"

Lotus answered, "She's spying on us."

"Who's spying?"

"Swallow."

Chen Zuoqian laughed. "What's there to see? And besides, she can't see us anyway."

Lotus replied in a severe tone, "Don't defend her; I can smell that slut's foul odor from miles away."

At dusk a crowd of people were sitting around in a circle in the garden listening to Feipu play a bamboo flute. Dressed in a silk shirt and silk pants, Feipu looked even more elegant and charming. He sat in the middle holding the flute while his listeners, for the most part his business companions, sat around in a circle. That crowd of people had become the center of attraction for everyone in the Chen household. The servants whispered back and forth as they stood on the porches observing them from afar. The rest of the people inside the rooms could hear the sound of Feipu's wooden flute through the windows, like the faint sound of gently flowing water; no one could ignore that sound.

Lotus was frequently very moved by the sound of Feipu's flute, sometimes so much that tears rolled down her cheeks. She wanted very much to sit down with that crowd of men and be much closer to Feipu. When Feipu took up his flute, he reminded her of a young man at college who used to sit alone in an empty room playing a zither; she could not remember that young man's face very clearly and did not have any hidden, secret affection for him. But she was easily transported by that sort of exquisitely beautiful scene; her emotions flowed forth like ripples on an autumn stream. She hesitated quite a while, then moved a rattan chair out onto the porch, sat down, and quietly listened to Feipu's playing. It was not long before the sound of the flute grew still and was replaced by the voices of the men talking. Lotus immediately felt it most uninteresting, and she thought to herself, "Talking is such a bore; it's nothing more than you lying to me and me cheating you; as soon as people start talking, they put on a hypocritical display of affection."

She stood up and went back into her room, where she suddenly remembered she also had a long flute, an heirloom left by her father, in her rattan suitcase. She opened the suitcase; it had not been in the sun for a long time and was already a little musty; all those abandoned and unworn schoolgirl dresses and skirts were neatly arranged in it as though all the days of her past were sealed there in dust, radiating tiny sparks from disappointed dreams. Lotus took out all the clothes, but did not see the flute. She clearly remembered putting the flute into her suitcase when she left home. How could it be missing?

"Swallow, Swallow, come here," she called toward the porch.

Swallow came in and said, "Fourth Mistress, why aren't you listening to the Young Master play the flute?"

Lotus asked, "Have you touched my suitcase?"

Swallow replied, "A long while ago you asked me to straighten up your suitcase, and I folded all your clothes, didn't I?"

Lotus asked further, "Did you see a wooden flute?"

"Flute?" said Swallow, "I didn't see one. Only a man can play a flute!"

Lotus stared straight into Swallow's eyes, laughed coldly, and said, "Then you must have stolen my flute, didn't you?"

Swallow replied, "Fourth Mistress, you shouldn't just insult people any old way; why would I steal your flute?"

"Naturally you'd have your own mischievous plans," said Lotus, "running around with a head full of clever schemes all day and still pretending to be little miss innocent."

Swallow said, "Fourth Mistress, you shouldn't wrongly accuse people like that. Go and ask Old Master, Young Master, First Mistress, Second Mistress, and Third Mistress when did I ever steal so much as a single copper from my masters?"

Lotus paid no more attention to Swallow's words; she stared contemptuously into Swallow's face, then ran into her little bedroom, stepped on her cheap wooden trunk, and ordered, "You talk so tough; open up and let me see!"

Swallow pulled at Lotus's leg and pleaded with her, "Fourth Mistress, don't step on my trunk; I really didn't take your flute!"

Looking at Swallow's frightened expression, Lotus was even more sure of herself; she picked up an ax from the corner of the room and said, "I'll hack it open and see; if it's not there, I'll buy you a new trunk tomorrow." She bit her lips, swung the ax down, and Swallow's trunk split right open as clothing, copper coins, and various sorts of trinkets spilled out all over the floor.

Lotus shook out all the clothes, but the flute was not there. Then, suddenly, she caught hold of a bulging, little white cloth package; when she opened it up, there was a small cloth figurine. The figurine had three fine needles stuck into its chest. At first she thought it was pretty funny, but she soon realized that the little doll-like figure looked an awfully lot like herself; on close inspection she saw that it had one word faintly written on it in black ink: "Lotus." She felt a sudden sharp pain in her chest, just as though she really was being pierced by three fine needles. Her face immediately went white. Swallow leaned back against the wall and stared at her in alarm. Lotus suddenly let out a shrill scream, jumped up, grabbed Swallow by the hair, and bashed her head repeatedly against the wall. She swallowed back her tears and shouted, "You trying to curse me to death? You trying to curse me to death?"

Swallow did not have the strength to struggle free; she just stood there limp and immobile, sobbing without end. Lotus grew tired, and while she was catching her breath she suddenly remembered that Swallow was illiterate. Who was it, then, who wrote her name on the cloth doll? This question distressed her even more. She squatted down and started wiping away Swallow's tears, then spoke in a gentle tone of voice. "Don't cry. It's all over now; just don't do it any more; I won't hold it against you, but you've got to tell me who wrote my name for you."

Swallow was still sobbing as she shook her head. "I won't tell. I can't tell."

Lotus said, "You don't have to be afraid; I won't make a big fuss about it. All you have to do is tell me, and I definitely won't get you in trouble." Swallow still shook her head. Then Lotus began to prompt her. "Was it Joy?" Swallow shook her head. "Then it must have been Coral, right?" Swallow still shook her head. Lotus swallowed back a breadth of cold air, and her voice was shaking slightly. "Then it was Cloud?" Swallow stopped shaking her head; she looked both despondent and ridiculous. Lotus stood up, looked up into the sky, and said, "You can know a person's face, but not her heart; I guessed it long ago."

Chen Zuoqian saw Lotus sitting woodenly on the sofa with red and swollen eyes, twisting a bunch of wilted daisies lying limply in her hand. He said, "You've been crying?"

Lotus answered, "No. You treat me so well, why would I cry?"

Chen Zuoqian thought a moment and said, "If you're feeling bored, we could walk around the garden, or we could go out for a midnight snack, too."

Lotus twisted the daisies again, tossed them out the window, and asked flatly, "What did you do with my wooden flute?"

Chen Zuoqian hesitated a moment and answered, "I was afraid you'd think of someone else, so I put it away."

The trace of a cold smile formed in the corners of Lotus's mouth. "All my heart is right here; who else would I be thinking about?"

Chen Zuoqian replied quite seriously, "Well, then, tell me who gave you that flute?"

"It's not a love token, it's an heirloom; my father left it to me."

"I was too suspicious," Chen Zuoqian said with a slight air of embarrassment, "I thought some young student gave it to you."

Lotus held out her hands and said, "Hurry up and bring it here; it's mine, and I want to keep it here."

Chen Zuoqian grew even more embarrassed. He walked back and forth rubbing his hands together. "This is terrible," he said. "I already had one of my servants burn it." He did not hear Lotus say another word as the room gradually grew dark. When he turned on the light, he saw that Lotus's face was white as snow and tears were flowing silently down her cheeks.

That night was a very unusual one for the two of them. Lotus curled herself up like a lamb and stayed far away from Chen Zuoqian's body; Chen Zuoqian reached over and caressed her, but did not receive any response. He turned the lights off a while, then turned them on again and looked at Lotus's face; it was as indifferent and unfeeling as a piece of paper. "You're going too far," he said. "I've almost got down on my knees and begged for forgiveness."

Lotus was silent a moment, then said, "I don't feel good." Chen Zuoqian said, "I hate it when people frown at me." Lotus turned over and said, "Why don't you go to Cloud's, she always smiles at you." Chen Zuoqian jumped out of bed and pulled on his clothes. "I will go then; thank God I still have three other wives!"

The next day, when Cloud came into Lotus's room, Lotus was still lying in bed. When Lotus saw her pull back the door curtain, she shuddered inexplicably. She closed her eyes and pretended to be asleep. Cloud sat down at the head of her bed, reached out and felt her forehead, and said, "You're not hot; probably not sick, just angry."

Lotus looked at her through half-opened eyes, "You here?"

Cloud just took Lotus's hand. "Come on, get up quick; lying around like this when you're not really sick, you're going to *make* yourself sick."

Lotus said, "What's there to do if I do get up?"

Cloud answered, "Cut my hair for me; I want to have a student cut like yours, too; liven myself up a bit."

Cloud sat on a round stool waiting for Lotus to cut her hair. Lotus wrapped an old dress around Cloud's neck, then took a comb and slowly combed her hair. Lotus said, "If it doesn't turn out right, don't blame me; it really makes me nervous to cut such beautiful hair as yours."

Cloud said, "It doesn't matter if it turns out badly; at my age, who cares about looking good?

Lotus just kept on combing Cloud's hair up and down. "All right, I'm going to cut it."

Cloud said, "Go on, cut it. What makes you so timid?"

Lotus answered, "Mainly because I haven't done this much; I'm afraid I'll cut you."

Having said that, Lotus started cutting. Lock after lock of Cloud's soft, black hair fell to the ground in time to the sound of the scissor blades snapping together. Cloud said, "You're very skillful, aren't you?"

"You better not praise me," said Lotus. "As soon as you praise me, my hand starts to shake." As she said that, she heard Cloud let out a loud, shrill, scream; her ear had definitely been snipped by Lotus's scissors.

Even some people out in the garden heard Cloud's frightening scream; Coral, her maids, and Feilan all ran over to see what had happened. They saw Cloud holding her bloody right ear; it hurt so much she was sweating. Lotus was sitting beside her holding a pair of scissors; her face, too, was white. On the floor there were a few locks of black hair. "What's happened to you?"

Cloud's tears started to flow, and she ran out into the garden holding her ear. Lotus stood there, dazed, by the side of that pile of hair; the scissors fell out of her hand with a thud. She mumbled as if talking to herself, "My hand was shaking; I'm not well." She pushed all the servants who had come to watch the excitement out the door. "What the hell are you doing here? Hurry up and call a doctor for Second Mistress!"

Coral remained in the room holding Feilan's hand. She smiled slightly as she looked over at Lotus. Lotus avoided her eyes, picked up a reed broom, and started sweeping up Cloud's hair when she heard Coral suddenly burst out laughing.

"What're you laughing at?"

Coral squinted at Lotus. "If I hated someone, I'd cut her ear off too, cut the whole thing right off."

Lotus frowned. "What do you mean by that? You think I did it on purpose?"

Coral laughed again merrily and replied, "Well, only heaven knows about that."

Lotus did not pay any more attention to Coral. She lay back down on the bed, pulled a blanket up over her head, and heard her heart beating wildly. She didn't know herself whether or not she was responsible for what those scissors had done; at any rate, everyone should believe she didn't mean to do it. Then she heard Coral talking through the blanket. "Cloud has the face of a saint and the heart of a scorpion; she dreams up more schemes in that narrow little mind of hers than anybody. I know I'm no match for her, but maybe you can take her on. I guessed that the first time I saw you." Lotus moved slightly under the blanket as she listened to Coral unexpectedly opening up.

Coral said, "You want to hear about how Cloud and I had our kids? Cloud and I got pregnant at just about the same time. When I was three months along, she sent someone to put abortion medicine in my tonic. But my fate was stronger than hers. The fetus didn't abort. Later on we went into labor at just about the same time. She wanted to have her child first, so she spent a lot of money on foreign labor-inducing shots; dilated her cunt so much it tore open. But my fate was still stronger than hers. I had Feilan first, a boy; but she went to all that trouble for nothing and had Yirong, no more than a cheap little bitch, and born three hours later than Feilan at that."

The autumn cold had already arrived. The women had all changed into their fall clothes; early in the morning and in the depth of night, the leaves fell all around, converting the garden into a single patch of dry brown. Some female servants were crouched around a fire burning leaves, and the stench of smoke filled the air. Lotus's window opened with a bang, and the servants saw that Lotus's face was flushed with anger. She grabbed a wooden comb and knocked on the windowsill. "Who told you to burn those leaves? Burning those beautiful leaves and making such a stink?" The servants gathered up their brooms and baskets, then a brave one of their number spoke up. "There's so many leaves, what're we going to do if we don't burn them?"

Lotus shouted as she threw her wooden comb down and

struck her. "I forbid you to burn them, I forbid it!" Then she slammed the window shut with another loud crash.

"Fourth Mistress's temper is getting worse and worse," the servant women told Joy. "She won't let us burn the leaves. Why's she so bad tempered?" Joy gave them a dressing down. "Stop your yammering; it's not your place to go around gossiping." In her heart, however, Joy was very angry. Formerly the leaves in the garden had always been burned several times a year. Was that old custom going to be forsaken just because Lotus had moved in? The servants stood by with their hands at their sides, and said, "Well, do we burn the leaves or not?" Joy answered, "Who said you're not to burn them? You go on and burn them for me; pay no attention to her."

The servant women burned the leaves once more, and Lotus did not show her face. But when the fire had burned down to ashes and everyone was gone, they saw her walk out of the south wing. She was still wearing a summer skirt, and the servants asked her how come she didn't feel cold with such a strong wind outside. Lotus stood there for a long time staring blankly at the pile of black ashes, then she went to the central courtyard to eat lunch. Blowing back and forth in the cold wind, her full skirt looked just like a white butterfly.

Lotus sat at the table and watched everyone else eat. She didn't once move her chopsticks. Her expression was calm and determined, and she folded her arms tightly in front of her body in order to ward off any attacks on her person. As it happened, Chen Zuoqian was away that day—a perfect opportunity for an outbreak of domestic trouble. Feipu spoke first. "Hey, why aren't you eating?"

"I'm already full," Lotus answered.

"You ate already?" Feipu asked again.

Lotus made a sound through her nose. "Huh, I smelled so much stinking smoke I'm already full."

Feipu didn't understand; he looked over at his mother. Joy's expression changed immediately as she told him, "You just eat your lunch; don't ask so many questions." Then she raised her voice and stared over at Lotus. "Fourth Mistress, I'd really like to hear what you have to say; what're we supposed to do with so many leaves piled up all over the ground?"

Lotus replied, "I don't know. What right do I have to manage household affairs?"

Joy said, "Every year we burn the leaves, and we've never had any trouble; why're you so much more delicate than everybody else? Can't even stand a little smoke."

Lotus replied, "The leaves will rot by themselves; do we have to burn them? Leaves aren't people, you know."

"What do you mean by that?" Joy asked. "What nonsense."

Lotus answered, "I don't mean anything, but there's still something I don't understand. Why do they have to bring the leaves into the back courtyard to burn them? Whoever likes to smell that smoke should have the leaves burned under her window."

Joy could not stand to hear any more; she slammed her chopsticks down on the table. "Why don't you look at yourself in a mirror, Lotus, and see what the hell you amount to in the Chen household? Acting as though somebody has been mistreating you."

Lotus stood up. Her gaze remained fixed on Joy's yellowish, waxen, slightly swollen face. Then she spoke, "You're right, what the hell do I amount to?" Lotus spoke very softly as though talking to herself. She smiled slightly as she turned and left the table; when she looked back her eyes were already brimming with tears; she said, "Heaven alone knows what the hell you all amount to!"

Lotus locked herself in her room the entire afternoon and would not even open the door when Swallow came to serve her tea. Sitting alone in front of the window, she saw that the big beautiful chrysanthemums in the vase on her dressing table were already wilted and black. She picked them up and wanted to throw them out, but didn't know where to throw them; the window was shut fast and couldn't be opened again. She walked around the room holding the flowers to her chest, thinking; finally, she opened up her clothes closet and put the flowers in there. Outside, the autumn wind was blowing again; it was a cold wind that blew the darkness little by little into the garden. She heard someone knocking on her door. She thought it was Swallow with the tea again, so she rapped on the inside of the door. "Get out of here, I don't want any tea." But the person outside said, "It's me; it's Feipu."

Lotus never imagined Feipu would come over. She opened the door and stood in the doorway. "What are you doing here?"

Feipu's hair had been mussed up by the wind; he smoothed back his hair, laughed a little nervously, and said, "They said you're sick, so I came over to see you."

Lotus sighed slightly. "Who's sick? If I want to die, I'll just die; it's too tiresome to be sick."

Feipu walked straight over and sat down on the sofa; he looked all around the room and suddenly said, "I thought you had a lot of books in your room."

Lotus held out her empty hands. "Not even one. Books are useless to me now." She was still standing as she went on. "Did you come to give me a lecture, too?"

Feipu shook his head. "How could I? I get a headache just watching scenes like that."

Lotus said, "Then you've come to patch things up? I don't think there's any need; someone like me deserves to be scolded."

Feipu was silent for a moment, then said, "My mother really didn't mean anything; it's just her nature to be stubborn and inflexible; you needn't quarrel with her; it's not worth it."

Lotus walked back and forth in the room; suddenly she laughed out loud. "I honestly didn't want to fight with First Mistress; I don't even know what got into me; don't you think I'm ridiculous?"

Feipu shook his head again, coughed, and said very slowly, "People are all the same; they don't know what their own emotions are all about."

The flute quite naturally came up in their conversation. "I had a flute once," Lotus said, "but unfortunately . . . I lost it."

"Then you can play the flute, too?" Feipu asked elatedly.

"No, I can't," Lotus answered. "I didn't have time to learn before I lost it."

"What if I introduce you to a friend who can teach you? He's the one who taught me."

Lotus laughed noncommittally, or as though she didn't know how to answer. At that moment Swallow came in with two bowls of sweet soup with red jujubes and white tremella; first she placed a bowl in Feipu's hands. Lotus said, "Just look how devoted this girl is to you; she prepared some refreshments without even being asked to." Embarrassed, Swallow blushed a deep red, put the other bowl down on the table, and ran out. Lotus called after her, "Swallow, don't run off, the Eldest Young Master wants to talk to you." Lotus covered her mouth and laughed out loud after she said that. Feipu laughed, too; he stirred his soup with a silver spoon as he said, "You're too harsh on her, too."

Lotus said, "You think she's easy to handle? That girl's despicable. Every time I have guests in here, she stands outside the door and eavesdrops on us. Who knows what sort of crazy ideas she's got in her head?"

Feipu sensed Lotus's displeasure and quickly changed the subject. He said, "I've always liked sweets, ever since I was a child: things like this red jujube and white tremella soup. It's really rather embarrassing; my friends all tell me only women like sweets."

Lotus's expression remained sullen, however, and she started to fiddle with her fingernails. Her nails were long and slender; painted with aromatic balsam oil, they looked like a row of pink fish scales.

"Hey, are you listening to me?" asked Feipu.

Lotus answered, "I'm listening. You were saying women like sweets and men prefer salty things."

Feipu smiled, shook his head, and stood up to take his leave. Just before he left he told Lotus, "You're an interesting person. I can't imagine what's in your heart."

Lotus replied, "I feel the same about you, too. I can't imagine what's in your heart, either."

On the seventh day of the twelfth lunar month, lanterns were hung up all around the Chen compounds. Chen Zuoqian celebrated his fiftieth birthday that day. From early morning on, an endless line of friends and relatives came into the garden to congratulate him. Chen Zuoqian sat in the living room and received his visitors wearing a new black robe that Feipu had given him, while Joy, Cloud, Coral, Lotus, and the children clustered around him exchanging pleasantries with the guests.

Just as the party was growing lively, a sudden, loud crash was heard; everyone looked in the direction of the noise and saw that a three-foot-tall vase had just smashed to pieces on the floor.

Feilan and Yirong had been chasing each other around the room and knocked the vase off its ornamental table. The two children stood there looking at each other, knowing they were in big trouble. Feilan was the first to recover from his initial fright; he pointed at Yirong. "She knocked it over. I didn't do anything."

Yirong quickly pointed her finger back at Feilan. "You were chasing me. You knocked it over."

Chen Zuoqian's expression was livid by that time, but the presence of his guests inhibited him from venting his anger.

Joy walked over and softly, but hoarsely, grumbled, "Whore's brats, whore's brats." She dragged Feilan and Yirong outside and gave them each a slap in the face. "Bad luck, bad luck." Then she pushed Feilan again. "Get the hell away from here." At that Feilan threw himself on the floor and started crying and screaming; his loud, high-pitched voice soon carried back into the living room. Coral ran out first. She took Feilan in her arms and glared at Joy. "Why don't you hit him again? Hit him again. You can't stand the sight of him anyway; you shouldn't miss this chance to hit him again!"

Joy replied, "What sort of talk is that? The child's done something wrong, and instead of teaching him a lesson, you actually try to protect him."

Coral pushed Feilan over in front of Joy and said, "Fine, I'll just hand him over to you to teach him a lesson. Go on, beat him, beat him to death. You'll feel much better if you beat him to death."

At that point Cloud and Lotus also ran out. Cloud pulled Yirong over to her and patted her on the head. "My little doll baby, why do you always give me so much trouble? Tell us, who really knocked over the vase?"

Yirong started to cry. "It wasn't me; I told you it wasn't me; Feilan knocked over the table."

Cloud said, "Stop your crying; if you didn't do it, what're you crying about? You two have ruined the Old Master's day of happiness."

Coral laughed coldly and said, "Third Little Sister, you're so young, how can you tell such a barefaced lie? I saw it all quite clearly; you knocked over the vase with your elbow."

The four females had nothing to say for a moment, but Feilan went right on crying and screaming.

After watching them for a while, Lotus said, "It's not worth all this fuss; wasn't it only a vase? If it's broken, it's broken; what can come of it?"

Joy looked askance at Lotus. "It's easy for you to say. Is this only about a vase? The Old Master likes everything to be auspicious. Taking on a bunch of heartless wretches like you, sooner or later you're going to ruin this fine old Chen household."

Lotus spoke up. "Huh? Why is it my fault again? Let's just say I was talking nonsense; who wants to worry about your affairs anyway?"

Lotus immediately whirled around and walked away from the fray. Walking toward the back garden, she ran into Feipu and some of his friends. Feipu asked her, "Why did you leave?"

Lotus rubbed her forehead and answered, "I've got a headache; every time things get too noisy, I get a headache."

Lotus really was getting a headache. She wanted a drink of

water, but all the water bottles in her room were empty. Swallow had taken advantage of helping out in the living room to ignore all her chores in Lotus's rooms. Lotus cursed, "The little bitch," under her breath as she went to the kitchen and lit a fire to boil some water herself. This was the first time she had done any such housework since joining the Chen household, and she was a little clumsy at it. After standing in the kitchen for a while, she walked back out onto the porch. She could see that the back garden was completely still and empty. Everyone had gone to join the party; only a certain loneliness remained behind, falling drop by drop. Like water dripping off the dead branches and dried leaves, it soaked right into Lotus's heart. Once again she saw the withered wisteria vine. Blowing in the wind, it emitted some sort of desolate murmur; the well was still eerily calling her. Lotus covered her chest. She felt as though she was hearing an apocalyptic voice from out of the void.

Lotus walked toward the well. She felt incomparably light, as though walking in a dream. The odor of decaying vegetation filled the air around the well; Lotus picked a wisteria leaf up off the ground, examined it carefully, and threw it into the well. She watched the leaf float like some sort of ornament on the dark blue surface of the stagnant water, obscuring part of her reflection; she actually could not see her eyes. Lotus walked all the way around the well, but could not find any angle from which to see her entire reflection; she thought it very strange. "One wisteria leaf, how could it . . . ?" Transformed into innumerable points of white light, some rays of the noonday sun danced slowly inside the old well. Lotus was suddenly seized by a frightening thought: a hand . . . there was a hand holding the wisteria leaf so as to cover her eyes. As soon as she thought that, she really seemed to see a pale white hand, dripping wet, reaching out to cover her eyes from the unfathomable depths at the bottom of the well. Lotus shrieked aloud with terror. A hand. A hand. She wanted to turn and run away, but it was as if her whole body were held fast to the side of the well, willing but unable to tear itself away. She felt herself lean over helplessly and stare into the well, like the stem of a flower broken by the wind. In another moment of vertigo she saw the water in the well suddenly bubble up as the sound of a vague and very distant voice penetrated her ears: "Lotus . . . come down here, Lotus. Lotus . . . come down here, Lotus."

When Cloud came looking for Lotus, she was sitting alone on the porch, holding Coral's Persian cat on her lap. Cloud said, "What are you doing here? The midday banquet's starting."

"My head's killing me," Lotus replied. "I don't feel like going."

"That won't do," Cloud said. "You have to go even if you're sick; it's a family occasion; the Old Master keeps asking for you to come back."

"I really don't want to go; I feel terribly sick; can't you all just let me sit quietly for a while?"

Cloud smiled and asked, "Are you angry at Joy?"

"No. I haven't the strength to be angry with anyone." Lotus made her annoyance obvious; she threw the cat to the floor and said, "I want to sleep for a while."

Cloud continued to smile. "Well then, you go on and sleep; I'll just go back and tell the Old Master."

Lotus slept deeply that whole day, but in her sleep she saw the well and the wisteria leaf in the middle of the well; it made her break out all over in a cold sweat. Who knew the meaning of that well? Who knew the meaning of that wisteria leaf? Who knew the meaning of Lotus's life? She got up later and sat for some time in front of the mirror, washing her face and combing her hair. She saw that her face in the mirror was as pale and lifeless as that dried-up leaf. The woman in the mirror was a stranger to her. She did not like that kind of a woman. She sighed deeply, and then she began to think of Chen Zuoqian and his birthday party; she began to regret her behavior. She scolded herself for acting so petty and spoiled; she knew full well that sort of behavior could only be detrimental to her life in that household. Then she hurriedly opened her closet and took out a silver-gray lambs-wool scarf, the birthday gift she had prepared long ago for Chen Zuoqian.

The evening banquet included only members of the Chen household. When Lotus went into the dining room, she saw that all of them had already sat down at the table. "They started without me," Lotus thought as she walked over to her chair.

Feipu greeted her from across the table. "You feeling better?"

Lotus nodded her head as she stole a look at Chen Zuoqian. His expression, cold, gray, steely, made her heart race. She picked up the woolen scarf and held it in front of him. "Old Master, this is my insignificant little gift."

Chen Zuoqian grunted and pointed toward a round table nearby. "Put it over there."

Lotus took the scarf over to the table and saw a big pile of birthday gifts given him by other family members. A gold ring, a fox-fur coat, a Swedish wristwatch, all tied with red silk ribbons. Lotus's heart beat rapidly again and her face felt hot and flushed. As she sat down again, she heard Joy say, "If it's a birthday gift, why didn't she know enough to tie it with a red silk ribbon?"

Lotus pretended not to have heard. She felt that Joy's carping was really hateful, but she certainly had been confused and distracted that whole day.

She knew she had already made Chen Zuoqian angry, and that was the one thing she did not want to do. She thought very hard of a way to make up for it. She had to let them see her special status in the Old Master's eyes; she must not appear inferior. She suddenly smiled sweetly over at Chen Zuoqian and said, "Old Master, today is your most auspicious day. I have very little money and cannot give you a gold ring or a fur coat, but let me make up for it with another kind of gift."

At that she stood up, walked over in front of Chen Zuoqian, put her arms around his neck, and kissed him twice on the face.

Everyone at the table stared speechlessly at Chen Zuoqian—who blushed a deep red. He looked as though he wanted to speak but could not get the words out. Finally, he pushed Lotus away and said harshly, "Have a little more respect in front of everybody."

Chen Zuoqian's reaction was actually quite natural, but Lotus had not expected it; confused, she stood there staring uncertainly at him; it was quite some time before she finally realized what had happened. She covered her face and didn't let them see her tears. She wept softly with a sound like tearing silk as she walked toward the door; the people at the table heard her say, "What did I do wrong? What did I do wrong this time?"

Even the serving women standing beside the table witnessed this birthday-banquet disturbance; they were acutely conscious that it would become a major turning point in Lotus's life in the household. That night, when two maidservants were taking down the birthday lanterns, one said, "Guess whose room the Old Master is sleeping in tonight?"

The other one thought for a while, but could not guess. Something like that depended only on his momentary preference, didn't it? Who could ever guess correctly?

The two women, Coral and Lotus, were sitting opposite each other. Coral had very carefully made herself up, penciling in dark eyebrows and applying an alluring shade of Beauty brand lipstick; and she was holding an expensive fur wrap across her knees. But Lotus looked as though she had just then gotten languidly out of bed; she held a cigarette between her fingers and was smoking it very slowly with a vacant look in her eyes. The strange thing was that neither of them spoke. As they listened to the ticktock ticktock of the clock on the wall, Lotus and Coral each harbored her own secret anxieties; they harbored them like two trees face-to-face in the wind. This is also a situation seen often in history.

Coral spoke first. "I've noticed you've been in a bad temper these past couple of days; are you having your period?"

Lotus answered, "What does it have to do with that? Mine is irregular; I never know when it's going to start or when it's going to end."

Coral said, "Such a clever woman, but you're not clear about that. Hasn't it come yet this month? You think you're pregnant?"

Lotus answered, "No, no. How could that be?"

"It's reasonable that you should be," Coral said. "Chen

Zuoqian is very good in that department. Put a pillow under your little waist at night. Really, I'm not fooling you."

Lotus replied, "Your mouth really doesn't have a lock on it, that you can say something like that."

Coral said, "That's all there is to say; what's there to hide about it? If you don't produce a child for the Chen family, hard times will come your way later. People like us are all the same."

"Chen Zuoqian hasn't even come around my way these days; let him please himself; I don't care."

Coral said, "You just aren't horny yet, but me, I'm different. I told him right out if he stays away from my place more than five days, I'll look for a bedmate. There's no way I can live like a widow. He has to work hardest where I'm concerned: he's afraid of me; he hates me; and he wants me too. But I'm not afraid of him.

"It's such a bore to talk about that," Lotus said, "and anyway I don't care. But I just don't understand what women amount to anyway; what sort of creatures are women? We're just like dogs, cats, goldfish, rats. . . . We're just like anything, anything except human beings."

"Don't keep on degrading yourself," Coral said, "and don't worry about Chen Zuoqian neglecting you. He'll come back to you; you're younger than all of us, you're intelligent, and you're cultured. He'd really be a fool if he abandoned you for Joy or Cloud; their waists are almost as big around as water buckets! What does it matter, anyway, that you kissed him in front of everybody?"

"You're really a pest," said Lotus. "I didn't mean that; I was talking about myself."

Coral said, "Don't think about that incident; it's not important; he's just a bit of a hypocrite. If it was in bed, it wouldn't matter if you kissed him on the face; even if you kissed him down there, he'd love it."

"Don't talk about it," Lotus said. "It really makes me sick."

"Well, why don't you come to the Rose Theater with me? Cheng Yanqiu is there in *Tears on a Barren Mountain.* How about it? Let's go relax a bit."

"I don't want to go," Lotus said. "I don't want to leave the house. I've only got one heart, and it feels the same no matter what; what good would it do to relax?"

Coral said, "Couldn't you just go along with me after I sat here all this time talking to you?"

Lotus said, "What fun is it if I go with you? Go ask Chen Zuoqian to take you; and if he's too busy, you can go ask that doctor to go with you."

Coral was speechless. Her face fell immediately. She gathered up her fur wrap, flung it around her neck, and stood up. She moved menacingly close to Lotus, stared at her, reached out and grabbed the cigarette from between Lotus's lips, threw it on the ground, and stomped on it. Then she said harshly, "That's nothing to joke about. If you talk such nonsense to anyone else, I'll beat your mouth to a pulp. I'm not afraid of any of you; I'm not afraid of anybody; anyone who wants to ruin me is dreaming!"

Feipu did indeed bring a friend to see Lotus, saying he was the flute teacher he'd hired for her. Lotus did not know what to do, however, because she'd never taken that talk about learning the flute seriously. She took a good look at the teacher. He was a young man with very light skin and a short haircut, like a student, yet not like a student, somewhat shy and reserved in his movements and gestures. He told her his name, and it turned out that he was the local silk magnate Gu's Third Young Gentleman. Lotus had watched them walk over hand in hand. The sight of two men walking hand in hand gave her a strange feeling of novelty and exoticism.

"What good friends you are," Lotus said with a smile. "I've never seen two grown men walking hand in hand before."

Feipu looked a little embarrassed. He said, "We've been friends since we were children; we studied in the same local school."

Looking at Young Master Gu, she noticed his face was even redder than Feipu's. Lotus thought this teacher was quite interesting; no telling what a man who blushed so easily was like. She said, "As old as I am, I've never made a good friend."

Feipu said, "That's not so strange; you probably look proud and aloof and not very easy to approach."

Lotus said, "That's unfair; I am alone, actually, but not proud; to be proud you have to have something to back it up with. What would I have to back up my pride?"

Feipu took his flute out of a black silk bag and said, "I want to give you this flute; Young Master Gu gave it to me, so now I'm 'borrowing flowers to present to the Buddha.' "

Lotus received the flute and looked over at Young Master Gu; he nodded his head and smiled. Lotus put the flute to her lips, blew out a random sound, and said, "I'm only afraid I'm too inept and won't be able to learn."

Young Master Gu said, "Playing the flute is very simple; as long as you put your heart into it, there's no reason why you can't learn."

"I'm only afraid I won't be able to put my heart into it; my heart's like a plate of sand; it's very hard to concentrate it in one place."

Young Master Gu smiled again. "Well, that does present a problem. I can only work on your flute playing; I can't take care of your heart."

Feipu sat down, looked at Lotus, then looked at Young Master Gu; his eyes filled with his own special tenderness.

"A flute has seven holes; one hole for each of the seven emotions. When you blend them together, it's especially graceful and especially sorrowful. A flute player has to have these two feelings: grace and sorrow." Young Master Gu looked very shyly at Lotus and asked, "Do you have these two feelings?"

Lotus thought a moment and replied, "I'm afraid I only have the latter one."

"If you have it, that's pretty good," said Young Master Gu. "Sorrow is one of the seven emotions, too. The only thing to fear is being empty, not having anything in your heart; then you couldn't play the flute well."

Lotus said, "Why don't you play something first and let me hear what this flute sounds like."

Young Master Gu did not refuse; he picked up the flute and started to play. Lotus heard a light, gentle, soft, and beautiful sound, at once like weeping and lamenting, come forth from the flute.

Feipu sat down on the sofa, closed his eyes, and said, "This is called 'Autumn Lament.' "

Just at that moment, Joy's maid Fortune came and knocked at the window, and called shrilly for Feipu. "Eldest Young Master, the mistress wants you to come to the living room and greet some guests."

Feipu asked, "Who is it?"

Fortune answered, "I don't know; the mistress wants you to hurry over."

Feipu frowned and said, "Tell the guests to come here to see me."

Fortune went on knocking on the window and shouting. "The mistress says you must come; if you don't, she'll take it out on me."

"What a pain," Feipu complained softly under his breath. He stood up helplessly and complained again. "What sort of guests? Damn it!"

Young Master Gu stood there holding his flute and looking at Feipu, then asked apprehensively, "What about the flute lesson; should I continue or not?"

Feipu waved his hand and replied, "You stay here and continue teaching. I'll just go see who it is."

When Lotus and Young Master Gu were the only ones left, they did not know what to say at first. Lotus suddenly smiled and said, "Liar."

Young Master Gu was startled. "Who's a liar?"

Then Lotus regained her composure. "I didn't mean you; I meant her."

Young Master Gu felt a little ill at ease. Lotus discovered that he was starting to blush again. She thought it very amusing that the scion of such a grand family also had a very thin skin; but a tendency to blush easily should be accounted a good quality in any case. Lotus looked sympathetically at Young Master Gu and said, "Please go on playing; you hadn't finished."

Young Master Gu looked down at his flute, placed it back in the black silk bag, and said softly, "It's finished; we've lost the mood now, so the tune is finished, too. A good tune is easily spoiled by a loss of mood; you understand? As soon as Feipu left, the flute wouldn't play well."

Young Master Gu soon stood up to say good-bye. Lotus saw him off as far as the garden and suddenly felt extremely grateful to him; fearing it would be unseemly to reveal it, she stopped, folded her arms in front of her chest, and made a deep ceremonial bow.

Young Master Gu asked, "When do you want to have your next flute lesson?"

Lotus shook her head. "I don't know."

Young Master Gu thought a moment and said, "Let's let Feipu arrange it. Feipu likes you very much; he often praises you to his friends."

Lotus sighed and thought to herself, "What good is it for him to like me? There's still no one in this world I can truly depend on."

Just as Lotus arrived back in her room, Cloud came bursting in, shouting excitedly that Feipu and Joy had started to quarrel. Lotus was surprised at first, then she laughed coldly and said, "I thought they would."

Cloud said, "Go and persuade them to stop."

"What would that look like?" Lotus responded. "They're mother and son; no matter how much they quarrel, what would it look like for me to tell them to stop?"

Cloud said, "You mean you don't know they're quarreling because of you?"

"Huh?" said Lotus. "That's even more bizarre. I don't have anything at all to do with them; what do they want to drag me in for?"

Cloud looked accusingly at Lotus. "Don't act so innocent. You know why they're quarreling."

Lotus's voice grew uncontrollably shrill. "What do I know? I only know she can't stand anyone being nice to me. Who does she think I am anyway? Does she think I'm going to do something with her son?" As she spoke, her eyes filled with tears. "It's so stupid, so hateful," she said. "How can she be so stupid?"

At that moment Cloud was cracking a melon seed between her front teeth. She pressed the just finished seed husks into Swallow's hand, shoved Lotus playfully, and said with a smile, "Don't be so angry. If you stand upright, you needn't fear a crooked shadow; if you've done nothing wrong, there's no need to fear a ghost knocking at your door; what're you afraid of?"

Lotus answered, "After you put it that way, it would seem I really do have something to fear. If you like to play the mediator, you go persuade them to stop. I'm not interested."

Cloud said, "Lotus, you certainly have a cruel heart; I've really seen it now." Lotus said, "You give me too much credit. No one's heart can be taken out and examined; but whoever has a cruel heart understands it best themselves."

Lotus ran into Feipu in the garden the following day. Feipu was walking along, listlessly playing with a cigarette lighter. He pretended he didn't see Lotus, but Lotus deliberately called to him in a loud voice. She stood there talking to him just like always. She asked, "Who was your guest yesterday? He made me miss my flute lesson."

Feipu smiled bitterly, "Don't pretend ignorance. The whole courtyard is buzzing today about my argument with my mother."

Lotus asked further, "What were you quarreling about?"

Feipu shook his head, methodically lit the lighter and blew out the flame, looked hastily all around, and said, "Staying at home too long gets on people's nerves. I want to go someplace again. It's better out in society where I'm free and I'm happy."

Lotus said, "I understand; after all that trouble, you're still afraid of her."

Feipu said, "I'm not afraid of her; I'm afraid of trouble, afraid of women; women are really frightening."

"You're afraid of women? Lotus asked. "Then why aren't you afraid of me?"

"I am a little afraid of you," Feipu replied, "but it's not so bad. You're different from them, so I like to go to your place."

Afterward Lotus recalled what Feipu had said so nonchalantly: "You're different from them." She felt Feipu had given her a sort of elemental comfort, faintly perceptible, like the winter sunlight, bearing with it a modicum of warmth.

Feipu rarely came to Lotus's room after that, and he seemed to be doing badly in business; he always looked gloomy and out of sorts. Lotus only saw him at the dinner table. Sometimes the image of Coral and the doctor's legs intertwined under the mahjong table would flit through her mind; she could not help secretly looking at her own legs under the table. Could she stretch them over toward his? When she thought about it, she felt both frightened and excited.

One day Feipu arrived unexpectedly, stood there rubbing his hands together and looking at his feet. Watching him stand there for so long without speaking, Lotus laughed out loud. "What've you got up your sleeve now? Why don't you say something?"

Feipu replied, "I'm going on a long trip."

Lotus said, "Don't you go on long trips all the time?"

Feipu answered, "This time I'm going to Nanjing to make a deal on some tobacco."

Lotus said, "What's wrong with that? As long as it's not opium."

Feipu said, "Yesterday an old monk examined my hexagrams and said that I'd have more evil than good fortune on this trip. Originally I never believed in that crap, but this time I actually believe it a little."

Lotus said, "If you believe it, then don't go. I hear there are an awful lot of bandits there; they cut off people's flesh and eat it."

Feipu said, "I can't not go. First off, I want to get out of the house. Secondly, I have to bring in some money. If the Chen family keeps on going this way, we'll eat up our entire fortune. The Old Master is a little muddleheaded now; if I don't take charge of things, who will?"

Lotus answered, "What you say makes good sense. You better just go. Besides, a grown man lying around home all day is hardly proper either."

Feipu silently scratched his head a moment and then suddenly blurted out, "If I went away and didn't come back, would you cry?"

Lotus instantly covered his mouth with her hand. "Don't curse yourself."

Feipu grabbed Lotus's hand, turned it over, examining it on both sides, and said, "Why can't I read people's palms? I can't make out anything at all. Maybe your fate is hard to decipher and everything is hidden."

Lotus pulled back her hand and said, "If Swallow sees us, she'll be gossiping all over the place." Feipu said, "If she dares, I'll cut out her tongue and make a soup with it."

As Lotus was saying good-bye to Feipu in the hall, she saw Young Master Gu pacing around the garden. She asked Feipu, "What's he doing outside?"

Feipu laughed and said, "He's afraid of women, too, just like me. He's going to Yunnan with me."

Lotus made a face: "You two are inseparable, just like husband and wife."

Feipu said, "Sounds like you're a little jealous. If you want to go to Yunnan, I'll take you along, too. Will you go?"

Lotus answered, "I would like to go actually, but it can't be done."

"Why can't it be done?"

Lotus poked him gently and said, "Don't act stupid; you know why it can't be done. Now go on, hurry up and leave."

She watched Feipu and Young Master Gu walk out through the moon gate and disappear. She was uncertain how she felt about this parting, disappointed or indifferent. But one thing was perfectly clear: With Feipu gone she would be even more lonely and isolated in the Chen household.

Lotus was smoking when Chen Zuoqian arrived. Her first reaction when she turned and saw him was to crush out her cigarette; she remembered he'd said he couldn't stand to see a woman smoke. Chen Zuoqian took off his hat and coat and waited for Lotus to hang them up. Lotus walked over hesitantly and said, "Old Master hasn't been here for a long time."

Chen Zuoqian said, "Why have you taken up smoking? As soon as a woman starts smoking, she loses her femininity."

Lotus hung his coat up, put his hat on her own head, and said jokingly, "This way I'm even less feminine, right?"

Chen Zuoqian just grabbed his hat off her head, hung it on the coatrack himself, and said, "Lotus, you're too audacious; when you start carrying on, you go too far; no wonder everybody talks about you."

Lotus responded immediately, "What do they say? Who talks about me? Is it other people or is it you yourself? I don't give a damn if people gossip like mad about me, but if Old Master can't tolerate me either, then I might as well die and be done with it."

Chen Zuoqian frowned and said, "All right, all right, why're all of you the same? All you can talk about is dying, as if you had such a miserable life. I hate that crap."

Lotus went over and put her hands on his shoulders. "If you don't like it, I won't mention dying any more, that's all. Who wants to talk about all these unhappy things when everything is just fine?"

Chen Zuoqian put his arms around her and sat her down on his lap. "Were you hurt that day? I was in a bad mood; I don't know why, but I felt irritated all day. I guess there's no way for a man to be happy about reaching his fiftieth birthday."

Lotus answered, "What happened that day? I forgot all about it."

Chen Zuoqian started to laugh; he squeezed her waist and said, "What happened that day? I don't remember, either."

After so many days, Chen Zuoqian's body felt very strange to Lotus, and he had the smell of mint oil about him. She guessed he had spent the last few days with Joy; she was the only one who liked to rub on mint oil. Lotus picked a bottle of perfume up from the table and carefully dabbed it around Chen Zuoqian's body; then she dabbed some on herself. Chen

Zuoqian asked, "Where did you learn that from?"

Lotus answered, "I can't have you smelling like them."

Chen Zuoqian kicked the blanket and said, "You're very possessive."

"I couldn't be possessive even if I wanted to be," Lotus said, and then asked suddenly, "Why is Feipu going to Yunnan?"

Chen Zuoqian answered, "He said he's going to take care of some tobacco business; I just let him do as he pleases."

Lotus asked further, "How come he's so friendly with that Young Master Gu?"

Chen Zuoqian laughed out loud and answered, "What's so strange about that; there are some things between men that you don't understand."

Lotus sighed silently. As she caressed Chen Zuoqian's skinny body, a secret thought suddenly came into her head: She wondered what it would be like if Feipu was lying there in bed beside her.

As a sexually experienced woman, Lotus could never forget what happened next. Chen Zuoqian's back was already drenched in sweat, but his efforts were still in vain. She was acutely aware that he had a deep look of fear and confusion in his eyes. "What's going on?" She heard his voice becoming timorous and weak. Lotus's fingers traveled up and down his body like flowing water, but the body under her hands seemed to have ripped apart and gone utterly limp; it grew more and more distant from hers. She understood that Chen Zuoqian's body had suffered a tragic transformation and she felt very strange. She didn't know if she were happy or sad; she felt quite at a loss what to do. She stroked Chen Zuoqian's face and said, "You're too tired; let's sleep a while first."

Chen Zuoqian shook his head and said, "No, no, I don't

believe it." "Then . . . what should we do?" Lotus asked. Chen Zuoqian hesitated a moment and said, "There's one thing that might work, but I don't know if you're willing to do it."

"As long as it makes you happy," Lotus said, "there's no reason I wouldn't do it."

Chen Zuoqian snuggled up to Lotus, biting her on the ear as he whispered something. Lotus didn't understand at first, so he said it again. Lotus understood that time; her face grew red with shame, and silence was her only answer. She rolled over on her side, stared at a dark corner of the room, and suddenly blurted out, "Wouldn't I be just like a dog then?"

Chen Zuoqian answered, "I won't force you. If you don't want to, then forget it."

Lotus still did not say anything; she just curled up like a cat. After a while Chen Zuoqian heard her sobbing softly. He said, "If you don't want to, you don't want to, that's all, but you don't have to start crying." He never imagined Lotus's sobbing would grow louder and louder; she covered her face and let herself cry without restraint.

Chen Zuoqian listened for a while and said, "If you cry any more, I'm leaving."

Lotus went on sobbing.

Chen Zuoqian pulled back the covers, jumped out of bed, and spoke as he put on his clothes. "I never saw a woman like you. A whore already, and you still want to have a chastity arch set up in your honor?"

Chen Zuoqian left in a huff. Lotus sat up in bed, stared into the darkness, and cried for quite a long time. She saw the moonlight shining on the floor through a crack in the curtain, a cold sliver of moonlight, very white and very dull. She heard the sound of her own crying ceaselessly reverberating in her ears; but outside, the garden was as silent as death. At that point she recalled what Chen Zuoqian said just before he left; she trembled violently all over, slammed her fist furiously into the bedding, stared at the darkness, and shouted, "Who's a whore? You're the real whores!"

Many different phenomena demonstrated that it was an unusual winter in the Chen household. When the subject of Chen Zuoqian came up randomly in the conversation of his four wives, they could not prevent an ambiguous expression from showing on their faces; they understood without speaking, and each harbored her own baleful secret. Chen Zuoqian spent every night in Cloud's room, and Cloud's daily demeanor was perfectly normal. When the other three wives observed Cloud, they didn't even try to hide the questioning look in their eyes. "Well Cloud, how ever do you manage to get the Old Master through the night?"

Those mornings Coral put on her theatrical robes and renewed her career under the wisteria vine. Every gesture and every note of her arias and dialogues were done very professionally; the people in the garden saw Coral's long sleeves flowing in the wind, the shadow of her dancing body resembling an enchanting apparition.

> It's the fourth watch in the morning;
> All along the river,
> Human voices are silent.
> A body clinging to a shadow,
> A shadow chained to a body—

I'm doubly sick at heart,
As I think back carefully:
I was only a beautiful face,
With an unlucky fate.
Pity me, bearing my shame and tears all these years,
Wrongly branded a whore and a·slut;
But now there's no escaping, backward or forward;
I might as well throw my waning life to the fishes.
Oh Tenth Sister Du, I'm ready:
Let my fragrance vanish, my jade body perish—
Since I have to die anyway,
I may as well die a bright, clear death.

Lotus listened entranced; she walked over toward Coral, grabbed her skirt, and said, "Don't sing any more; if you go on singing, my soul will fly away. What were you singing?"

Coral raised her sleeve and wiped the rouge from her face, sat down at the stone table, and could only pant. Lotus gave her a silk handkerchief and said, "Look at the way your face is made up with red spots here and white spots there; you look just like a ghost."

Coral said, "There is only a breath's difference between people and ghosts; people are ghosts and ghosts are people."

Lotus said, "What did you just sing? It made me very sad listening to it."

"Tenth Sister Du," Coral answered. "That was the last opera I sang before I left the opera troupe. Tenth Sister Du is about to commit suicide, so of course she sings sorrowfully."

"When will you teach me to sing that piece?" Lotus asked.

Coral stared at Lotus a minute. "You say it so lightly; you

want to commit suicide, too? Whenever you decide to commit suicide, I'll teach you."

Lotus was so surprised she could not speak; she just looked dumbly at Coral's greasepaint-smudged face. She discovered that she did not hate Coral; at least she did not hate her now, even though her words were deliberately hurtful. She knew quite well that Coral, Joy, and herself now had a common enemy in Cloud. But she did not care to express it openly.

Lotus walked to the side of the abandoned well, bent over, and looked down into it; then suddenly she laughed and said, "Ghosts, there really are ghosts in here! Do you know who died in this well?"

Coral remained seated at the stone table. She said, "Who else could it be? One of them was you, and one of them was me."

Lotus said, "Coral, you're always making those macabre jokes; it makes my scalp shiver."

Coral started to smile and said, "Are you afraid? You haven't committed adultery; what are you afraid of? All the women who committed adultery died in this well. It's been that way in the Chen household for many generations."

Lotus took a step back and said, "How horrible. Were they pushed in?"

Coral waved her long flowing sleeves, stood up, and said, "If you ask me, who should I ask? Why don't you go ask those ghosts yourself?" Coral walked to the edge of the well, looked in, too, then chanted in an operatic falsetto, "Wrongfully . . . murdered . . . ghosts . . . ahhhhh . . ."

They talked for a while, off and on, by the side of the well and somehow got around to Chen Zuoqian's secret malady. Coral said, "No matter how good an oil lamp is, there always comes a day when it burns out; I'm only afraid it can't take any more oil. The female principle is too powerful in this garden; it would only be what fate ordains if it injures the masculine principle. Now this is really great: Chen Zuoqian, Old Master Chen, sits on the pot but can't shit; but we're the ones left high and dry, sleeping in empty rooms every night."

As they went on talking, they came again to Cloud. Coral's face was distorted in anger as she cursed her. "She shakes that cheap meat of hers in front of the old man all the time; look how she loves to shake it; she's just dying to lick his asshole and swear it tastes as sweet as it smells. She thinks she can make trouble for all of us; you wait and see how I fix her good some day, make her scream for help."

But Lotus's mind was wandering; whenever she came near that abandoned well, she could not escape those nightmarish hallucinations. She heard the water bubbling up deep inside the well, carrying to the surface the voices of some lost souls; she really heard them. And she also felt a cold vapor, emitted by the well, enveloping her body and spirit. "I'm afraid," Lotus yelled out, as she turned about and ran.

She heard Coral hollering after her, "Hey, what's wrong with you? If you tell on me, I'm not afraid; I didn't say anything."

One day Yiyun came home from school alone, and Cloud immediately suspected something. She asked, "Where's Yirong?"

Yiyun threw her book bag on the ground and said, "She got beat up; she's in the hospital."

Cloud took two male servants and hurried off to the hospital without even asking for any more details. When they returned, it was already dinnertime. Yirong had a bandage on her head, and Cloud had her carried up to the dinner table. Everyone at the table put down their chopsticks and gathered around to look at Yirong's head injuries.

Yirong was Chen Zuoqian's favorite child; he took her on his lap and asked, "Tell me who hit you; tomorrow I'll skin him alive."

Yirong grimaced as she said a boy's name. Chen Zuoqian was enraged. "Whose brat is he? How dare he hit my daughter?"

Cloud wiped her tears as she spoke. "What can you find out by asking her? You won't get to the bottom of this until you find that boy tomorrow and ask him. What heartless little beast would attack a girl so viciously?"

Joy frowned slightly and said, "You go on and eat now. Children are always fighting at school; she's not seriously injured; she'll be all right after a few days rest."

Cloud responded, "First Mistress, you're putting it too lightly; she was almost blinded. How can a girl's tender body stand such a beating? And besides, I really don't blame that boy so much; the one who makes me angry is the one who put him up to it. Otherwise, since they weren't enemies, why would that boy jump out from behind a tree and start hitting Yirong with a club?"

Joy was busy pouring chicken soup into her bowl as she said, "Second Mistress is too suspicious. What reason is there to be so suspicious when children have a falling out at school? Don't start suspecting and accusing people; it's unpleasant for everybody."

Cloud replied coldly, "The real unpleasantness will come

later. How can I just let this go? I'll be damned if I don't get to the bottom of it."

No one expected it the next day when Cloud brought a boy into the dining room; he was rather fat, and his nose was running. Cloud said something softly to him, and the boy walked around the table looking closely at each person's face; suddenly he pointed at Coral and said, "It was her; she gave me a dollar."

Coral looked up and rolled her eyes, then stood up, pushed back her chair, grabbed the boy by the collar, and said, "What did you say? Why would I give you a dollar?"

The boy shouted as he struggled to escape her grip, "You did, you gave me a dollar to beat up Chen Yirong and Chen Yiyun."

Coral slapped the boy hard across the face and cursed, "Bullshit! I don't even know you, you little bastard. Who told you to frame me?"

At that point, Cloud moved in and separated them; feigning a smile, she said, "Even if he picked out the wrong person, I've got a good idea what's going on now." Having said that, she took the boy out of the dining room.

Coral looked extremely angry; she threw her spoon on the table and said, "Shameless."

Cloud was standing right there and retorted, "Whoever's shameless knows it full well. Do I have to reveal the whole sordid business?"

Chen Zuoqian had finally heard enough; he shouted angrily at them, "If you don't intend to eat, then get the hell out of here; all of you get the hell out of here!"

From the beginning to the end of this incident, Lotus remained an outsider; she observed them coldly and didn't say a word. She had guessed right off Coral's role in the affair. She understood a woman with Coral's character: In love or hate she would be violently unrestrained. She felt this whole incident was both cruel and ridiculous, completely irrational; but the strange thing was she sympathized with Coral, not with the innocent little Yirong, and even less with Cloud. She reflected to herself that women are so strange; a woman can understand other people perfectly, but can never completely understand herself.

Lotus had her period again, but at no time did it make her feel as anxious and uneasy as that time. That flow of dark purple menstrual blood represented a merciless assault on her person. She was perfectly aware that her chances of becoming pregnant were becoming hopeless on account of Chen Zuoqian's impotence and indifference. If her barrenness became a certainty, then would she not become as lonely as a single duckweed leaf blown around the Chen family garden?

Lotus discovered she was becoming increasingly sentimental; she burst into tears easily and often. She was crying as she walked to the toilet to dispose of her menstrual wrappings. "Lazy bitch!" she cursed, when she saw a piece of crude toilet paper still floating in the toilet. Swallow never seemed to be able to use the new flush toilet properly; she always forgot to flush after using it. Lotus was just about to flush it down when an extraordinarily intuitive feeling of suspicion gave her an idea. She found a long-handled brush and held her nose as she poked at the toilet paper. When the paper was unfolded to its original shape, the indistinct image of a woman appeared on its surface. Although it was soaked and blurred, the woman's image could still be easily made out at a glance, and it had been painted with God knew what sort of dark red blood.

Lotus understood immediately: The image was of her; Swallow had found another method of secretly cursing her. "She wants me to die so bad, she threw me in the toilet." Her entire body trembled as she fished the paper up out of the toilet; she did not care at all how dirty it was; all the blood in her body was boiling with rage at Swallow's evil behavior.

She held the toilet paper as she burst into the little side room where Swallow was lying on the bed napping.

Swallow said, "Fourth Mistress, what are you doing?"

Lotus threw the toilet paper down in front of her, and Swallow said, "What's that?" When she saw it clearly, her face turned gray, and she started stammering, "I didn't do it."

Lotus was so angry she couldn't speak; she glared at Swallow in despair born of rage. Swallow shrank back on the bed and did not dare to look at her. Then she said, "I was just fooling around; it's not you."

Lotus said, "Who did you learn this sort of evil business from? Are you trying to kill me so you can be a wife in my place?"

Swallow did not dare make a sound; she took that toilet paper and started to throw it out the window, but Lotus yelled at her, "Don't throw it away!" Swallow turned to argue. "But this is filthy; what do you want to keep it for?"

Lotus walked around the room with her arms folded. "If I keep it, of course I have a reason. It's up to you, I'll give you two choices. The first one is public: Take the filthy thing and let the Old Master see it, let everybody see it. I don't want you to serve me; what sort of service is this? You're trying to murder me. The other one is private."

"How private?" Swallow asked timidly. "I'll do anything you ask, but don't send me away."

Lotus smiled. "To keep it private is very simple: All you have to do is eat it."

Swallow started. "Fourth Mistress, what are you saying?"

Lotus cocked her head to look out the window and then repeated with a pause after each word, "All . . . you . . . have . . . to . . . do . . . is . . . eat . . . it."

Swallow went limp all over, fell off the bed onto her knees, covered her face, and started to cry. "It would be better if you just beat me to death."

Lotus said, "I don't feel like beating you; beating you would soil my hands. And you better not accuse me of being too harsh, either. This is known as 'using someone's own methods to control them'; it's written in the classics and can't be wrong."

Swallow, still on her knees, leaned against the wall and continued crying.

Lotus said, "This time you want to stay clean. If you won't eat it, then get out; take your bedding and get out."

Swallow cried for a long time, then suddenly wiped her eyes and choked as she spoke. "I'll eat it. I'll eat it." Then she picked up that piece of soiled toilet paper, stuffed it in her mouth, and let out a ghastly sound of dry gagging.

Lotus looked on coldly. She experienced no real sense of satisfaction; for some unknown reason she felt terribly disappointed and nauseated. "Cheap little hussy." She glanced disgustedly at Swallow and walked out of the side room.

Swallow took sick the next day; she was seriously ill. The doctor came and said she had typhoid. When Lotus heard the news, she felt a secret pain in her heart, as though she had been cut with a dull knife. The news got out somehow, and all of the servants were gossiping about how Lotus made Swallow eat a piece of toilet paper. They said they'd never have guessed from her appearance that Fourth Mistress was more vicious than anybody; they also said there was probably no way to save Swallow's life.

Chen Zuoqian had Swallow taken to the hospital. Lotus hid in her room when they carried Swallow out; but she peeked through a slit in the window curtains and saw her lying on the stretcher, near death. Her bare scalp was visible because so much of her hair had fallen out; it was a dreadful sight. Lotus felt Swallow's dry, jaundiced eyes were looking right through the window curtain and piercing her heart. Later on Chen Zuoqian came to Lotus's room and found her standing there frozen in front of the window. He said, "You're too vicious; you've got everybody gossiping about it and ruining the Chen family's reputation."

Lotus replied, "She's the one who was vicious to me first, cursing me to death every day."

That only made Chen Zuoqian angry. "You're the mistress and she's only a bondservant; how can you descend to her level?"

Lotus was speechless for a moment, but after a while she said weakly, "I didn't mean to make her sick, either; she did it to herself; can you blame it all on me?"

Chen Zuoqian waved his hand and said impatiently, "None of you are easy to deal with; I get a headache every time I see one of you. None of you better give me any more trouble."

After he finished talking, Chen Zuoqian walked out the door; he heard Lotus speak softly behind him. "Good God, how am I supposed to live then?"

Chen Zuoqian looked back, nodded to her, and said, "Any way you want to. You can live any way you please; just don't make any more servants eat toilet paper."

An old female servant called Mama Song came to wait on Lotus. According to what Mama Song herself said, she had been working in the Chen household ever since she was fifteen, well over half her lifetime; why, she had raised Feipu from the time he was a child, and also the Eldest Young Mistress who's now studying in college, she raised her, too. Listening to her bragging about her great seniority in the household, Lotus tried to tease her. "Then you must have raised Old Master Chen since he was a boy, too, huh?"

But Mama Song didn't get the joke; she just smiled and answered, "Oh no, not him. But I did see him marry four wives with my own eyes. When he brought Joy, his First Mistress home, he was only nineteen; he wore a big gold pendant on his chest, and First Mistress had one, too, weighed every bit of half a pound. When he brought Cloud, his Second Mistress, home, they changed it to a small gold medal. And when Third Mistress, Coral, came in, they only wore a few rings on their fingers. By the time he brought you here, we didn't see you wearing anything special. You can see from this that the Chen household is declining day by day."

"If the Chen household is declining day by day, what on earth are you doing here?" Lotus asked.

Mama Song sighed and answered, "I'm used to serving here. If I went back to my old home and lived a leisurely life, I just couldn't get used to it."

Lotus covered her mouth and laughed, then said, "Mama

Song, to tell the honest truth, some people in this world really are fated to be servants."

Mama Song said, "Isn't it the truth? As soon as people are born, they're fated to be masters or servants; if you don't believe it, you still have to believe it. Just look how I wait on you every day; even if someday the sky falls down and the earth caves in, just as long as we're still alive, I'll be waiting on you, but you'll never be waiting on me."

Mama Song was a foolish and garrulous old servant woman. Lotus often grew tired of her, but on many excruciatingly dull nights, when she sat wearily alone for hours in the lamplight, she had to have someone to talk to. She would call Mama Song into her room, and the two of them, master and servant, would talk about the most trivial and uninteresting things, and Lotus would soon feel bored again. As she listened to Mama Song prattle on, her thoughts would wander to some strange and distant place. Actually, she was not listening to what Mama Song was saying; she was merely observing that Mama Song's pale yellow lips wriggled like insect larvae. She felt this way of getting through the nighttime hours was ridiculous. "But," she asked herself, "if I don't spend the time this way, what else can I do?"

One time they started talking about the women who died in the abandoned well. Mama Song said the last one had died forty years ago; she was a concubine of the Elder Master, Chen Zuoqian's father. She even said she had waited on that concubine for about half a year.

"How did she die?" Lotus asked.

Mama Song squinted her eyes mysteriously. "Wasn't it something to do with men and women? The family's shameful secrets can't be told outside, otherwise the Old Master will get after me."

"If you put it that way," said Lotus, "then I'm an outsider, too? All right, don't talk about it; you go on to bed."

Mama Song looked at Lotus's expression, then smiled as she asked, "Fourth Mistress, you really want to hear about such filthy things?"

"You just talk," Lotus answered, "and I'll listen. What's so terrible about that?"

Mama Song lowered her voice and said, "A tofu peddler! She was playing around with a tofu peddler."

"How on earth with a tofu peddler?" Lotus asked blandly.

Mama Song went on. "That fellow's tofu was very famous, so the cook had him deliver tofu, and the two of them met by chance. They were both young and hot-blooded, and they hit it off after exchanging a few flirtatious glances."

Lotus asked, "Who seduced who first?"

Mama Song giggled and replied, "The devil only knows; it's hard to say exactly how things developed; anyway, the man hit on the woman and the woman hit on the man."

Lotus inquired further, "How did anyone know they were carrying on?"

"By spying on them!" Mama Song said. "Elder Master hired a detective to follow them. It was her fault, too, for not lying well enough. She went to that tofu peddler's house and stayed there until after dark without coming out. At first that detective didn't dare disturb them; but after a while he was too hungry to wait any longer, so he kicked open the door and shouted, 'You two may not be hungry, but I am!' "

When she reached that point, Mama Song burst out laughing. Lotus watched Mama Song laughing her head off, but she did not laugh; she sat upright and simply said, "Disgusting." She lit a cigarette, took several greedy drags, and asked suddenly, "Then after she committed adultery, she jumped into the well?"

Mama Song's face took on a deeply secretive expression, and she replied softly, "God knows. Anyway, she died in the well."

Because of that story Lotus began to feel a nameless terror; she did not dare to sleep with the light off. When she turned off the light, everything around her was dark and terrifying. She seemed to see that abandoned well bounding over from under the wisteria vine to come to rest right under her window; she saw the pale luminosity of that hand reaching through her window, dripping wet and beckoning to her.

No one knew that Lotus was terrified by the stories of the abandoned well, but Joy did come to know about her sleeping with the light on. Joy said on many occasions that even the richest family would be impoverished if they didn't turn off the lights at night. Lotus simply pretended not to hear her. She discovered that she had already wearied of verbal fighting among the Chen women; she didn't feel like defending herself, didn't feel like gaining the upper hand, and didn't feel like expressing any interest in the trifles they usually disputed. The things she thought about were all so aimless and irrelevant that even she herself could not make any sense out of them. She felt that if she had nothing to say, she would just keep still. Everyone in the Chen household discovered that Lotus had become silent and uncommunicative, and they guessed it was because she was no longer favored by Old Master Chen.

It was almost time to celebrate the New Year, and there was a buzz of activity throughout the Chen household: slaughtering cattle and pigs, and bringing in all the New Year goods. Outside Lotus's window there was a hubbub every day. Lotus was sitting alone in her room when she suddenly remembered her own birthday; her birthday was only five days after Chen Zuoqian's: the twelfth day of the twelfth lunar month. It had long since gone by, but she only then remembered it; she couldn't help feeling let down. She gave Mama Song some money and sent her out to buy some prepared meats and a bottle of Sichuanese rice wine.

Mama Song asked, "Fourth Mistress, what's the occasion today?"

Lotus simply said, "Don't give me any trouble; I want to see what it feels like to get drunk."

After that Lotus found a small wine cup, placed it on the table, and sat down to stare at it, just as though she were looking at a tiny baby of twenty years ago being held to the breast of a mother she never knew. The events of the intervening twenty years were not very clear to her mind; she only remembered her father's blood-soaked hand still trying to reach up and stroke her hair. Lotus closed her eyes, and her mind once again was a complete blank; the only thing she was clear about was the concept of her birthday. Her birthday. She picked up the wine cup and examined the bottom; there were a few brown specks of dirt. "The twelfth of the twelfth month," she said to herself. "How could I forget such an easy day to remember?"

No one in the world besides herself knew that the twelfth day of the twelfth month was Lotus's birthday. No one but herself was going to come and give a birthday party for her.

Mama Song was gone a long time before she finally came back and placed a package of salted pork lungs and intestines on the table. Lotus said, "Why did you buy those filthy things? Who wants to eat that?"

Mama Song looked Lotus up and down very strangely and suddenly blurted out, "Swallow's dead. She died in the hospital."

Lotus was very shaken, but she calmed herself down and asked, "When did she die?"

"I don't know," answered Mama Song. "I only heard she called out your name just before she died."

Lotus blanched slightly. "Why would she call out my name? Do they think I killed her?"

Mama Song said, "Don't go getting angry; I only told you what I heard people say. Life and death are fated by Heaven; you're not to blame."

"Where's her body now?" Lotus asked further.

"Her family took it back to their village," answered Mama Song. "The whole family was weeping and wailing; it was really pitiful."

Lotus opened the bottle of wine, sniffed the aroma, and said dryly, "There's nothing much to cry about; when you're alive you suffer; when you die it's all over. Dying is better than living."

Lotus was sitting alone sipping the warm rice wine when she heard some indistinct but familiar footsteps; the door curtain was thrown open with a loud flap, and a dark man burst into the room. She turned and looked at him for a long time before she finally recognized Feipu. Hurriedly, she covered the meat and wine with the tablecloth so as not to let Feipu see them; but he had already seen them, and he shouted, "Well, well, so you're actually drinking wine."

"What are you doing back?" Lotus asked.

"If I don't die, I'm always going to come home sometime," answered Feipu.

Feipu had changed a great deal in the many days since she'd last seen him; his face was dark, he looked a little more robust, but his face expressed exhaustion. Lotus noticed he had dark rings under his eyes, and she could see thin threads of blood in his cornea; these features were as if stamped from the same mold as cast his father Chen Zuoqian's face.

"Why did you start drinking wine; you trying to drown your sorrows in wine?"

"Can sorrows really be drowned out with wine? I was giving myself a birthday party."

"It's your birthday? How old are you?"

"Who cares how old I am; each day I get through is another day. You want a glass of wine? Wish me a happy birthday."

"I'll have a glass and hope you live to be ninety-nine."

"Nonsense. I certainly don't want to live that long; save your flattery for the Old Master."

"How long do you want to live, then?"

"I guess it depends on the situation; whenever I get tired of living, I'll just stop living; it's as simple as that."

"Then I'll drink another glass so that you can live a fairly long time. If you die, then I won't have anyone here to talk to."

The two of them slowly sipped their wine and talked once again about Feipu's tobacco business. Feipu said with self-derision, "The chickens flew the coop and the eggs were smashed; I'm certainly not made for doing business. I not only didn't make any money, I actually lost several thousand; but I did have a hell of a good time this trip."

Lotus said, "Your life is already happy enough as it is. What do you have to be unhappy about?"

Feipu quickly responded, "Don't you go telling the Old Master; otherwise he'll give me another lecture."

Lotus said, "I certainly don't care to meddle in your family's affairs. And besides, he treats me like a worn-out old cleaning rag now; he doesn't even look at me any more. Why would I want to tell him anything you did wrong?"

After drinking so much wine, Lotus's speech was no longer very composed. She let her voice reveal her feelings for Feipu, and Feipu naturally sensed the change. He started feeling very soft and gentle; his face grew red and hot, and from his belt he detached a small pouch with a brightly painted dragon-and-phoenix picture. He handed it to Lotus. "I brought this back from Yunnan. I want to give it to you as a birthday present."

Lotus glanced at the little pouch, smiled ambiguously, and said, "Only a woman can give such a pouch to her sweetheart; how can you change things around this way?"

Feipu was slightly embarrassed; then he suddenly grabbed the pouch out of Lotus's hand. "If you don't want it, then give it back to me; somebody else gave it to me in the first place."

Lotus said, "You're a fine hypocrite, trying to trick me with a souvenir from someone else; won't it dirty my hand if I take it?"

Feipu put the pouch back on his belt, and said awkwardly, "I didn't really plan to give it to you; I was only fooling you."

Lotus frowned slightly. "I'm used to being fooled; everybody comes here to fool me, and now you come to have some fun fooling me, too."

Feipu lowered his head, looked up occasionally to steal a furtive glance at Lotus's expression, and then remained silent.

Suddenly Lotus asked, "Who gave you the pouch?"

Feipu's knees bounced up and down a couple of times, and he said, "You better not ask that."

The two of them sat there, vacantly sipping their wine. Lotus turned the wine cup around playfully on her palm and looked at Feipu sitting directly opposite her. His head was lowered, his youthful crop of hair was thick and black, his neck stuck straight out, strong and proud, and a few fine blue veins twitched slightly in his eyes. Lotus felt a liquid warmth in her heart. An unfamiliar desire swept like a spring breeze throughout her body; she felt out of breath, and the image of Coral and the doctor's legs intertwined beneath the mahjong table once again occupied her mind. She looked at her own long, lovely legs, resembling finely turned rolls of thin gauze, as they slid warmly and passionately toward their goal—Feipu's feet, knees, and legs; now she was powerfully aware of his physical presence. Her expression grew misty as her lips parted weakly and trembled slightly. She heard the sound of something being torn apart in the air, or perhaps the sound was only coming from somewhere deep inside her body.

Feipu raised his head; a look of passion poured forth from his eyes as he stared at Lotus. His body, especially his legs, remained stiffly poised in his original posture. He did not move a muscle. Lotus closed her eyes; she listened to her irregular heart beat—one fast, one slow—as she leaned her legs fully against Feipu's and waited for something to happen.

It seemed as though several years went by in an instant. Then Feipu pulled his knees back, crouched sideways against the back of his chair like someone who'd been beaten up, and said in a hoarse voice, "This is no good."

Lotus mumbled like one just waking from a dream, "What's no good?"

Feipu raised his arms slowly and bowed slightly. "It's no good. I'm still afraid." His face twisted in pain as he spoke. "I'm still afraid of women. Women are too frightening."

Lotus said, "I don't understand what you mean."

Feipu just rubbed his face and said, "Lotus, I like you, I'm not kidding."

"You like me, but you treat me this way."

Feipu was nearly choking; he shook his head, and his eyes constantly avoided Lotus's gaze as he spoke. "I can't change; Heaven is punishing me; generations of Chen men have always lusted after women, but when it came to me, I just couldn't do it. Ever since I was little, I thought women were frightening. I'm afraid of women. I'm especially afraid of the women in our family. You're the only one I'm not afraid of, but I still can't do anything. Now do you understand?"

Lotus had long since started to weep. She turned her head away and spoke very softly. "I understand; you don't have to explain. I don't blame you at all now, really, I don't blame you at all."

Lotus got drunk after Feipu left. Her face was flushed as she danced aimlessly around her room smashing things left and right. Mama Song came in but could not control her; all she could do was call for the Old Master. When Chen Zuoqian came into the room, Lotus threw her arms around him; her breath reeked of wine, and she babbled incoherently. He asked Mama Song, "Why did she start drinking?"

"How should I know?" answered Mama Song, "If something was troubling her, would she tell me?"

Chen Zuoqian sent Mama Song to Joy's room to fetch some medicine to cure drunkenness, but Lotus started yelling, "I forbid you to go! I forbid you to tell that old witch!"

Chen Zuoqian threw Lotus down on the bed in disgust. "Look at yourself! You're acting crazy! Aren't you afraid people will laugh at you?"

Lotus jumped up again, hooked her arms around Chen Zuoqian's neck, and pleaded, "Old Master, stay with me tonight. Nobody cares about me. Love me tonight, Old Master."

Chen Zuoqian answered in exasperation, "How could I love you in this state? I'd be better off loving a dog."

Joy heard that Lotus was drunk and came right over. She chanted, "Amitabha Buddha preserve us," a few times in the doorway and then rushed in and pulled Lotus and Chen Zuoqian apart. She asked Chen Zuoqian, "Should I give her some medicine?"

Chen Zuoqian nodded his head.

She tried to hold Lotus's mouth open and force some medicine down her throat, but Lotus pushed her and sent her staggering across the room.

"All of you grab her," Joy shouted. "Show this drunken bitch who's boss here!"

Chen Zuoqian and Mama Song both took hold and restrained Lotus; but just as Joy got the medicine into her mouth, Lotus spat it out all over Joy's face.

"Old Master, why don't you stop her?" Joy demanded. "This drunken bitch is trying to start a rebellion."

Chen Zuoqian held Lotus firmly around the waist, but then Lotus simply collapsed against him.

"Old Master," she said, "please don't go. I'll do anything you want tonight; I'll stroke it; I'll suck it; I'll do anything you ask me to, only please don't go."

Chen Zuoqian was too furious to talk.

Joy could not stand to hear any more. She rushed over and slapped Lotus across the face. "Shameless slut! Old Master, look what's come of your spoiling her so!"

The south wing was thrown into a terrible uproar; people

ran over across the garden to enjoy the spectacle. Chen Zuoqian had Mama Song block the door and not let anybody in to see the show. Joy said, "She's brought enough shame on herself already, and you're still afraid of somebody seeing her? How can she face anyone from now on?"

"You shut your mouth!" Chen Zuoqian barked. "I think you need a little sobering-up medicine, too."

Mama Song put her hand over her mouth to stop herself from laughing, then walked over to the porch to block the door; she saw a crowd of people standing outside the window gawking. She saw the Eldest Young Master, Feipu, walking slowly toward her with his hands in his pockets. Just as she was wondering whether or not to let him in, he turned around and walked off in the opposite direction.

After the first big snowstorm, the barren and desolate winter garden was covered with a layer of rabbit-fur snow while the tree branches and the house eaves were transformed into exquisitely carved crystals, glittering and transparent. Some of the youngest children of the Chen household ran out into the yard early in the morning to build a snowman; then they had a snow fight, chasing each other around under Lotus's window. Lotus even heard Feilan's high-pitched bawling after he had fallen down in the snow. The light from the snow also reflected blindingly through the windowpane. Then there was the never-flagging sound of the clock ticking on the wall. Everything was palpably real, but Lotus felt as though she had returned from a trip to the Heavenly Kingdom; she could not believe that she was still living and that she would have to live for another day in the same old manner.

She had seen the dead Swallow during the night; in death, Swallow was a bald-headed woman. She had seen Swallow standing outside, pushing in on her window, she kept pushing and pushing on her window. Lotus was not the least bit afraid. She was waiting for Swallow's cruel revenge. She lay there very calmly. She knew the window would soon open.

Swallow crept in silently wearing some sort of hairpiece rolled up like a rich woman's chignon.

Lotus asked her, "Where did you buy that hairpiece?"

Swallow answered, "The God of Death has everything."

Then Lotus saw Swallow take a long hairpin out from the back of her chignon and stab at her chest with it. She felt a sudden jab of pain and quickly fell into a dark abyss. She knew she had died; she was absolutely certain she had died, and she was dead for such a long time it seemed as though ten years had gone by.

Lotus pulled a robe over her shoulders and sat there on the bed; she did not believe her death was only a dream. She noticed there really was a long hairpin stuck into the brocade bed covers; she picked it up and held it on her palm. It was cold as ice. This, too, was no dream, but an absolute certainty. "Why am I still alive, then? Where did Swallow disappear to?"

Lotus discovered that the window was partly open, just as in her dream. The air rushed in from outside, fresh and chilly, but she could still sniff out the lingering odor of death left behind by Swallow. It had snowed, and only half the world still remained. The other half was invisible; it had been silently wiped away. Perhaps this was simply an incomplete death.

"Why did I die halfway and then stop?" Lotus asked herself. "It's really strange. Where's the other half, then?"

Coral walked out of the north compound. As she walked

across the snow wearing a black mink coat, the healthful glow of her expression and the beauty of her glorious deportment virtually transformed the color of the air around her. As she walked by Lotus's window, she called to her, "Drunken lady, are you sobered up now?"

Lotus asked, "Are you going out in all this snow?"

Coral knocked on the window, "Who's afraid of a little snow? As long as I can be happy, I'll go out even if it's snowing daggers."

As Coral walked by with her hips swaying, for some unknown reason Lotus looked at her and called out, "You better be careful."

Coral looked back and threw her a winsome smile.

Her smile made a deep impression on Lotus. That was the last time Lotus saw Coral's captivating smile.

It was afternoon when Coral was brought back home by two male servants. Cloud walked behind them cracking melon seeds all the way. The way in which events reached this conclusion was quite simple: Cloud caught Coral and the doctor in bed at a nearby Inn. Cloud threw Coral's clothes outside and then gloated, "You stinking whore, did you think you could get away from me?"

Lotus watched Coral leave and come home on the same day, but it was not the same Coral in the morning and the afternoon. As Coral was dragged into the north compound, her hair was disheveled, and her eyes glowed with anger as she cursed everyone who was dragging her along. She cursed Cloud, "If I live, I'll skin you alive, and if I die, I'll still cut your heart out and feed it to the dogs."

Cloud did not say a word, but just kept on cracking melon seeds.

Feilan picked up one of Coral's shoes and shouted, "Your shoe fell off! Your shoe fell off!" all the way home.

Lotus did not see Chen Zuoqian. After a while Chen Zuoqian went to the north compound alone; by that time the north compound was already locked.

Lotus had no heart to go next door and investigate; she was extraordinarily depressed as she listened carefully for any sounds from Coral's room. She was very anxious to know how Chen Zuoqian would punish Coral, but not the slightest sound came from the adjacent room. A male servant stood outside the door with a ring full of keys, locking and unlocking the door. Chen Zuoqian came out again, stood there a moment gazing out at the snowy garden, shook his hands, and walked toward the south compound.

"What a lot of snow; still, a timely snow promises a good harvest," Chen Zuoqian said, and his face was much calmer than she expected. Lotus even sensed a certain feeling of genuine calm in his expression. Lotus leaned against the bed and looked straight into Chen Zuoqian's eyes; she saw a cold glint there that made her uneasy and fearful. She asked, "What are you all going to do to Coral?"

Chen Zuoqian took out an ivory toothpick and picked his teeth before he answered. "What can we do to her? She knows herself what has to be done."

Lotus said, "Why don't you give her a chance?"

Chen Zuoqian laughed and said, "What has to be done will be done."

Lotus couldn't sleep all night; her thoughts were tangled in confusion. She listened constantly for movement in the adjacent room while she thought only of her own situation. Every time she thought of her own life, however, everything was a complete void, as elusive as the snow outside her window; half of it was real, but the other half melted into illusion. At midnight she suddenly heard Coral singing her Peking opera. She could hardly believe her ears, so she held her breath and listened again. It really was Coral, singing her Peking opera on her night of suffering.

Sigh for a beautiful woman,
Born under an unlucky star,
Her perfect love match,
A river flowing east.
A heartless lover sends no news,
Crying on the flowers and weeping to the moon,
Only increase my dark sadness.
Tears on my pillow accompany the rain on the steps,
Falling ceaselessly on the other side of the window.
Beyond the mountains are still more mountains;
When will his great sword return?
I want to be a stone sentinel watching for my man;
I long to send a message, but it's much too hard.
I still have this pillow of horn and our brocade quilt,
Bright as white silk,
But I'm afraid sleeping alone there's no cure
For a half-cold bed.

The atmosphere in the back garden was very strange throughout the night. Lotus kept tossing and turning, and found it very hard to sleep. Later on she heard Feilan crying and yelling; it seemed like someone was carrying him out of the north compound. Suddenly Lotus could no longer remember what Coral's face looked like: She only saw the image of Coral and the doctor's legs intertwined under the mahjong table; that picture flitted constantly in front of her eyes, and she vaguely recalled their image as thin as paper blown in a cold wind. "How pitiful," Lotus mumbled to herself as she heard the first morning rooster crow out beyond the garden wall. After that the entire world was once again as still as death. "I'm going to die again," Lotus thought. "Swallow is going to push open the window again."

Lotus lay there in a daze, half-asleep and half-awake. Just at the crack of dawn, she was startled by the confused sound of many footsteps. The sound of the footsteps went from the north compound in the direction of the wisteria vine.

Lotus pulled the curtain back just a little and saw the shadowy figures of several people moving in the darkness; they were carrying someone over toward the wisteria vine. Lotus could sense that it was Coral; Coral struggled silently as she was being carried toward the wisteria vine. She had been gagged and could not make a sound. "What are they going to do?" wondered Lotus. "What are they carrying Coral over there for?"

In the darkness the men reached the edge of the abandoned well; they surrounded the well and were busy for a moment. Then Lotus heard a deep hollow sound as though a huge white splash echoed out of the bottom of the well. Someone had been thrown into the well. Coral had been thrown into the well.

Everything was completely silent for about two minutes until Lotus let out a wild, blood-curdling wail. When Chen Zuoqian burst into her room, he saw her standing barefoot in the middle of the floor, frantically tearing her hair out. Lotus went on wailing distractedly; the look in her eyes was dull and lifeless, and her face resembled nothing more than a sheet of white paper. Chen Zuoqian guided her over onto the bed; he clearly understood that this was Lotus's final day; that young college girl Lotus was no more. Chen Zuoqian pressed the blanket down over her body and asked, "What did you see? What did you see?"

"Murder," Lotus answered. "Murder."

"Nonsense," Chen Zuoqian said. "What did you see? You didn't see anything. You're out of your mind."

Later that morning the Chen household was rocked by two startling stories. Third Mistress Coral had thrown herself into the well to drown her shame, and Fourth Mistress Lotus had gone insane. Everyone generally agreed that Coral's death was perfectly natural and reasonable; licentious women and adulterous wives never come to a good end. But why would the young, perfectly healthy, and refined Fourth Mistress Lotus suddenly lose her mind? Those who were most familiar with the inner workings of the Chen household said that was very simple: "The fox mourns the death of the hare." Creatures of the same kind grieve for one another, that's all.

In the spring of the following year, Chen Zuoqian, Old Master Chen, took his fifth wife, Bamboo. When Bamboo first entered the Chen compound, she often saw a young woman sitting alone under the wisteria vine, or, sometimes walking around and around the abandoned well; as she walked, she talked down into the center of the well. Bamboo saw that she was very clean, pretty, and refined, not at all like a madwoman.

She asked the women around her who she was, and they simply told her, "She used to be the Fourth Mistress; something's wrong with her mind."

Bamboo said, "She's very strange. What's she saying to the well?"

They repeated Lotus's words for her: " 'I won't jump, I won't jump.' She says she won't jump into the well."

Lotus says she won't jump into the well.

NINETEEN
THIRTY-FOUR
ESCAPES

Perhaps my father was a mute fetus. His profound reticence left my family shrouded in a murky gray fog for fully half a century. During this half-century, I was born, came to maturity, flourished, and grew old and decrepit. The vital blood and semen of father's Maple Village continues to circulate through my body; perhaps I was also a mute fetus. I, too, am profoundly reticent. I was born under the sign of the tiger, and left home and came to the city the year I turned nineteen. Thinking back on the years of my youth, how like a tiger cub I was, crouched under the eaves of my father's house, my whole body glowing with a dim blue sheen as I gazed deep into the penumbra of the family fog that grew ever thicker the longer it drifted along, following the changes of the sun and moon. Living under that penumbra were the last eight surviving relatives of my clan.

Last winter I stood under a streetlight in the city examining my shadow. I realized this was going to become a habit that would grow and spread throughout my body. The city light is always as white and still as snow. I discovered that my shadow was wildly and weirdly elongated on the sidewalk, like a reed blowing in the wind; I was being followed by my shadow; I pushed my shoulders forward and leaned into the metallic pole of a high-voltage neon lamp. Looking back at my shadow on the ground, I saw that in the dead of night in the city it took on the image of a fugitive. Some sort of congenital fear and trembling made me cover my head and scurry away. I am like my father. As I ran wildly through the urban night's eerie light, my father's shadow was shouting and chasing me from behind in a surrealistic pursuit that transcended the nature of ordinary matter. I understand: Running for my life that time was an escape.

I am acutely aware that strange experiences like these are always related to recollections of the past. As I recall, on many evenings in the past my father stood in front of my high metal bed, with one hand stroking my face and one hand held to his forehead, while he turned his head back and stared at our shadows changing shape on the floor; several years went by in this way, and I grew to be twenty-six.

You are my good friends. Let me tell you, I am my father's son; I am not called Su Tong. In the city I have developed many habits inherited from my father that I unfurl before your eyes like a white funeral flag. I like to study my shadow. Last winter, after drinking some sorghum wine with you, I knocked over a bottle of red ink, and drew pictures of my eight relatives on the wall. I also wrote a poem that I intended to insert between the pages of the leftover history book of my youth. It was a nonsensical and incoherent poem in defense of myself. In the poem I imagined the glorious years of my clan's past; I imagined also the red and black lines of misfortune slashed across their veins. Several beginnings and endings appeared one after another. In the end I broke down in tears; I lost my voice; I smeared the red ink over the paper with all my might, smeared the poem until it was impossible to distinguish the words. I remember the first few lines were written with extraordinary difficulty:

> *My old Maple Village home*
> *Has been silent for many years,*
> *And we*
> *Who have escaped here*
> *Are like wandering blackfish*
> *For whom*
> *The way back is eternally lost.*

If I go now and push open the door to my father's house, I will only see my father and my mother; my other six relatives are not at home. They are still out wandering somewhere like blackfish in the mud. They have not yet arrived at that wood-framed house.

My father likes dry straw. Throughout the four seasons of the year, his body gives off the crisp, pure, pungent aroma of dry straw. That pungent aroma is born out of the places where his skin is wrinkled and folded. In spring and autumn the people on the street always see him staggering home from the suburbs, balancing two baskets of dry straw on a pole as he dodges in through our front gate. That lovely, soft, yellowish-brown straw is stacked into piles, and kept in both the main room and the small room I once lived in; father regularly lies down on those piles of straw and loudly curses my short, delicate mother.

There is no way I can explain a person's reluctance to part with his straw, just as there is no way I can explain the principles of Heaven and the rules of human morality. If I trace back my bloodline, perhaps our clan's ancestral home was strewn with this kind of straw; perhaps my eight relatives all dropped into this world on that straw in our ancestral home, carrying with them this peculiar memory. When my father looks at those piles of straw, he can transform himself into a wizard. When he picks up a handful of straw and examines it closely in the last rays of the afternoon sun, he can smell the breath of his deceased father. Grandmother Jiang, Grandfather Chen Baonian, Elder Brother Dingo (Gouzai), and the little woman Huanzi are all given form and substance from that straw.

But it's not my destiny ever to see these relatives. As I said before, my father was, perhaps, a mute fetus. When I first learned that all of us together made up one particular link in the great teeming chain of human life, my heart was filled with sweet sadness; I wanted to explore the springs of my bloodline; I used to pester my mother for stories about my ancestors. But my mother did not know any; she was not from Maple Village. "Why don't you go ask your father," she said, "when he's been drinking."

My father was unusually quiet when he was drunk and he would, at such times, generally sleep in the same bed with my mother. On nights like that the look in my father's slightly bloodshot eyes was distant and mysterious. He would stretch out his arm and hold my mother tightly; press his mouth, reeking of liquor, up against my ear; and slowly spit out the names of those relatives: Grandmother Jiang, Grandfather Chen Baonian, Elder Brother Dingo, little woman Huanzi. He would also repeat over and over again: "Nineteen thirty-four. Do you know?" Then he would tell me in a loud voice, "Nineteen thirty-four was a year of disaster."

Nineteen thirty-four.
Do you know?
Nineteen thirty-four was a year of disaster.

For a certain period of time my history book was filled with the year 1934. Nineteen thirty-four burst forth with powerful rays of purple light that arrested all my thoughts. It is a faraway age that can never exist again. For me it is also a growth ring on an ancient tree; I can sit straight up astride it and reexperience the vicissitudes of life in 1934. If I sit straight up astride it, the first thing I will see is my grandmother, Jiang, floating out of history.

Grandmother Jiang's long, skinny feet pressed firmly and motionlessly into the cold, muddy, wet rice paddy. She was a perfect picture of a rural woman in early spring. Her face was completely splattered with mud; her cheekbones stuck out prominently; and she hung her head to listen to the sounds of the baby in her womb. She felt herself to be just like a wild, uncultivated mountain. After the men had hacked and cleared it, they planted sons and daughters in her body one after another, just like trees. The sound of the unborn child was like the wind blowing and shaking her, blowing and shaking a wild, uncultivated mountain.

The spring sun comes up very early in my old Maple Village home; the first white rays of sunlight trickle down in a winding path following the hilly landscape just slightly enough to warm a group of long-term workers in the wet rice paddy. Grandmother Jiang was a most unusual long-term worker. She worked for the wealthy landlord Chen Wenzhi's family, soaking all day in Chen Wenzhi's ten-mile-long unbroken stretch of wet rice paddy, transplanting at least ten thousand rice seedlings.

Grandmother Jiang constantly felt the presence of the black brick building on the northern hillside; a small patch of sunlight that had been dyed black undulated rhythmically up and down her back. The shadow of the man standing on the roof of that far-off black brick building belonged to Chen Wenzhi. He was gazing at Grandmother Jiang through a pair of Japanese binoculars. That spring Grandmother Jiang wore only a backless undergarment of red cloth, shaped like a round bib, which revealed her strong, slim, masculine-looking back. Her back gave off a consistently warm vapor; but the scene was hazy from a distance, and Chen Wenzhi kept wiping the lenses of his binoculars with his shirt-sleeves.

Grandmother Jiang's movements were unusually beautiful; relying on her long arms and legs, she planted the rice seedlings in a powerful and unconstrained manner, a manner pleasing both to the eye and the mind. Chen Wenzhi sighed over Grandmother Jiang's work in the paddy fields; he stood on the roof of the black brick building for the entire morning secretly observing Grandmother Jiang's each and every move, his sallow, deeply wrinkled face covered with an expression of obsession. After midday, Grandmother Jiang waded out of the paddy field; she threw a short coat haphazardly over her shoulders and walked along in the midst of the other long-term workers, shaking out two dripping-wet bunches of rice seedlings; her round red undergarment was swelled out noticeably; through his binoculars, the wealthy landlord Chen Wenzhi could also see that Grandmother Jiang was pregnant.

The women of my clan are all extremely good at bearing children. Then, in 1934, Grandmother Jiang was pregnant once again. My father was just then longing to enter this world, and I was lying in wait, peeping out at them from the mouth of another side grotto of history. That was the form the chain of humanity took when it was fastened upon my body.

That black brick building always stands out prominently when I imagine the life of Maple Village and its environs in the early years. Whether that black brick building existed or not is meaningless; what is important is that it has already become a powerful symbol accompanying my image of Grandmother Jiang; or, one could say that the black brick building is merely a stage prop given to me by Grandmother Jiang in order to call forth my amazing powers of imagination.

All of the old people of the Chen clan who actually saw Grandmother Jiang tell me she was an ugly woman. She didn't own a backless undergarment of red cloth shaped like a round bib, and she didn't have the big breasts of a peasant woman to fill out such an undergarment, either.

Grandfather Chen Baonian was eighteen when he took this

big-footed woman of Jiang Family Village as his wife. They made their bows to Heaven and Earth and were married on the third day of the first lunar month. The people of Maple Village gathered in the Chen family's ancestral temple and drank up three big pots of congee made of vegetables and red beans fried in lard. Chen Baonian also crowded around the iron pot and drank; while he was waiting with unbearable anxiety, a red bamboo wedding palanquin came slowly into view. Chen Baonian's face was red as a beet when he threw down his bowl and shouted out joyously, "Chen Baonian's cock has someplace to live now!"

And so Grandmother Jiang stepped down from her red bamboo wedding palanquin accompanied by a burst of raucous laughter on the part of the people of Maple Village. She, too, heard Chen Baonian's joyful cheer. As Chen Baonian took Grandmother Jiang's stiff, sweaty hand and walked toward the ancestral temple, he discovered that this woman from Jiang Family Village, whose face was veiled by a red scarf, was a full head taller than he was; his gaze traveled down her body, resting at last on her feet; wearing a pair of embroidered cloth shoes, her feet were large and sturdy as she stepped blindly, with her toes pointed outward, into the Chen family's ancestral temple.

A murky gray spike of green bristle grass grew out of Chen Baonian's heart; all the time he was bowing in front of his ancestors' spirit tablets, he kept curling up his sharp little finger and furiously digging his fingernail into the palm of his bride's hand. Chen Baonian's expression was calm while he was doing this, and he cocked his head to hear the woman's voice. The woman only murmured noncommittally from somewhere deep in her throat; just then, Chen Baonian smelled on her body the rank odor of a sacrificial animal in heat.

This marriage was one act in the history of my clan that took place sixty years ago; to this day it still deserves to be recollected. They say Grandfather Chen Baonian left home seven days after his marriage and went into the city to look for work. Chen Baonian had two round bundles of thin green bamboo strips draped over his shoulders as he staggered un-steadily out of Maple Village at dawn. All along the road he gluttonously wolfed down a pile of hard-boiled eggs he had brought in his pocket, eating all the way to Horsebridge. In the town of Horsebridge a crowd of various sorts of craftsmen who were opening up early saw Chen Baonian hurrying down the road; he looked completely shameless with the fly of his long black pants open and his colorful semen-spattered underpants showing through. Someone shouted, "Chen Baonian, button your fly!"

"Meddlesome dog," answered Chen Baonian, "it's easier to get it in and out with my fly open!" He threw some eggshells on the stranger's head and walked angrily out of Horsebridge. Ever since then, when the people of Horsebridge talk about Chen Baonian, they always recall this vulgar greeting he once gave them.

Seven days passed in primordial darkness with the door bolted. The door opened on the seventh day, and the married woman from Jiang Family Village stood in the doorway and poured a wooden bucket of water out on Maple Village. After that the women of Maple Village swept into my ancestral home like a swarm of bees and buzzed furiously all around Grandmother Jiang. They saw that the window facing south had been nailed shut by that bastard Chen Baonian. My ances-tral home was dark and dank. Grandmother Jiang sat on the edge of the bed and glanced furtively with brightly shining eyes at everyone. The smell of a sacrificial animal in heat permeated the entire room. She was afraid to talk as she clumsily held an article made of bamboo between her knees and began to work. The women saw clearly that the bamboo article was Chen Baonian's "bamboo woman"; that big-breasted bamboo woman used to "sleep" on the corner of the bed. Grandmother Jiang suddenly smiled at everyone, pursed her lips together, and pulled a strip of bamboo up out of the bamboo woman's head; the more she pulled, the longer it grew, and the bamboo woman's head slowly unraveled and fell to the floor. Grandmother Jiang's slender fingers were very strong and dexterous; right from the beginning she made a deep impression on the people of Maple Village.

"Your man is a master bamboo craftsman. A good bamboo man has a thick money belt with coins clinking all around his waist," all the Maple Village women told grandmother Jiang.

Grandmother Jiang sat on the bed thinking about Chen Baonian, the master bamboo craftsman. His hands were honed as sharp as his bamboo knife; when he touched her, she felt the pain of their cutting edges; she thought that she was just another strip of bamboo being cut and planed by Chen Baonian. All you bitches of Maple Village, do you know that Chen Baonian is also a little sorcerer who can predict women's futures? He says that in ten years the women of Maple Village are all going to be killed off; in the future the woman he married from Jiang Family Village will be a pestilential star of evil blazing down on the history of Maple Village.

Chen Baonian had never read *The Hemp-Clad Adept's Miraculous Physionomia*. His amazingly acute sensitivity to female physiognomy derived from various secret revelations and personal life experiences. In the past, whenever he encountered a woman with a round face and fat buttocks, his eyes would flush with red and he would doggedly pursue her, not returning until his curiosity was satisfied. On the first night after Chen Baonian took a wife, the moonlight flowed like water into my ancestral home; he sat astride Grandmother Jiang's body looking down at her face and sighing incessantly. His hands, like bamboo knives, planed across Grandmother Jiang's soundly sleeping face. Her high, protruding cheeks were scraped by Chen Baonian's bamboo-knife hands until they bled.

Grandmother Jiang was finally awakened by the pain. Chen Baonian's hands pressed down on her face like a powerful curse, penetrating the deepest recesses of her mind and body. She tried with all her might to push him off, but Chen Baonian sat bolt upright and immovable like a shaman gradually entering a demonic trance. She saw the man's pupils grow very deep, and in the deepest spot a swirl of clouds were roiling around like an ocean. The man spoke to her in a low, deep voice. "You are a star of evil."

Chen Baonian repeated his prediction on each of those seven dark nights.

I once went to old Bamboo Town on the lower reaches of the Long River, and followed the dilapidated old city wall looking for the ruins of Chen's Bamboo Goods Store. Today this city has long since lost its unsullied country air and its sweetly arresting aroma from the bamboo strips lying everywhere. I stood there with a red canvas pack on my back in the shade of the city wall; my gaze wrapped around the gravel road, like a wild kudzu vine hanging down off the wall, and the people walking on it. Which of you white-haired old people ever saw my grandfather Chen Baonian?

Grandfather Chen Baonian was in Bamboo Town all eight times it was reported to him that Grandmother Jiang was pregnant. The boy he would send to the countryside to collect bamboo strips told him, "Your old lady's pregnant again, her stomach's as big as a ball."

Chen Baonian inhaled slowly like he had a toothache and asked, "How big exactly?"

The boy pointed to the sesame oil shop next door. "As big as a sesame oil pressing vat."

"About eight months?" mused Chen Baonian.

The boy said, "Why do you have to ask yourself how many months? Every time you go home and shoot off that hundred-shots-a-hundred-hits pistol of yours, not one bullet's ever fired in vain."

Chen Baonian finally smiled wryly and sighed. "That bitch's really got a fire in her belly."

I can imagine Chen Baonian's momentary confusion concerning women and their procreative powers. His bamboo goods shop was illuminated by the bright blood of Grandmother Jiang's female nature; all the bamboo chairs, mats, baskets, and plaques hanging on the walls and from the rafters or piled on the floor vibrated in unison, conducting the plain and vigorous cries of women and children to assail his nerves. Would the only birth that he ever witnessed, that of Elder Brother Dingo, rise up again before Chen Baonian's eyes? At that time my grandmother Jiang was a primitive and totally inexperienced mother. She lay on a pile of golden-yellow straw in the ancestral home, her sallow face silently solemn, her two hands clinging tightly to a bunch of dry straw. Chen Baonian leaned against the door; he saw Grandmother Jiang squeeze yellow drops of juice from the dry straw she held in her hands. He felt his whole body tremble, his energy totally sapped, but bright flames danced about in Grandmother Jiang's eyes; those flames kept burning through the entire birth process, right up until Elder Brother Dingo dropped out wailing onto that pile of straw. This scene was as wondrous and moving as a sunset by the riverside. Chen Baonian watched with his own eyes as the house mice, nurtured by generations of the Chen family, jumped out from the corners of every room and danced joyfully in a circle around that bloodstained pile of straw; his wife wore a wan smile as she nodded respectfully in the direction of those magical mice.

My grandfather Chen Baonian spent all of 1934 in this town developing his hidden potential by eating, drinking, whoring, and gambling to his heart's content, without once returning to my old Maple Village home. The curtain of night was falling when I came upon the ruins of Chen's Bamboo Goods Store in a narrow, dilapidated hundred-year-old lane; an old-fashioned dusky streetlight shone once again on a man from Maple Village; I looked bemusedly all around. Clearly that wood-framed house had long since sunk into the depths of history; could I still discover the traces of my grandfather Chen Baonian's depravity in Bamboo Town half a century ago?

Among my deceased relatives, Dingo, the Chen family's eldest son, first strode into my family history and came to people's attention in the role of a manure collector. Dingo's glory shown forth with sudden brilliance in 1934. He was fifteen that year, short of stature, but with grandmother Jiang's slender arms and legs, he looked like a clever little monkey.

The people of Maple Village liked to raise dogs. When the dogs were lonely, they gathered in packs and roamed the countryside, depositing their shiny black droppings on all the winding country roads. Elder Brother Dingo carried a bamboo basket around all day chasing after that pack of dogs and busily collecting their manure. Even if the dog droppings hid themselves in the tall grass several miles away, they could not escape Dingo's sharp eyesight and keen sense of smell.

This all began in 1934. Grandmother Jiang told Dingo, "After you fill a basket with dog manure, go find somebody with land; a basketful of dog manure will bring in two coppers; they love to use dog droppings to fertilize their fields. When you make enough coppers, Mom will buy you a pair of rubber overshoes; when winter comes, the soles of your little feet will be warm as toast."

Dingo stared lovingly at his little bare feet a moment, then raised his head and smiled at his mother as she was grinding husks with a stone roller. His mother's eyes were fixed on the deep hole in the round grinding stone, following the ground-up chaff as it rolled painfully around. Dingo smelled the cold, indifferent fragrance given off by those dark brown flakes. That pair of warm rubber overshoes suddenly grew very large in his imagination; he leaned happily over his mother's grinding stone and shouted, "Have Dad buy a pair of rubber overshoes and come home!"

Grandmother Jiang watched her son spinning around on the grinding stone like a top, but she went right on demonically pushing the stone. In dizzy confusion Grandmother Jiang slapped her son on the butt and muttered, "You go pick up the dog droppings; there'll only be rubber overshoes when you've collected enough dog droppings."

"Do I still have to pick 'em up when winter comes and it starts to snow?" asked Dingo.

"Yes. The ground is white after the snow, and the dog droppings are even easier to spot."

Dreams of a pair of rubber overshoes made 1934 a busy and fulfilling year for Dingo. He carried out a rebellion against Grandmother Jiang. He did not hand over the coppers he earned from the sale of dog manure to her, but put them in a wooden box instead. Driving away a number of magic mice, he hid the wooden box away from prying eyes in a crack in the wall. Sometimes awakening in the middle of the night, Dingo would get up from his grass mat, tiptoe between the sleeping bodies of his family members, and go examine that wooden box. In the darkness his sleepy little face was quite touching; he could not resist handling those coppers, and the coins clinked quietly together. Dingo would sigh like an old man full of deep emotion as many fantasies filled his mind. A whole boxful of copper coins gave off bright golden rays that lit up the face of this country boy.

As I look back on my family's history, I see that the disaster of 1934 was visited also upon Dingo: One morning that wooden box suddenly disappeared. After Dingo scratched in that hole in the wall until his fingernails were broken and bloody, he turned into a mad dog. He tied several of his younger brothers and sisters together and tortured them with a bamboo whip to try to get them to confess the whereabouts of that wooden box. The crying and shouting of the little boys and girls in my ancestral home disturbed the entire village.

Grandmother Jiang heard news of the commotion and

hurried home from the fields to find Dingo ruthlessly whipping his younger brothers and sisters. The look of wild cruelty in Dingo's eyes made her shiver all over. Was this the curse Chen Baonian hammered into her body? Grandmother Jiang suddenly realized that evil is a large part of the original nature of the human race; it is as natural as the movements of the sun and moon. She leaned against the door and looked around at her children; once again she wondered if she were not a tree with an empty nest in the middle of its trunk, shaking back and forth as the wind and rain buffeted it from all directions.

After the loss of the wooden box, my family was shrouded in pain and depression. Dingo sat all day on a pile of straw in the corner of the room examining his surroundings. He seemed to hear that box of copper coins clinking together somewhere in the hidden recesses of the ancestral home. He suspected his family members of hiding the wooden box. Several times Grandmother Jiang felt her son's gaze sweep by and stop stubbornly on her tired face like a thorn thrust painfully into her flesh.

"Aren't you going out to collect dog manure?"

"No."

"You do want those rubber overshoes, don't you?"

Grandmother Jiang suddenly lunged over, grabbed Dingo by the hair, and said, "Come over here feel your seven-month-old younger brother in Mom's stomach Mom doesn't want him with the money saved she'll buy you the rubber overshoes make a tight fist and hit Mom hard as you can in the stomach hit as hard as you can . . ."

Dingo's hand made contact with Grandmother Jiang's abdomen, ever protruding like an overhanging cliff. He saw his mother's face flush deep red with excitement as she bent over toward him. She wore a seldom-seen smile as she took his hand and said, "Dingo hit me knock away your younger brother and Mom'll buy you the rubber overshoes." This primitive temptation made Dingo jump up; he sobbed as he delivered three blows into his mother's full, hard abdomen; Grandmother Jiang closed her eyes and uttered three anguished cries from the depths of her womb.

The fetus that was beaten by Dingo was my father.

Afterward I heard about what happened to Dingo's wooden box and could not help feeling depressed about this glorious yet bizarre story. I heard that in 1935 when the south was inundated by a great flood, my old Maple Village homeland was turned into a watery wasteland. As Grandmother Jiang was escaping in a bamboo raft, she saw that wooden box suddenly float up out of the foundations of the ancestral house; seven or eight half-drowned mice were swimming out toward deep water, gingerly escorting the box. Grandmother Jiang recognized the box and those mice. She was amazed that the Chen's venerable family mice were so amazingly strong that they could actually carry Dingo's copper coins down deep into the foundations of the house. She thought those copper coins must certainly be speckled with green rust from down there under the water; if you went down and dredged them up, they would no longer smell of Dingo and dog manure. Where did those family mice intend to take that waterlogged wooden box anyway?

As I once told my father, I really admire those magical family mice that lived in our ancestral home. I also like my fifteen-year-old dog-manure-collecting uncle Dingo.

All his life my father never forgot those three blows he suffered while still in his mother's womb. Perhaps he always hated his now-deceased elder brother Dingo. From January to October of 1934, my father grew bigger and heavier, like a bamboo root growing under the earth. He began jumping around, preparing to vault out of his mother's womb. The year had reached the time for the season to race through its rapid revolution; Maple Village's two hundred acres of early rice had gone from green to brown. The background of the Maple Village countryside in autumn was a panorama of golden brown, washed over by a warm southerly breeze blowing through 1934's foliage with a mixture of odors well worth savoring.

To this day it is still a mystery why the rules of morality were overturned everywhere in Maple Village that autumn. It was the harvest season in the countryside. The cocks crowed at midnight and the pigs thrashed around in their pens at dawn. In times past there was no sex anywhere in Maple Village in October, but this year was a mystery. Perhaps that warm southerly wind confused the entire network of sexual desire in Maple Village. Why did the men and women cutting rice in the fields throw down their sickles in droves and drift off into the waves of ripe rice without leaving a trace, huh? What sort of a wind would you say that was, anyway?

Grandmother Jiang, dragging around her ponderous body, was in a daze in that kind of wind. She heard the wanton clamor of men and women, full of happiness and lusty vitality, carry over from the depths of the waves of ripe rice to surround her and her fetus. With one hand she gently caressed the baby in her womb while she tightly clenched her other hand into a fist and pressed it against her lips; a dry wail suddenly forced its way out between the cracks in her fingers and rose steadily higher like sesame flowers blooming from the bottom up; those who heard it were terrified. They said when my grandmother

Jiang started to wail, she surpassed the female ghosts in the graveyard; her wailing was charged with a mysterious and tragic significance.

The hill of tawny earth in the northeast corner of Maple Village and the black brick building on the hilltop were still in the background. Grandmother Jiang and my father inside her just stood there like that in a historical tableau of fifty years ago.

Chen Wenzhi was in extremely high spirits during the rice-harvesting season; he swallowed a large amount of opium every day and then roamed around his three hundred acres of rice paddy looking like a red-crowned crane. From the roof of his black brick dwelling, Chen Wenzhi looked far out over the autumn scene; those Japanese binoculars of his were constantly following Grandmother Jiang. In the warm southerly wind of a beautiful autumn day, he secretly observed the entire process as Grandmother Jiang gave birth to my father. As reflected in the glass lenses of his binoculars, Grandmother Jiang's movements were as furtive as those of an old doe. She was pushed and pulled front and back by wave after wave of rice stalks, her whole body a dazzling golden yellow, as she made her way in the direction of an old pile of straw on the raised earthen ridge between the paddy fields. Afterward she lay down silently on that pile of straw, put a clump of her stringy and disheveled hair in her mouth, and sucked it while her pupils burned painfully like two small suns. It was a beautiful October day with a warm southerly wind. Chen Wenzhi watched a woman give birth for the first time. Just before she gave birth to a new life, Grandmother Jiang's tired body grew abundant and richly beautiful, burning without inhibition like a wild chrysanthemum made large by the sun's light.

In the instant my father dropped onto the straw, the

brightness of his blood rose heavenward and filled the autumn sky around Maple Village. The powerful and unrestrained sound of his crying shook the binoculars out of Chen Wenzhi's hands; this threw the black brick building into an uproar. After the binocular lenses were shattered, Chen Wenzhi slowly grew limp and then collapsed there on the roof; he looked weak and desperate. When the servants rushed over and picked him up, they discovered his white silk pants were soaked through with brightly shining semen.

I realize that this fellow Chen Wenzhi was a strange demonic character, forever wrapping himself, lianalike, around the leaves and branches of my clan history. Half the people of Maple Village had the surname Chen, and the Chen family's clan record mentions a tenuous blood relationship between my family and that of Chen Wenzhi. It is of no real importance whether Chen Wenzhi and Chen Baonian's fathers were related as fifth-generation cousins on the paternal side or as sixth-generation uncle and nephew; what is important is that Chen Wenzhi's family was famous far and wide throughout the nineteenth century for its great wealth—while generations of my family lived in thatched huts and were prey to both cold and hunger. My grandfather Chen Baonian traded his younger sister, Phoenix, to Chen Wenzhi in exchange for five acres of land. I imagine Maple Village morality was repeatedly eroded and corrupted, generation after generation, in just this manner.

Phoenix was like a leaf of incomparable beauty fallen off our lush, old, many-branched family tree and turned into slime. They say she was the prettiest woman ever in our clan; she spent two years as Chen Wenzhi's concubine and gave birth to male triplets, all of whom Chen Wenzhi's family buried one by one in their bamboo grove. Some people saw those male babies being buried alive; their appearance was both lovable and misshapen: Their heads were extraordinarily soft; their hair was thick and golden yellow; and none of them could cry. After the news leaked out, all of Maple Village was in a state of shock for several days. Off and on they heard Phoenix's grief-stricken sobbing coming from the Chen family's bamboo grove; then, later that night, she started insanely shaking each stalk of bamboo, taking advantage of the midnight moon to try to destroy the Chen family's vast expanse of bamboo.

At that time Chen Baonian was seventeen years old and had not yet taken a wife; he stood there shivering in the freezing cold by the stone mill just outside the bamboo grove, stamping his feet continually and shouting at his younger sister, "Phoenix, don't ruin the bamboos, you mustn't ruin the Chen's bamboos!"

He did not dare run over in front of Phoenix and stop her; he just stood by the stone mill in the early spring cold and shouted, "Phoenix, dear Little Sister, don't ruin the bamboo; Elder Brother's a pig and a dog; his conscience isn't worth shit; don't ruin any more bamboo!"

This strange stalemate between brother and sister came to a close with Phoenix's violent death. Phoenix crumpled slowly to the ground in the bamboo grove, still shaking the bamboos.

It was a strange death. Some recall that in death her face was reddish violet, like a flower pressed in remembrance between the pages of our family history. Fifty years ago, relatives and friends in Maple Village wanted to help Chen Baonian carry Phoenix's coffin into Chen Wenzhi's home; but Chen Baonian just buried his face in the white shroud and sobbed continuously. He said, "There's no use; I knew she wouldn't live past today; no matter how, she would have died anyway. I had her fortune told. Neither Chen Wenzhi nor I is to blame; Phoenix's fate was simply to die and not to live, that's all."

Fifty years later I have captured my great-aunt Phoenix like a flash of radiant purple light in our family history. Phoenix was just a beautiful firefly flitting rapidly by in front of my face; how, then, did I capture her purple radiance? Phoenix's strange triplets differentiate her from Grandmother Jiang; when I think of those three misshapen male babies buried in the bamboo grove, and then recall the theories of birth and heredity I once studied, a suspicious assumption darkens my eyesight—I can't look any more deeply into my family history.

I now require Chen Wenzhi's reappearance.

In all of the extensive Maple Village Chen clan, only Chen Wenzhi's branch was rich, and only the grandfathers and grandsons of his branch had monstrous characters for several generations. Each one had his particular perversion, and their lives lasted about the same number of years; they all only lived to be about forty. The people of Maple Village believed that Chen Wenzhi and his ancestors' early demise was retribution for their overindulgence in alcohol and sex. They monopolized virtually all the beautiful women in the Maple Village area for nearly two hundred years. Those women who entered the Chen family compound, with its five deep, dark courtyards, were like beautiful wild horseflies sadly and indifferently stinging the bodies of the Chen men. After they had sucked the morbid, mildewed blood and semen from the Chen men, they lost their original beauty; then they were pushed into the firewood house in the back courtyard to chop firewood or cook the meals; and their faces were permanently imprinted with the mark of a Chen family concubine: a dark black plum-blossom tattoo.

Occasionally a woman with a plum-blossom tattoo would be driven out of the Chen household to prowl the vicinity of Horsebridge; she would put on a melancholy smile to entice the town craftsmen. When the people of Horsebridge saw a woman with a plum-blossom tattoo, they would walk over and circle around her to ask her about life and death in the Chen household. And to ask her about a mysterious white jade crock.

I have to describe for you the Chen Wenzhi family's white jade crock.

I have not seen, nor could I ever see, that white jade crock. But right now I see Chen Wenzhi's family in 1934; I see that white jade crock placed on a long table in the living room. That crock contained an extraordinary medicine of great interest to the people of Maple Village. The unofficial local history of my old home, the *Immortal Isle Gazetteer*, has the following to say about this extraordinary medicine:

A family treasure not displayed to outsiders. Believed to have been concocted by a shaman from the eastern mountains from the blood and semen of virgin boys and girls. It increases male potency, fortifies the kidneys, or perhaps extends one's lifespan.

Even the women with the plum-blossom tattoos were completely unable to explain the Chen family's unique medicine;

they only speculated that the extraordinary medicine in the bottom of the white jade crock was almost finished.

In the late summer and early autumn of that year, Chen Wenzhi ran hurriedly around like an ant on a hot frying pan; he sent his servants away and walked all around people's houses craning his neck this way and that; he also stole a large number of brightly colored undershorts hanging on people's clotheslines, stuck them in his breast pockets, and ran home to inspect them single-mindedly in private. In that pile of undershorts there was one pair that belonged to Elder Brother Dingo who, when he could not find them, figured the wind blew them away. So he picked up a piece of square cloth printed with a blue flower pattern, tied it around his waist, and went out to collect dog droppings.

Dingo, carrying his manure basket, went looking for dog droppings until he arrived at the foot of Chen Wenzhi's black brick building. He did not know that someone was watching him from the roof. Suddenly he heard Chen Wenzhi's steward shouting at him from up there. "Dingo, Dingo, come up here and do something for us, and we'll give you whatever you want."

Dingo raised his head, looked up at that jet black building, and thought for a moment. "You want me to push the grindstone?"

"That's right, push the grindstone. Come on," the steward said with a smile.

"You'll really give me anything I want?" As soon as Dingo said this, he threw down his dog-manure basket and ran into Chen Wenzhi's house.

The following incident took place in the granary in the Chens' back courtyard. Baked in the noonday sun, the enormous granary gave off an appetizing aroma. As soon as Dingo was pulled in there by the steward, his head started to swim; he had never in his life seen such a huge granary with so much raw grain. He could vaguely make out a number of village boys and girls thirstily sitting there on those piles of rice, crunching away on the raw grain.

"What about the grindstone? Where's the grindstone?"

The steward patted Dingo on the head, screwed his mouth up strangely, and said, "It's over there. You don't have to push it. It'll push you."

Dingo was shoved into a dark place deep inside the granary. Where was the stone grinding wheel? Instead he saw Chen Wenzhi sitting there straight and proper on an armchair made from amboyna wood, his whole body spattered top to bottom with golden flecks of grain. On his knees he was holding a white jade crock. Chen Wenzhi smiled at Dingo with extreme tenderness; he noticed that the contours of Dingo's little face, a wonderful combination of Chen Baonian and Grandmother Jiang's various characteristics, were both attractive and guileless. He asked Dingo, "Why hasn't your mother gone into the fields these past few days?"

"My mother's going to have another baby."

"Your mother's . . ." Chen Wenzhi bent over suddenly and tore off the cloth hiding Dingo's privates. Dingo jumped and screamed; at that point he saw clearly some kind of strange, thick, foul-smelling liquid pour out of the white jade crock as it rolled on the ground. That fetid odor made Dingo want to vomit; but as he crouched down to gather up his blue flowered cloth he felt Chen Wenzhi's slender, bony hands pulling at his crotch. Faced with this bizarre gesture from the most powerful person in Maple Village, Dingo was shocked into immobility;

he wanted to cry, but his tears just wouldn't come.

"What're you trying to do, what're you trying to do?!"

At that instant the smell of dog manure that clung to Dingo's body filled the air like fog. Dingo smelled the pungent odor of dog manure on his own body. His round eyes opened wide, and he shook like a weed in Chen Wenzhi's hands. After his early adolescent semen flowed like a bubbling spring onto Chen Wenzhi's palms and was poured into the white jade crock, Dingo started sobbing loudly, sobbing and shouting incoherently, "I'm not a dog I want rubber overshoes give me rubber overshoes give me rubber overshoes!"

After it was all over, Elder Brother Dingo really did walk out of Chen Wenzhi's house carrying a pair of rubber overshoes. He returned to the hill of tawny earth and saw the purple rays of the twilight sun shining on his dog-manure basket; the village was engulfed in smoke from cooking fires, and that pack of wild dogs roaming up and down the northwest hillside was biting and scratching and barking without cease. Dingo ran staggering along, carrying that pair of rubber overshoes; he noticed the scent of dog manure on his body was growing stronger, and he began to dread the smell of it.

That night Grandmother Jiang walked all over calling Dingo until she arrived at the desolate burial ground; there she saw her son lying on a clump of knotweed holding on his chest a pair of black rubber overshoes, an item seldom seen in Maple Village. Dingo had fallen asleep, his eyes constantly twitching as though he were frightened. In his dreams the expression on his little face kept changing very rapidly. To the usual odor of dog manure on Dingo's body was now added the smell of fresh semen. Grandmother Jiang picked Dingo up apprehensively, looked down at him, and discovered that her son was already old. That pair of black rubber overshoes her son held tightly to his chest was like an evil star that had just fallen into Grandmother Jiang's home.

In 1934 the news that Maple Village exported twenty thousand stalks of large southern bamboo to all parts of the country was printed in the famous Shanghai daily *Shenbao*. And it was also that year that the number of bamboo craftsmen working in my old hometown grew as wildly as bamboo shoots in spring. At least half of the men in the area abandoned their work in the fields and took up the big-handled bamboo knife to make big money. The sound of thin bamboo strips being cut resounded from almost every house in Maple Village. All the while Chen Wenzhi's hundred and fifty acres of wet rice paddy was untended and full of weeds. Maple Village was consumed by an uncharacteristic atmosphere of restless impatience.

This massive change in occupation and general round of disturbance was set in motion by my grandfather Chen Baonian's rise to fame and fortune. People just back in the village after transporting bamboo to town told the others, "Chen Baonian has made it big. All the bamboo couches, mats, plaques, bushel baskets—even the hand baskets and short benches Chen Baonian makes—are now going for a good price. And everybody in town knows the Chen Baonian brand. Chen Baonian's built a wooden house. Chen Baonian has gold rings on both hands. He goes to the brothels to sniff heroin and fuck the women, and as he's leaving, shit, he just takes off a gold ring and throws it on the bed."

Surprisingly enough, Grandmother Jiang only heard this news after everyone else. She had walked all over anxiously looking for people to ask about Chen Baonian. She would ask, "Do you know just how much money Chen Baonian's made? Is it enough to buy a hundred and fifty acres of land?" These people she asked all looked contemptuously at the filthy, emaciated woman and said absolutely nothing. Grandmother Jiang would stand there puzzled a moment and ask again, "Is it enough to buy a hundred and fifty acres?" Then somebody would suddenly laugh derisively at Grandmother Jiang and answer, "Chen Baonian says he'll spend whatever money he makes and he won't give you a single copper."

"We could buy that hundred and fifty acres," Grandmother Jiang now mumbled to herself. She sighed as she stroked downward across her shriveled-up breasts until her hands came to rest on her greatly protruding abdomen. When her fingers touched her skin where it pressed against the back of my father's head, they intertwined, and she cradled the baby in her womb with infinite tenderness. "That bastard Chen Baonian."

Grandmother Jiang's lips quivered as she bowed her head and became entranced by her own daydreams, as various and rapidly changing as the clouds. The people then felt Grandmother Jiang's barren expression both beautiful and ludicrous.

Actually I imagine that Grandmother Jiang was partly insane by this time. She constantly followed the men who had gone into town and seen Chen Baonian, staring with a burning gaze at their pockets and waistbands. Her lips trembled, as she asked, "Where's Chen Baonian's money, then?" She held up her open palms and hovered around those men like a ghost. The men felt sparks of sadness as they shooed Grandmother Jiang away with a wave of their hands.

Right up to the time father was born, Grandmother Jiang never received any money from town. The new bamboo craftsmen in Maple Village gradually followed in Chen Baonian's footsteps and crowded into town. Nineteen thirty-four was the year of escape for Maple Village's bamboo craftsmen; it is reported that by the end of that year men from Maple Village had set up bamboo goods shops in every single town on the lower reaches of the Long River.

I imagine Maple Village's wide yellow mud road probably came into being at that time. Grandmother Jiang watched with her own eyes as that road was transformed from a narrow path to a broad thoroughfare and from desolation to prosperity. That autumn she stood by the side of the road with a scythe in her hand, aimlessly studying the men leaving home; 139 new and old bamboo craftsmen packed up their bags and set out on that yellow mud road, leaving their old Maple Village homes behind. That year Grandmother Jiang's memory was extraordinarily acute; she memorized the face and voice of virtually every one of those men. From that day on, that wide yellow mud road was like a huge python coiling around Grandmother Jiang's memory of her old home.

From that time on, that yellow mud road also extended into my family history. The people of my clan crowded together with their Maple Village neighbors like a line of ants on the move; countless pairs of bare feet strode upon the road of their ancestors, hurriedly departing in the direction of unknown cities and towns. Several decades later I faintly perceived the sound of those rebellious feet tramping through history, and I was helplessly confused. Women of my old home, why were you unable to keep your men at home to live and die with you? Women should not have been left behind like Grandmother Jiang was, to sink or swim in the bitter sea. Maple Village should not have become a village of women.

The one hundred and thirty-ninth bamboo craftsman was Chen Yujin. Grandmother Jiang would always remember that Chen Yujin was the last one. She was standing by the side of the yellow mud road at the time. Chen Yujin and his wife came running by frantically—one after the other. Chen Yujin was running away with a coil of bamboo strips around his neck and a bamboo knife in his hand; his wife was chasing after him in her bare feet with her hair all disheveled. The incredible shrieks, like the autumn wind, emitted by Chen Yujin's wife seemed to help her run faster. She caught hold of her husband.

After that Grandmother Jiang witnessed a hand-to-hand struggle between Chen Yujin and his wife for that bamboo knife. Grandmother Jiang heard Chen Yujin's wife's hoarse and thunderous harangue. She shouted, "You silly fool going into town who's going to cook for you who's going to wash your clothes who's going to screw you if you don't want it I still do let go I'll cut off your fingers go on into town and make bamboo goods *then.*"

The morning the pair of them fought over the bamboo knife was so long and drawn out it was suffocating. The man looked utterly hopeless, and the woman's voice was full of anxious indignation. As Grandmother Jiang observed with reverent fascination this drama being played out on the yellow mud road, she felt an unbearably stifling sense of depression; she picked up her straw basket and had started to return home when she heard Chen Yujin roar like a caged animal. Grandmother Jiang turned around just in time to see every detail as Chen Yujin swung his bamboo knife down in a murderous attack on his wife. As the knife's cold glint flashed in all directions, deep red blood spurted up like fiery flames, mottled and misty. The vibrant, young, beautiful body of Chen Yujin's wife was rent apart with a terrible noise as she collapsed facedown in the middle of the yellow mud road.

How, then, did the blood spilled on the yellow mud road that morning come to spread out in the shape of a lotus flower? The shattered spirit of Chen Yujin's wife filled the early autumn mist and gave off an almost imperceptible sweetness. My grandmother Jiang jumped onto the road, raised her scythe, stepped over a pool of blood, and set out after the wife killer Chen Yujin as he made his escape. The yellow mud road buckled under the weight of Grandmother Jiang's feet as she ran haltingly along with her round eyes staring angrily ahead. But the name she yelled out, as she chased Chen Yujin, actually belonged to our family. The people in the fields heard her call Chen Baonian's name. "Chen Baonian . . . murderer . . . Chen Baonian . . . grab him . . . !"

I know that 139 Maple Village bamboo craftsmen crossed the great river downstream and entered the prosperous cities and towns of the south. It was these 139 bamboo craftsmen who lighted the torch of the bamboo goods business and pioneered a completely new handicraft industry in the southern cities. A wave of bamboo goods shops run by the men of Maple Village gradually washed over the banks of the riverine south. My grandfather's Chen's Bamboo Goods Store was famous for a while in the city in 1934. I've heard it said that Chen's Bamboo Goods Store employed the cream of the local riffraff—thugs, and undesirable characters of every conceivable stripe, and that these hoodlums could resist any and all disasters, natural or man-made. That gang of criminal craftsmen gathered under Chen Baonian's banner of command, each one with

an agile mind and strong hands, was just like a flood-foment-
ing dragon slithering into a mighty ocean. Chen Baonian loved
them like his own life; he felt vaguely that he had picked up
pieces of filthy nondescript firewood, set them ablaze, and the
flames rendered him fearless in the face of his feelings of
loneliness and cold.

By 1934 Chen Baonian could already pass himself off as a
highly skilled craftsman and a socially astute proprietor. His
shop engaged in a number of very fashionable but shady
enterprises; when his bamboo goods had passed through the
hands of eighteen apprentices, they took on a cachet of splen-
did perversity that rendered them irresistible on the bamboo
goods market.

When I studied the history of the rise of Chen's Bamboo
Goods Store, I was captivated by the dark shadows of those
eighteen apprentices. Once, in the vicinity of the ruins of
Chen's Bamboo Goods Store, I interviewed an old man nick-
named the little blind man. He died three years ago in a fire.
The neighborhood people said when the little blind man died
he was senile; his little room was littered with bamboo goods
from years ago; late one night all those bamboo articles just
caught fire; the little blind man was buried like an ancient
mummy in bamboo ash half a yard high. He represented the
final glory of Chen's Bamboo Goods Store.

Many anecdotes concerning the relationship between my
grandfather and the little blind man were still in circulation
for my reference.

The story goes that the little blind man came from an
extremely harsh background; he was a foundling from the
brothel on the south side of town. He could not even figure out
himself how he managed to grow up. When he stared at you

with his one good eye, you would discover a faint flower-shaped spot of blood covering the pupil of his blind left eye. The little blind man often recalled, like a dream of past glory, the origin of that spot of blood. When he was five years old, he fought with a dog over a piece of smoked meat that had fallen from its hanging place under the eaves of someone's home. He bit into the smoked meat first, but the dog's vengeful claws scratched him deep in the eye.

He had met Chen Baonian while sitting on his own dilapidated rickshaw. Once again he told the story of how he got the bloody spot in his eye, and Chen Baonian was extremely moved. Similarly unhappy memories related to dogs brought them together; every time Chen Baonian came out of the brothel on the south side of town, he would climb onto the little blind man's rickshaw; under the flickering glow of the little red lanterns, they would reminisce about many instances concerning the lives of dogs and men. Later on, the little blind man sold his beat-up rickshaw, took a case of rice wine to Chen's Bamboo Goods Store, kowtowed to the master, and started to learn the craft. He quickly became Chen Baonian's favorite apprentice. He was like a dark bitter plum blooming wildly and alone around the periphery of my clan history.

The amazing 1934 robbery of three grain-transportation ships, pulled off by Chen's Bamboo Goods Store gang, was engineered by the little blind man and Chen Baonian. There was a crop failure that year, and famine was everywhere throughout the cities and the countryside; still, nobody could figure out why, with their business booming and the cash pouring in, Chen's Bamboo Goods Store gang would want to rip off three ships full of coarse, unpolished rice. From my investigations into the lives of Chen Baonian and the little blind man, I'd guess this was because of a dream they both had about food in their youth—when they could never get enough food to fill their stomachs.

If you were born with a burning desire to steal food, you might have joined Chen's Bamboo Goods Store gang as they stormed those grain ships in 1934. Like more than a hundred bamboo craftsmen just in from the villages, you would have hid yourselves on the wharf, in between the grain sacks, waiting until after midnight for the moon to go down. When you saw the little blind man, the leader of the grain raid, jump onto the grain ship with an awl-shaped bamboo knife between his teeth, and then, with that bloody spot blazing away in his solitary eye, whirl around like a madman with a huge sack of grain, you, too, would have yelled and jumped onto the grain ship, cleaned out all the grain in less than an hour, pushed the ship's crew into the river, and made them cry for mercy.

This incident occurred among the numberless affairs of human life half a century ago; it seems genuinely credible. I believe it was only a signal for one sort of social change, a beacon of light *or* darkness. They say that after the raid on the grain ships, a bamboo craftsmen's gang naturally came into existence in the town. They clustered around Chen Baonian's bamboo goods store like the myriad stars honoring the moon, and their trademark was that sharp, exquisitely serviceable awl-shaped bamboo knife.

That awl-shaped bamboo knife is worth celebrating; the little blind man invented it the night before they plundered the grain ships. Since it was shaped like a small traditional dagger, you could drill a hole and hang it on your belt or just slip it into your pants pockets. The little blind man selected the dry bamboo from Maple Village to carve out this easily concealed weapon. He then showed it to Chen Baonian. "How do you like this baby? I'm going to carve one for everyone. The best way to make it to the top in this world is probably with a knife."

My grandfather Chen Baonian immediately fell in love with that knife. From then on, all through the second half of his life, he always carried one of those sharp, exquisitely serviceable awl-shaped bamboo knives. Chen Baonian, Chen Baonian, did you ever think of the end of the world when you stuck an awl-shaped bamboo knife in your belt and blustered your wretched way around the city?

One day in the countryside, Dingo was called into the bamboo grove at the head of the village by an outsider, a man who came to Maple Village to collect bamboo. He told Dingo that Chen Baonian had sent him something. Deep in the bamboo grove, that outsider solemnly presented Dingo with an awl-shaped bamboo knife.

"Your dad sent it to you."

"For me? What about my mom?" Dingo asked.

"It's for you. Your dad wants you to wear it."

As Dingo received the knife into his hands, he felt along with it the provocative and richly exotic aura of the city. He seemed almost to see Chen Baonian's face reflected in the delicately thin edge of the knife; the image was vague but strong. The bamboo knife was very light and covered in a pale green luster; Dingo carefully examined this mysterious object in the sunlight, stabbed it a couple of times into the palm of his hand, heard the faint throbbing sound of his blood flowing under the pressure, shouted out loud, "Wah!" from the pain, and finally smiled down at the knife. He was afraid others would see it, so he carried the knife home hidden away from their prying eyes at the bottom of his manure basket.

That night Dingo stared at his father's awl-shaped bamboo knife in the moonlight for a long time without sleeping. Dingo's naive imagination was so strongly called forth by the light from that bamboo that it flowed like a torrential stream across the dirt floor of his old home. He imagined the city where all the bamboo craftsmen lived, imagined the buildings, the women, the foreign motorcars, the department stores, and his father's shop in the city; all the time he was mumbling vague exclamations of ecstasy. Grandmother Jiang was finally awakened; she crawled over to Dingo's straw bed, reached out her hand reeking of smoke from the wood cooking fire, and felt Dingo's forehead. She felt her son fall limply onto her breasts like a feverish puppy. Her son's eyes opened wide and bright; there were two strange awl-shaped lights glowing there like coals in the dark.

"Ma, I want to go into the city and be a bamboo craftsman with Dad."

"Dear Dingo, your forehead's really hot."

"Ma, I want to go into the city and be a bamboo crafts-man."

"Dear Dingo don't talk nonsense and scare your mom you're only fifteen you can't even hold a big-handled bamboo stripper you still haven't been married and had children how can you go into the city the city that miserable place good people go there and their hearts turn black evil people go there and pus flows out of the soles of their feet and their heads are covered with sores you let Chen Baonian rot his stinking dogs-won't-eat-cat's-won't-lick bones in the city don't even think about going into the city Dingo."

Actually this was a night of disastrous change in the history of my family. That night our old home's countless family mice vigilantly opened their red eyes wide and squeaked wildly, as if in harmony with Dingo's every sigh. In the darkness that thatched hut was shaken by a powerful rhythm. Hot vapor rose continuously from Dingo's body as he stuck his head out from under the covers; he heard the family mice squeaking and searched for them intently, but didn't even catch a glimpse; nevertheless, his constantly throbbing heart was already communicating with those Chen family mice. In the split second when the family mice suddenly grew quiet, Dingo stood up from his straw bed like a sleepwalker, mechanically picked up his manure basket, and opened the wattle door.

A road made for night flight lay there bathed in the rich autumn moonlight.

A road made for night flight stretched out toward the depths of 1934.

Dingo scrunched up his shoulders as he scampered along the yellow and mud road in his bare feet; fireflies flitted by on all sides; leaves and dry grass scudded along at knee level on the night wind; and a mysterious undercurrent eddied around in the boundless black expanse of rice paddy, floating Dingo's light little body along as though he were an escaping minnow. The moonlight and the water shimmered together. Dingo turned his head back and gazed from afar at his Maple Village, just then bathed in the merciless pale light of this September night. Not a dog barked; perhaps the dogs were used to hearing Dingo's footsteps. The entire village was a single dark stillness—solid, dejected, with only some thatch on a few rooftops, like Mom's hair, blowing in the wind. He pictured vaguely to himself Mom and that bunch of younger brothers and sisters crowded together on the big bed at home, soundly sleeping a dreamless sleep, their breaths, reeking of poorly digested grasses and ferns, blending in the stale air; Dingo slowed his pace, suddenly howled several times like a wolf, then, just as suddenly, stopped.

That night he discovered an amazingly large number of dog droppings on the yellow mud road. Dog droppings sped neatly by his tear-filled eyes like pieces on a chessboard. Dingo collected the dog droppings as he walked along, took off his short padded jacket, and wrapped them in it; by the time he reached Horsebridge, the jacket was about to burst. Dingo relaxed his grip, and the whole contents tumbled out on top of the horse bridge; he never even turned his head to watch the dog droppings roll away.

The next morning the first thing my grandmother Jiang saw when she opened the door was that pair of black rubber overshoes Dingo left behind. In the early autumn frost the black rubber overshoes were covered with a crystalline substance resembling salt. They were sitting in a puddle of water. Dingo's footprints were still visible from just in front of the door to the yellow mud road, rising and falling as they wound their way forward as if freighted with a heavy load of care, the ten-toe prints looking like ten pitiful little lima beans. Grandmother Jiang ran along, with her hair flowing wildly behind, all the way to Horsebridge, calling after Dingo. When someone showed her that bundle of dog droppings on the bridge, she picked up the icy cold dog manure and started to wail. She threw the dog manure at the people standing around watching. She headed home alone. All the way back she saw countless piles of dog droppings directing their beautiful black luster at her. The more she cried, the more beautiful the black luster of the dog droppings became. Later on, she began to hide from them; she could not stop vomiting whenever she smelled that odor.

I can recite a poem by an unknown southern poet. This poem moves me just like a lament. Last year, when my father was seriously ill, I stood with my back to him and told him the story of a father and a son; poetry is most enchanting recited in a sickroom when you are surrounded by the odor of medicine.

> *Father and I*
> *Are walking shoulder to shoulder;*
> *The autumn rain's stopped a while;*
> *Seems like many years*
> *Since the last cloudburst.*
>
> *We walk in the rain and the*
> *Intervals between the rain;*
> *Our shoulders are clearly touching,*
> *But we need not utter a single word;*
> *We just came out of the house,*
> *So we need not utter a single word;*
> *This is what comes*
> *Of living together for a long time.*
>
> *The dripping water sounds like*
> *Slender twigs snapping off;*

Father and I walk along peacefully,
Cherishing our ineffable affection.

My father understood. His hearing was always sharp. Looking at the outline of my back, he suddenly laughed out loud. I turned around to discover on my father's pallid face the particular expression worn by descendants of the Chen clan at the beginning of their lives: a highly transparent happiness and an anxiety as dark as storm clouds. In the snow-white hospital room, I saw my father as he appeared when he was a baby, and I heard quite clearly the dripping of the rain of history snapping off the slender twigs of individual lives mentioned in the poem. That day my father escaped his mute condition and spoke loudly to me. I stared at him just as though staring at an infant, and thus I prayed for my father to be reborn.

Was father born at the wrong time? Or did uncle Dingo's three blows shake him out of his mother's womb too soon? Father came into this world with six purple birthmarks, and bore his way right into the middle of the plague of 1934.

In 1934 cholera raged in the 350-square-mile area around Maple Village, and the rural scene was very dismal. In his bamboo-plaited cradle, handed down by the ancestors and long since turned black, my father sensed the cholera germs in the air. He was always reaching up vainly and grabbing at nothing, and the sound of his crying was both heartrending and nerve-racking. After the ancestors' cradle received my father, it started to screech mournfully like an old zither; everyone in the family grew restless and easy to anger with that sound reverberating around them; the children broke into countless fights playing around the cradle.

Right after she gave birth, Grandmother Jiang's life was thrown into dark confusion. She washed all her dirty, blood-spattered clothes in the pond, then set her son down in a big wooden basin and looked down at him; she saw a mysterious and highly irregular shadow flash across the infant's face.

Eight days after he was born, father refused to feed at Grandmother Jiang's breasts. Grandmother Jiang was in a constant state of anxiety; she scratched her heavily swollen breasts until they were covered with scars, terrified that her milk had been poisoned through infection with the rampaging plague. Grandmother Jiang had a brilliant idea: She squeezed some of her milk out into a large bowl and fed it to a dog. Then she carried the bowl and followed the dog all the way out to a place beyond the edge of the village. Gradually she noticed the dog's head bob off to one side as it collapsed beside a stream. The dog was the wealthy landlord Chen Wenzhi's soft, golden-haired sheepdog. Chen's dog tried with all its remaining strength to lap a little water, but just could not reach the stream.

Grandmother Jiang was very shocked by the dog's low, desperately frenzied moans. She broke the bowl, hurriedly buttoned up her previously unbuttoned blouse, and ran as fast as she could from that dying dog. She felt vaguely that her breasts, with which she had nurtured eight children, had now so perfectly stored and refined all the elements of hatred and ruination that they'd become as powerful as iron or stone. She suddenly suspected her own breasts had broadcast the plague germ throughout the Maple Village area.

That night Grandmother Jiang dreamed her body was blasted to pieces and transformed into the Plague Goddess of popular legend, floating through the length and breadth of Maple Village like a spirit, singing dirges all the way while poisonous vapors spewed from every pore. The dream lasted a long time, and Grandmother Jiang cried and laughed until she was nearly dead. The children all woke with a start and sat up on the grass bed to study their mother. Did the children understand? Grandmother Jiang liked this dream. She did not want to wake up.

One day, in her dream, my father's cradle grew quiet. Actually the infant's little face was red. His pulse was as tenuous as a thread; only his last feeble cry drew Grandmother Jiang over to him. As she dreamed, Grandmother Jiang's eyes were clear, bright, and trancelike. She picked up the infant's feverish body and swept him out the door like a gust of wind. In the dream mother and child were running lightly and swiftly through the rice paddy in the night. The stars in the sky above my old Maple Village home were clean and bright, and the air was filled with drops of sticky dew. The dew was fresh and sweet as it dropped into the open mouth of the parched and starving infant. My father greedily sucked the dew without cease. His precarious little life was also cleansed and renewed by those thousands of dew drops and once more burst out in green leaves and branches.

My father always believed that half a century ago Grandmother Jiang had discovered the miracle of nurturing infants with night dew. It is an everlasting miracle, and it also counts as a miracle in the vast, long, and mysterious historical record of my clan. This miracle made it possible for my father to survive that year of disaster by drinking in the natural essence of the countryside.

When his descendents trace my father's life line, they will see two black circles representing 1934. My Maple Village relatives and neighbors who could not escape the epidemic were as numerous as weeds flattened into the ground. The spirits of those who died so suddenly seeped deep into the soil of Maple Village and howled wildly. All was deep, dark, and gloomy between heaven and earth as the spirits of the living and the dead melded together as one body, like a vast expanse of duckweed blown here and there by the wind and struggling to stay afloat in a stagnant pool. In the space of three days five of Grandmother Jiang's six children joined the army of dead souls.

They were the first group of my clan relatives to perish.

They were placed in a straight row on a straw mat, their five little faces burned black as charcoal from the choleric fever. Their eyes still stared blankly at their mother just as they had the day before. Grandmother Jiang burned incense all night in my family's ancestral home; the incense smoke curling heavenward bathed the five dead children in the delicate aroma of primitive simplicity. Grandmother Jiang sat on the floor with her arms wrapped around her knees and kept the ritual vigil for her children's spirits. She heard a bell ringing all night in the darkness, calling her children. When the sun came out the next morning and the incense smoke had dissipated, Grandmother Jiang began the burial. One by one she laid the five children out in a horse cart, the boys facedown and the girls faceup, and covered their heads with deep green bamboo leaves. Then she strapped my father on her back and set off in the cart.

My family's burial cart lumbered slowly along the yellow mud road. There were dozens of burial parties scattered along the length of the road. Funeral horns blared out dark and mournful music, sending shock waves through 1934. Women's high-pitched songs of mourning filled the air everywhere, and among them was my grandmother Jiang's unique melody. At many points in her funeral song were interspersed folk airs of farewell to a young lover; these rendered her strange song richly anecdotal. Grandmother Jiang rode the horse cart around for a long long time trying, unsuccessfully, to find a suitable burial spot. She was amazed to discover that both sides of the yellow mud road had become a virtual mountain range of grave mounds, with no empty space remaining; countless new graves had sprung up like piles of dog droppings in Maple Village.

Later on, she stopped the horse by the side of a pond. Getting down from the cart, Grandmother Jiang leaned against the horse's side and looked all around, at a loss what to do. She did not know how, but she walked away from that huge crowd of people come to bury their dead; the water in the pond was all blackish-green silence, and weeds grew luxuriantly by the side of the pond without a trace of human existence. From all directions she heard the indistinct sound of far-off funeral horns lingering in the air; suffused with the sound, the village seemed infinitely large. The morning breeze blew my grandmother Jiang's thoughts into a confused tangle; her eyes gradually filled with a dark, visionary fire. She grasped the horse's bridle and pulled it into the pond. When her bare feet stepped into the thick mud on the bottom of the pond, the cold was so piercing she cried out. She began to drop her children one by one into the water; after the five children sank to the bottom of the pond, a long, unbroken chain of colorful bubbles appeared on the surface. As Grandmother Jiang stared at those bubbles, her feet began to slide gradually toward the deeper water. At that point my father, strapped on her back, suddenly began to cry; his crying moved Grandmother Jiang like a voice from heaven. With her body half-submerged, Grandmother Jiang turned her head and asked my father, "What's wrong with you? What's wrong?" My infant father gazed up at the blue sky and went on bawling, boldly and uninhibitedly. Grandmother Jiang was stopped in her tracks; she pulled wildly at her hair, looked toward the south, and shouted, "Chen Baonian Chen Baonian come back right now!"

Chen Baonian was sitting in the city, four hundred miles away from Maple Village, holding the catlike little woman Huanzi on his lap and staring intently at the street outside his bamboo goods shop. Out there was the city of 1934. My grandfather Chen Baonian was pondering the meaning of his dream. He had dreamed that five little bamboo baskets fell from the rafters, bounced over into his arms, and burst into flames. He was burned until he woke up.

He did not want to return home. He was far away from the plague, far away from the epidemic of 1934.

I've heard that while the plague was raging a black-robed sorcerer made an appearance near our old home. He set up a stand in Horsebridge and went to work exorcising evil spirits and suppressing demons. An unending line of people came from every direction to consult this master. Grandmother Jiang carried my father on her back into Horsebridge to see for herself what the black-robed sorcerer looked like. When she saw a young man from the north, dressed in a black robe, standing between a demon-headed sword and a piece of yellow picture-mounting paper, she experienced a brightness before her eyes, and her whole body felt inspired. She pushed and shoved with all her might through the crowd, making her way forward, losing a straw sandal in the process. She gazed at the sorcerer and shouted at the top of her voice, "Star of evil, where's the star of evil?"

Grandmother Jiang's hoarse, raspy voice was lost in a cacophony of other people's voices. Thousands of Maple Village residents appeared before the black-robed sorcerer that day, kowtowing and seeking the spirits, hoping that he could reveal to them the cause of the plague devastating the countryside. The black-robed sorcerer sang and danced, waving that ancient, copper-colored demon-headed sword. Up and down went the sword until finally it landed on the ground. Grandmother Jiang saw the sharp point of the sword oozing blood and pointing southwest down the yellow mud road. "Just look, all of you." The crowd stood on tiptoes and gazed off to the southwest. All they saw was a dense milk-white vapor rising over a far-off stretch of hillside. The scene was obscure yet full of grace. Only a single black brick building could be seen crouching there like some huge beast lying in wait for the people of Horsebridge.

The black-robed sorcerer's words overwhelmed Horsebridge:

In the southwest lies a font of evil,
Concealed within a jade crock.

If the jade crock is not emptied,
The plague will never end.

My Maple Village friends and neighbors seethed with agitation. They stared at the black brick building with eyes full of grief and indignation; this amazing moment of magic instantly enlightened them; the eyes of the old and the young, males and females, all saw the plague germs rising heavenward from out of the black brick building; purple bacteria were even then rushing to attack Maple Village. They knew the discharge from the font of evil was the origin of the plague.

Chen Wenzhi!

Chen Wenzhi!   Chen Wenzhi!

Chen Wenzhi!   Chen Wenzhi!

Grandmother Jiang saw that jade crock high up in the sky, rendered large and visible by the sorcerer's magic. She seemed to hear the sound of the font of evil boiling up out of the jade crock. Everyone in Maple Village except Dingo had only heard rumors about Chen Wenzhi's jade crock, but never actually seen it; it was the mysterious black-robed sorcerer who allowed them to experience the radiant splendor of the jade crock. That day Grandmother Jiang and her now-enlightened rural neighbors chewed repeatedly on the name of the rich landlord: Chen Wenzhi.

It was in just this manner that the curtain was raised on the drama of two thousand Maple Village disaster victims burning down Chen Wenzhi's family granary. When the affair was over, the black-robed sorcerer had quietly disappeared, and nobody knew where he had gone. In the spot were he set up his stand, a sweat-speckled black robe, blowing back and forth in the breeze, hung on an ancient scholar tree.

For years after that, Grandmother Jiang loved to remind others of that once-in-a-hundred-years conflagration. She remembered that the granary had been full, with nine huge piles of grain. When the fire took hold, the granary went up in golden splendor, the smoke giving off a rich, aromatic fragrance. The sweet-scented smoke from the burning grain caused everyone's eyes to water profusely. Chen Lichun, a man whose wife and children had all died of cholera, went crazy at the sight of those flames; he slithered around like a snake on the nine burning volcanoes of grain, wiping the tears from his cheeks while dancing around like a shamaness calling down the gods. Everybody stamped their feet and shouted for joy at Chen Lichun's performance.

Chen Wenzhi's black brick building was thrown into a chaos of nervous trepidation. Members of the Chen family crowded onto the roof crying to heaven and earth, their despair so great they didn't want to go on living. Supported between two maids, Chen Wenzhi's body, skinny as a stick of kindling, stood like a heron in a thunderstorm—not moving a muscle. His Japanese binoculars were already broken; even by squinting his eyes, he was unable to make out clearly the faces of the people swarming around the granary. "Why can't I see who they are? Who are they?" *They* flowed back and forth like waves before Chen Wenzhi's eyes, setting fires and turning the granary into a bright red conflagration. Later on Chen Wenzhi recognized among the arsonists a woman with a baby on her back. The woman's entire body glowed a bright, flaming red, like the body of the Fire Goddess, as she pushed her way between the men, climbed on top of the last remaining pile of grain, and set it ablaze with a rope soaked in pine oil.

"I set a pile of grain on fire, too," Grandmother Jiang later told everyone. "I started the fire, too." She really missed that all too hurriedly disappearing black-robed sorcerer. She was thoroughly convinced that the great conflagration had burned off the plague of 1934.

The year I was eighteen, pouring over the classics of Mao Zedong in my family's attic, I immediately associated his *Report on an Investigation of the Peasant Movement in Hunan* with the residents of Maple Village burning down the Chen family granary. Looking way back in time to my grandmother Jiang's 1934 transformation into a Fire Goddess, I believe Grandmother Jiang's revolution against the rich landlord Chen Wenzhi will one day become a glorious page in the history of my family. Like Grandmother Jiang, I, too, miss that mysteriously magnificent black-robed sorcerer. Who was he? Where is he now?

Maple Village's once famous Pool of Corpses came into existence shortly after the epidemic struck.

The Pool of Corpses was about a mile and a half from my ancestral home. It was originally a reed pond; when Dingo was eight years old, he used to play around there while tending a flock of white geese. I was sick at heart when I investigated the origin of the Pool of Corpses. All the old people of Maple

Village told me the first bodies submerged in the pool were those of Grandmother Jiang's five dead children. They still recalled that the tracks left at the side of the pool by Grandmother Jiang's horse cart were so deep they remained for quite a long time. Those who came later to bury their dead walked in her cart tracks.

Eighteen handicraftsmen who wandered around the Maple Village area were buried in that pool. In death their spirits expressed their anger by keeping their corpses' eyes open; their naked bodies stretched out facedown in the water, one on top of the other; a solid patch of purple and green, horrifying to look at, sent the putrid odor of death soaring up into the sky. They say on this account the purslane shoots grew in unusual profusion around the banks of the Pool of Corpses, making it a wonderful place for the residents of Maple Village to dig up edible wild herbs.

Every morning the purslane shook with dewdrops, and the women of Maple Village, bamboo baskets in hand, rushed to the banks of the pool. They walked around the rim of the pool, fighting over the wild herbs. Plague and famine forced these women to become ferocious and brutal. They fought and wrangled by the Pool of Corpses nearly every day. My grandmother Jiang once cut and wounded a neighbor of hers with a scythe, and she herself also had a scar on her forehead in the shape of a saw tooth. Later, in the long river of her life, the scar always reflected the light of that unique experience, one responsible for Grandmother Jiang's outlook on the world.

I envisage the women of Maple Village all transformed into wild female beasts; but would they, many years later, gather at the entrance of the village to bask in the sunlight, old and gentle, and think back on 1934? The scars on their faces would move people as much as commemorative medals, and cause later generations of Maple Villagers to be filled with profound respect for their aged grandmothers.

I seem to see Grandmother Jiang running through the bitter wind and pestilential rain of 1934 with my young father on her back, and the scar on her forehead glistening brightly in the shape of a saw tooth. Images of my grandmother, the Pool of Corpses, and its purslane plants regularly flashed before my eyes; but I have no power to comprehend the bizarre suffering my grandmother experienced beside the Pool of Corpses.

Why, my grandmother, did you come that day to the edge of the Pool of Corpses and stare, deep in your own silent thoughts, at the dead bodies? Dead, black water covered your children and eighteen handicraftsmen. The wild herbs by the side of the pool had already been grazed bare by people and dogs. You smelled the sweet, putrid odor of death and shivered with happiness. It was a day deep in the middle of autumn, and you vaguely heard the muffled roar of distant thunder rolling over from the edge of the sky. The beat-up old bamboo basket you'd placed on the ground shook with frightened anticipation of the bizarre suffering you were about to endure.

Grandmother Jiang was actually waiting for rain; waiting for the rain to fall and the purslane by the side of the Pool of Corpses to shoot up anew from out of the ground. At that precise moment a strange red wedding palanquin appeared on the raised path between the fields. The red palanquin swooped down like a hawk in the direction of the Pool of Corpses. Four sedan bearers she'd never seen before smiled at her, put down the palanquin, walked over to Grandmother Jiang, and picked her up effortlessly. "Get in the palanquin, you ugly woman."

Grandmother Jiang shouted and struggled to free herself from the grip of the four men. She shrieked, "Are you men or demons?"

The four men laughed as they tossed Grandmother Jiang into the palanquin like a bundle of dry sticks.

Inside the palanquin all was black and red, red and black. She felt herself brush up against a stiff, wet body. Moldy, musty dust and the faint sound of a man's feeble breathing permeated the inside of the palanquin as Grandmother Jiang raised her head and saw Chen Wenzhi. A reddish glow danced crazily around Chen Wenzhi's waxy yellow face. Chen Wenzhi put his hands carefully on grandmother Jiang's board-stiff shoulders and said, "Chen Baonian will never come back; you come with me."

Grandmother Jiang shrieked as she held Chen Wenzhi's cheeks up with both hands to prevent his heavy head from collapsing onto her breasts. She heard Chen Wenzhi's heart beating like a leaf in the wind, with a will but no strength, in his dry, shriveled, cotton-soft chest. She dug the sharp points of her ten fingernails deep into Chen Wenzhi's skin, causing him to cry out like a wild cat. As Chen Wenzhi's black blood dripped onto Grandmother Jiang's hands, he mumbled softly, "Come on with me, and I'll put a plum-blossom tattoo on your face, too."

As the red palanquin shook back and forth for all it was worth, an exhausted Grandmother Jiang gradually fainted away into its black mists and red waves. Outside, the four sedan bearers heard a desolate sound. "I want to wait for the rain I want to dig for herbs!"

. . .

Grandmother Jiang dimly realized that she had been thrown into the water, but she could not open her eyes. Her ravished body started to float like a goose feather. Once again she heard the muffled sound of thunder at the edge of the sky; but why didn't it rain? She opened her eyes as it was nearing dusk and discovered that she had been sleeping in the Pool of Corpses. The putrid odor given off by the decaying flesh of the dead surrounding her stuck thick as glue to her half-naked body. The well-known and the unknown dead gathered together at her feet in strange and various postures, their brownish purple bodies greeting the brilliant rays of the deep autumn sunset. A swarm of rats darting across the Pool of Corpses leapt hysterically by in front of her chest. Grandmother Jiang crawled up numbly and made her way past one after another of the rapidly rotting corpses. She wondered to herself, "Why doesn't it rain?" It probably would not rain because the sun appeared at dusk. Sharp, thin rays of evening light poured into the fields, piercing her eyes painfully. Grandmother Jiang raised a muddy hand and covered her face. She was not the least bit afraid of the dead floating in the Pool of Corpses; she thought she was already a female ghost herself.

When she crawled up on the bank of the pool, Grandmother Jiang saw there was a bag of something in her beat-up old bamboo basket. After she opened it up and saw what it was, she half shouted and half sobbed to heaven. It was a bagful of snow-white polished, uncooked rice. She thrust her hand into the bag, grabbed a handful of rice, crammed it into her mouth, and hurriedly swallowed it down. She told herself, "Heaven left it for me," then walked quickly home, carrying her beat-up old bamboo basket and laughing all the way.

When I discovered the indissoluble bond that was established between the Pool of Corpses and Grandmother Jiang, I came to believe the dark shadow of death lay across the fate of our clan. Death was one vast, ink-blue, arched roof towering over Grandmother Jiang's relatives, from our old home in Maple Village to the small towns of the south.

That a huge star of evil has been pursuing my clan fills me with disappointment, heartache, and anger.

Old Dingo arrived in the city on the ninth day of the tenth lunar month in 1934. He had walked four hundred miles in his bare feet to stand in front of his father Chen Baonian's bamboo goods store, his face covered with dirt and his hair hanging down to his shoulders.

The bamboo craftsmen saw a young man, looking like a beggar, tottering back and forth as he stuck his head in at the main door; the stench of sweat mingled with dog manure streamed into the store. He extended one hand toward the bamboo craftsmen, and they thought he was begging for money; but the young man's tightly held fist opened up, and in the palm of his hand he held an awl-shaped bamboo knife.

"I'm looking for my dad," Dingo said, after which he leaned against the doorframe and collapsed onto the floor. His mouth hung open with exhaustion; it was impossible to tell if he was trying to smile or about to cry. Sitting with his back against the doorframe, he peed in his pants; his piss was bright red as it trickled across the floor of Chen's Bamboo Goods Store, and spread out in a gurgling pool at the feet of the bamboo craftsmen.

Later on, Dingo would remember it was the little blind man who first rushed over and embraced him that day. The little blind man kept exclaiming wildly at the stench emanating from his body. Dingo cringed limply against the little blind man's chest, staring up at him through tear-filled eyes; the expression of elation in the little blind man's lone eye fascinated Dingo, with its profoundly mysterious flower-shaped spot of blood. Dingo reached his arms around the little blind man's neck momentarily, heaved a long sigh, and fell into a deep sleep.

They say Dingo slept for two days and two nights after he arrived at the bamboo goods store. On the third day Chen Baonian picked him up three times and threw him down on the bed before he finally woke up. The first thing Dingo blurted out when he woke up was a peculiar question: "Where's my dog-manure basket?" He felt around in the little upstairs room and then asked Chen Baonian again, "My mom? Where's my mom?"

Chen Baonian was stumped for a moment, then he slapped Dingo in the face and said, "Aren't you awake yet?"

Dingo covered his face and looked his father over carefully. He had arrived in the city. His city life began in just this fashion.

Chen Baonian did not let Dingo study bamboo working. He took him over and made him acquainted with their big city-style rice crock; then he took a big bamboo ladle out of the rice crock and gave it to Dingo. "Dingo, wash ten big ladles of rice every day and boil it in the big kettle until it's good and dry; in the city we eat whenever we feel like it. No more stealing my bamboo knife; when you make it to eighteen, Dad'll teach you all the secret tricks to making eleven kinds of bamboo implements. If you go on stealing this and stealing that, though, Dad'll beat you every day until you're eighteen."

Dingo sat near the back door of the bamboo goods store keeping watch over a huge iron kettle of boiling rice. He was wearing Chen Baonian's oilskin apron, and in his hand he always clutched a yellowing strip of bamboo; his thoughts were confused and his expression was blank. In the autumn of 1934 the city was shrouded in an indistinct sheet of white mist; the people, houses, and smokestacks were quite close to Dingo, and yet they appeared remote and illusory. Dingo folded his strip of bamboo, section by section, and tossed it on the street near the door of the bamboo goods shop. He saw a woman standing on the back steps of the sesame oil shop across the street and looking his way. She was wearing a flashy blue cheongsam, her two arms were bare, and she stood there with her hands on her hips. You could not decide if she was a woman or a girl; she was quite small but very voluptuous, her expression being at once seductive and childlike.

This is the first time the little woman Huanzi appears in my family history. Inevitably she appears in front of Dingo, the two of them being separated by the wet, humid city street and a huge pig-iron kettle. I think this has concrete historical implications; the little woman Huanzi was fated to become a singularly important guest in our clan, one who established an eternal connection with us.

"Are you Chen Baonian's little Dingo? Is your mom pregnant again?"

The little woman Huanzi began to come to life in my painting as she suddenly walked across the street and made her way around the big iron kettle while the sweet, warm fragrance of flowers wafted out from beneath her blue cheongsam. Her white shoes were just then stepping lightly but noisily on those strips of bamboo Dingo had scattered in the street. Dingo concentrated his entire gaze on those white shoes and the scattered bamboo strips; the blood was racing back and forth down below his abdomen in the manner typical of Maple Village men; he covered the bulging crotch of his coarse cloth pants and reached out with his other hand to touch Huanzi's white shoes.

"Don't step on the bamboo strips don't crush the bamboo strips."

"Your mom, is she pregnant again?" Huanzi moved her white shoes slightly and put her hand on the top of Dingo's hedgehoglike head. Dingo's fifteen-year-old body trembled like a blade of grass under Huanzi's touch. With that touch of her hand, Dingo recognized all the women in the world. He closed his eyes and, with Huanzi's inducement, thought of his mother in the countryside.

Dingo said, "My mom's pregnant again, going to have it soon." My grandmother Jiang's swollen abdomen loomed up before his eyes; that was the abdomen he had struck so hard, which was soon going to give birth to another fuzzy little baby. Dingo ran his trembling gaze over the blue cloth covering Huanzi's abdomen and thought there must be a beautiful flower hidden deep within its soft loveliness. Was Huanzi pregnant?

Dingo began his urban life just at the time my grandfather Chen Baonian's bamboo implements business grew extraordinarily prosperous. Every day mountainous piles of bamboo articles were heaped up on the floor and then transported by a fleet of wooden carts to the river wharf and the train station. Dingo snuck across the workshop from his post in front of the big kettle, leaned against the window frame, and looked out admiringly at all those bamboo goods carts. He saw Chen Baonian moving around and about the piles of bamboo goods in front of the door, the pale green color of bamboo flashing across his face. Seen through the window frame, Chen Baonian appeared as though cut in half. Dingo discovered that Chen Baonian's short, stocky legs and well-developed upper body were those of the ordinary Maple Village man, well-known to him; but his dark face had been transformed by the city: Its vigorous heroic spirit already betrayed obvious traces of male weariness. Dingo discovered his dad was a tall smokestack that had risen in the city; his mom could not see this smokestack at all.

All the old bamboo craftsmen I met were still moved by Dingo's thefts of that bamboo knife. They said little Dingo's eyes lit up as soon as he saw that bamboo knife; he liked the big-handled bamboo knife that had been handed down by Chen Baonian's ancestors so much he was damn near obsessed. He stole the knife more times than they could count. And every time Chen Baonian took it back from him. The old bamboo craftsmen always remember the time Chen Baonian and his son were chasing each other around after that knife. At that time Chen Baonian became unusually angry and violent; when he took back the knife, he turned it around in his hand, and pummeled Dingo in the face with the long handle. While he was hitting him and listening attentively to the tearing and cracking of Dingo's skin and bones, Chen Baonian's eyes gave off that cruel and tyrannical glow characteristic of the men of our clan. They said the strangest thing was that Dingo wasn't the least bit afraid of that knife handle; he stood stiffly against the wall facing Chen Baonian. And even when his face turned blue from the blows, he still didn't cover up. "Never saw a father and son like those two never . . ."

Tell me why Dingo was always trying to steal that knife
Then tell me why Chen Baonian was afraid he would
The big-handled bamboo knife
Is lost

I never saw that big-handled bamboo knife handed down to my ancestors. I don't know. I'm only thinking of the element of bamboo in the blood of the Maple Village men. If my grandfather Chen Baonian and my uncle Dingo were both stalks of bamboo, if all their emotions were stalks of bamboo, everything would surpass our thoughts about it. I would not need to enter into the empty spaces left behind by previous generations, and I could still compose my family history. I, too, would be transformed into a stalk of bamboo.

But I can't help liking my bamboo stalk of an uncle, Dingo. I fantasize seeing the little upstairs room in the Chen's Bamboo Goods Store in the city of old, where Dingo and his friend, the little blind man, once lived. In the black of night the window of that little upstairs room gave off a faint red glow; that red glow came from their eyes. When you gaze up at that little upstairs room, you are bound to be moved; you will see that up above people's heads there are still other people; they are watching us from that little upstairs room that will never exist again; they are hanging there in the empty sky of 1934.

By looking through the small window of this upstairs room, Dingo was able to take in Chen Baonian's entire workplace at a glance. From the dark interior of his little room, Dingo's face, always festering and swollen, looked like a restless red poppy. He stood by the window keeping watch over the bamboo workshop as night fell. He was awaiting the arrival of the little woman Huanzi from the sesame oil shop. When Huanzi came over, she always carried her white shoes in her hand and walked barefoot through the piles of bamboo implements on the workshop floor beneath Dingo's window; she jumped nimbly over the room full of bamboo implements like a cat in heat, and pushed open the door to my grandfather Chen Baonian's room.

As soon as she pushed open that door, my family history was bathed in a bright multicolored light. My uncle Dingo was burned by the intensity of that light; he pushed his injured face hard against the cold bamboo wall and rubbed until it hurt. "Mom? Where's my mom?"

Dingo stared at the door to Chen Baonian's room; he heard the sound of Huanzi's cat-like screeching, moist and warm, flow out the door and float across the bamboo workshop. This was not the sound Grandmother Jiang made when she and Chen Baonian embraced in their nakedness on the straw mat in their old home; Dingo knew she remained as dumb as a withered tree. The sound gradually swelled and rose up to Dingo's little room. He started to get dizzy. His hands began to churn like boiling water across the crotch of his coarse trousers. "Mom, oh Mom, where are you?"

Dingo's body thrashed restlessly as he curled up in a circle like a snake; he screwed up his scar-streaked face and finally discharged his manhood.

Now I understand that little upstairs room. Dingo's friend the little blind man also lived there. I have also reflected on the factor's contributing to Dingo's frenzied masturbation. Perhaps my reflections are totally authentic. An image of the dark red flower-shaped spot of blood in the little blind man's lone eye materializes in front of me. Generations of my clan ancestors found it hard to escape unnatural sexual temptations. I think that, inspired by the blaze of that flower-shaped spot of blood, Dingo simply imitated his friend the little blind man. At any rate the old bamboo craftsmen remembered in 1934 the little upstairs room of the bamboo goods shop was splattered everywhere with blotches of white and yellow semen.

I must repeatedly thrust the little blind man into my composition. He is an indistinct black embellishment on the branch of my clan that extended into the city, and he causes me both curiosity and confusion. My grandfather Chen Baonian and my uncle Dingo were both strongly attracted to him, and now the attraction has come down to me as well; when I looked for the little blind man at the site of the old bamboo goods shop, I visited the home of nearly every single bamboo craftsman. I felt terribly distracted and depressed when I heard he had perished in a fire. I told those old bamboo craftsmen I would really have liked to see that solitary eye of his.

Continue to compose. Was Dingo's crime of spying on Chen Baonian and the little woman Huanzi's fornication a tragedy instigated by the little blind man? Dingo crawled over above the door to his dad's room and peered down inside; he saw the white calves of his father and the little woman Huanzi's legs on the bamboo bed, and at the head of the bed hung the ancestral big-handled bamboo knife. The little blind man had told him to "go on and get yourself an eyeful, but whatever you do, don't call out"; but Dingo suddenly yelled down from his perch on top of the door frame, "Huanzi, Huanzi, Huanzi . . . !" He fell down off the door while he was still yelling. Chen Baonian dragged him into the room. Looking at Chen Baonian standing there naked with his face pale and livid, Dingo experienced no fear at all; but when he saw Huanzi standing on the bamboo bed in her blue cheongsam, his eyes filled with hot tears. Huanzi spoke as she buttoned her dress. "Dingo, you little bastard!"

Chen Baonian hung Dingo up from the rafters the whole night; his expression showed no pain; he just kept looking up at the window of the small upstairs room.

The little blind man trained Dingo's fifteen-year-old sexual desires. His influence on Dingo was already total. I tried to summarize that unique influence and education, and discovered they formed a rounded, black life curve:

money

women   women

birth   death

This black curve weighed most heavily on Dingo's body; he hung suspended in midair, stranded prematurely in the orbital point known as women. They say that Dingo contracted typhoid fever because of this. Old people always used to believe that young men contracted typhoid for such reasons. In the winter of 1934 Dingo lay sick in bed in his little upstairs room, counting his black hairs one by one as they fell from his head. The stench of Maple Village dog manure still clung to his hair. He braided his hairs into a string he could thread through the hole in one of the awl-shaped bamboo knives made by the little blind man; thus that awl-shaped bamboo knife with a tassel of hair gave off an odor of typhoid there in his little upstairs room. Whenever Chen Baonian came up to that little room, he always smelled that peculiar odor. When he reached his hand under Dingo's warm, filthy blanket to measure the strength of his son's life, he could not prevent his mind and heart from being filled with a host of boundless and indistinct memories. An earlier Chen Baonian reappeared in Dingo's body. Chen Baonian stroked the front of Dingo's gradually balding head and said, "Dingo, you're really sick; do you still want Dad's big-handled bamboo knife?"

Dingo remained silent under his covers. Chen Baonian spoke again. "What do you want?"

Dingo suddenly choked up, and his body writhed painfully under his cotton-padded blanket. "I'm about to die. . . . I want a woman. . . . I want Huanzi!"

Chen Baonian raised his fist, but then lowered it again. He saw the flames of death already dancing on his son's face. As he escaped into the distance away from that little upstairs room, he could still hear Dingo's hoarse voice shouting behind him, "I want Huanzi Huanzi Huanzi!"

That winter the bamboo craftsmen regularly saw the little blind man carrying the deathly ill Dingo outside to sit in the sun. The two of them went across the bamboo workshop, shoved open the back door, and sat down together in the sunlight. At midday the little woman Huanzi always hung her clothes out behind the sesame oil store to dry. Various colorful and beautiful articles of Huanzi's clothing fluttered on a bamboo pole. The whole city was transformed into a blue cheongsam noisily sprinkled with drops of water from Huanzi's hands. The little woman Huanzi poked her moon-shaped face out from behind the blue cheongsam, looked all around charmingly, laughed gaily as she glanced over at them, and shook out her dripping wet blue cheongsam. Huanzi knew there were two sick men sitting there near the back door of the bamboo goods shop. (I heard it said that the little blind man suffered from gonorrhea from the age of eighteen to forty.) She sprinkled her coquettish allure in front of them like raindrops.

I am so unfamiliar with the winter of 1934. I have absolutely no confidence in my ability to describe the activities of my elders in the family history of that winter. I heard that my grandfather Chen Baonian also carried Dingo on his back to sit in the sun. Then he must have sat with Dingo while they stared at the little woman Huanzi hanging out her clothes. What sort of a scene did it make when these three people stared at each other from opposite sides of that blue cheongsam, and what should it have looked like when the winter sunlight of 1934 shone down on them? Do I know?

I do, however, know what happened to two of them in the end. I know that Chen Baonian finally said to his son, "Dingo, I'm going to give you Huanzi, so don't die. I'm going to send Huanzi into the countryside. All you have to do is go on living, and Huanzi will be your wife."

Chen Baonian said this to Dingo while sitting near the back door of the bamboo goods store. That afternoon Dingo was already clinging to life by just a few feeble breaths. Chen

Baonian heated a pot of warm water and washed Dingo's head with it. Chen Baonian washed Dingo's head repeatedly with Beauty brand perfumed soap, so that the smell of dog manure nearly disappeared completely and his head gave off an urban fragrance. I also know that when the little woman Huanzi stood there that afternoon behind her bamboo pole wringing out her dripping wet blue cheongsam, a stream of light blue water washed down the street.

For many years my father kept the wooden door to our house open day and night. He always believed our relatives were out there wandering on the road and seemed to be keeping the door open just to welcome them on their arrival. The dry straw he kept in the house was divided into six piles. He said the smallest pile was for Elder Brother Dingo, who died young; but he had never seen Elder Brother Dingo. What if, when Dingo's ghost came to lie down in our house, he was enormously large? Father once told me after people die they are much bigger than when they were alive. Last year, before my father entered the hospital, he divided up the piles of straw; he told us the largest pile of straw was for Grandmother Jiang and Chen Baonian.

I watched him as he divided the piles of straw for our deceased relatives; when he came to the sixth pile of straw, he hesitated; he held that pile of straw in his arms and did not know where to put it.

"Who's is that?" I asked.

"Huanzi's." Father said, "Where should I put Huanzi's straw?"

"Put it beside Grandfather's, I guess."

"No." Father looked at Huanzi's straw. Then he went into his own room. I watched him stuff Huanzi's straw under his bed.

Where is that little woman Huanzi now? My family's straw is waiting just the same for her arrival. She was a city woman. Why did she enter the history of my Maple Village family? My father and I had no way to explain it. What I cannot forget is the significance of this enigmatic pile of straw. Can you tell for certain why this pile of straw was hidden under my father's bed?

The old people of Maple Village told me that Huanzi appeared in Horsebridge at sunset one snowy day. Her delicate little body was thickly wrapped in fashionable city clothing, and she was happily walking along on the snow-covered mud road. A man accompanied her. The man was wearing a dog-skin cap and a woman's scarf that together completely covered his face, revealing only a pair of colorless eyes. Some people recognized from the man's walk that it was Chen Baonian.

This was the most secret return to the countryside of any of Maple Village's bamboo craftsmen. Many people clearly observed Chen Baonian and Huanzi hurrying toward home, but afterward they discovered that Chen Baonian had disappeared in the twilight. My grandmother Jiang stood in the doorway and watched the little woman Huanzi walk through the snow toward our ancestral home. In the snow Huanzi's blue cotton-padded coat had a powerful bright blue sheen that hurt Grandmother Jiang's eyes. I can still hear clearly the sound of those two women talking together for the first time, fifty years ago.

"Who are you?"

"I'm Chen Baonian's woman."

"I'm Chen Baonian's woman. Who are you really?"

"If you put it that way, I don't know who I am. I'm pregnant; it's Chen Baonian's child. He dragged me here to have it. I didn't want to come he tricked me into coming."

"You're three months gone I could tell at a glance."

"Did you have one this year? I brought a whole lot of children's clothes guess you can have some of them."

"I don't want your children's clothes did you bring Chen Baonian's money with you?"

"I brought a whole lot of money all of these coins are stamped with Chen Baonian's red seal take a look."

"I know his coins all have his red seal he didn't give me any money this year five children died this fall."

"Let me in the house all right I'm about to freeze to death Chen Baonian he didn't want to come back."

"It's just as cold whether you go inside or not did he want you to have the baby in the countryside?"

(At the same time, I hear the sound of Chen Baonian's footsteps crunching the snow behind our ancestral home. Is Chen Baonian listening too?)

The first thing Huanzi saw as she entered my house was six slow-burning ropes of artemisia hanging down the side of the wall; the acrid smell of vegetable ash lingered in the air inside the house. Huanzi pointed to the ropes and asked, "What's that?"

"Ropes to call back the spirits of the dead. When someone dies, the living have to call their spirits back for them. Don't you know that?"

"Did six of your children die?"

"Chen Baonian died, too." Grandmother Jiang gazed attentively at the artemisia ropes for a moment, then walked to the cradle in the corner of the room, picked up her baby, smiled slightly, and spoke to Huanzi. "Only one survived; all the rest died."

The baby that lived was my father. When the little woman Huanzi leaned her face down to him, the accompanying scent of the city also brushed against his little cheeks. He wrinkled his lips together as if to cry but didn't; in an instant his lips broadened out into his very first smile. Thus my father learned how to smile when he smelled the flavor of the city brought in by Huanzi. His little hand reached out tentatively to touch her face; Huanzi's maternal instincts were completely awakened. Shrieking and trembling, she opened her mouth, nibbled the baby's little hand, and mumbled inarticulately, "I love children so much I dreamed I had a little boy just like you, sweetie."

Recalling the history of Grandmother Jiang and the little woman Huanzi's life under the same roof was one of the most difficult tasks in the composition of my family history. Not since my ancestor's of five generations ago had there ever been a case of polygamy in my clan; but our Maple Village neighbors and relatives told me those two women really did live together through the winter of 1934. Huanzi's blue dress was often washed and dried and fluttered repeatedly in the wind outside our ancestral home.

They said when the pregnant Huanzi walked along the narrow rural roads of Maple Village cradling my infant father, her abdomen was already very heavy. Huanzi was a city woman who dearly loved children; she also loved both the wild and the domesticated dogs that roamed east and west all over the place; she would regularly spit the chewing gum out of her mouth for them to eat. You would not know where Huanzi wanted to go when she walked along carrying one child in her womb and one in her arms; she wandered up and down the village whenever the sun came out; when she passed by any men, she would smile seductively at them. You would see her walking slowly into the depths of the bamboo grove, lightly patting the baby as she crooned a lullaby and glanced apprehensively all around at the scenes of Maple Village in winter. When Huanzi showed up in the bamboo grove, our rural neighbors discovered that she bore a remarkably close resemblance to my deceased great-aunt Phoenix. In the shade of the bamboo leaves their expression and demeanor were astonishingly similar.

Huanzi and Phoenix were the most beautiful women in my family. It's a shame they did not leave behind a photograph; there is no way I can judge whether they really were so alike. They were both scarlet phoenix birds under my grandfather Chen Baonian's wing. One was Chen Baonian's younger sister, and the other was originally not a relative of my clan; she was my grandfather Chen Baonian's neighbor, the female proprietor of the sesame oil shop in the city. Was she my great-aunt Phoenix's sister after all? My grandfather Chen Baonian, which bird did you really want? There is no way for later generations to know any of these things.

I would love to dive beneath the surface of Grandmother Jiang's rock-strewn mental field in order to study that pickled cabbage soup she prepared for Huanzi. All winter, while Huanzi waited out her period of confinement in my house, she received bowl after bowl of pickled cabbage soup from Grandmother Jiang's hands, and she drank them all down to the last drop. She smacked her lips and told grandmother Jiang, "I just love this soup. The only thing I like to eat now is this soup."

As Grandmother Jiang served her the soup and stared at Huanzi's daily enlarging abdomen, her expression was rather dull, and she kept repeating, "Its wintertime; the wild herbs are all gone; there's nothing I can give you but this pickled cabbage soup."

The cabbage was pickled in a big crock. Whenever Huanzi felt like eating, she just stuck her hand into the salty black brine, pulled up a handful of pickled cabbage, and ate it out of her hand. One day Huanzi pulled up a handful of pickled cabbage, but was suddenly unable to swallow it down; tears spilled out of her eyes as she angrily threw the pickled cabbage on the floor, stamped her feet, and bellowed out, "Why's there nothing in this house but pickled cabbage pickled cabbage pickled cabbage?"

Grandmother Jiang walked over, picked up that handful of pickled cabbage, put it back in the crock, and spoke severely to Huanzi. "It's wintertime; there's nothing I can give you but pickled cabbage. If you don't want to eat it, you can't just throw it on the ground."

"What about the money? What about Chen Baonian's money?" Huanzi asked. "Get me something else to eat."

"Chen Baonian's money is gone. I bought Chen Baonian an acre of land. Too many people have died in the Chen family, and we don't even have a burial ground. People can go on living without eating vegetables; but if there's no burial ground, there's no point in living."

Under Grandmother Jiang's cold, implacable gaze, Huanzi

covered her face and sobbed. She felt the skin on her face had already grown coarse and sallow. This was the punishment Chen Baonian's old home meted out to her. Still sobbing, Huanzi thought for the first time of the tragic direction of her entire life. She cried softly, "Chen Baonian Chen Baonian you rotten bastard," as she walked once more towards the big crock full of pickled cabbage. In utter despair she pulled out a handful of pickled cabbage and crammed it into her mouth; her almond eyes opened wide as she swallowed that handful of pickled cabbage all the way down to the pit of her stomach, where it caused a powerful spasm of nausea. Huanzi began to vomit from somewhere deep within her entire life; she vomited out a small stream of bitter black bile that splattered all over her beautiful blue cotton-padded coat.

I know that Huanzi's trip to Horsebridge to sell her ring in exchange for meat took place right after that fit of vomiting. They say it was a square-shaped gold ring my grandfather had given her; she threw it down on the butcher's counter without the slightest twinge of regret, picked up a piece of pork, and left Horsebridge. That was the second time the people of Horsebridge had seen the little woman Huanzi from the city. They all say she was as skinny as a cat, and when she walked she seemed barely able to support her three-months pregnant body. She walked along the yellow mud road running the length and breadth of Maple Village carrying that piece of pork, but when she met young men she didn't ever forget to cast her flirtatious city-woman glances in their direction.

A large rock quickly grew up out of the middle of that yellow mud road I have described so often before; that rock, harboring its seemingly murderous intent, tripped up Huanzi; she cried out in alarm as her pregnant body tumbled toward the ground like a felled tree. That piece of pork flew into the air at the same time. Huanzi's cry of alarm reverberated, pathetic and remote, over the yellow mud road as dusk fell. In that instant she seemed to become conscious of the heaven-sent disaster directed at the baby in her womb. She fell over into the deserted rice field, protecting her midsection tightly with both hands, but she still suffered an excruciating pain in her abdomen. She felt it clearly and unmistakenly as the little life in her womb slipped out and was lost. She was suddenly transformed into a hollow woman. Huanzi sat on the ground sobbing and crying out in a weak but shrill voice; she watched as a pool of red washed forth in waves from under her body. She reached out frantically as that bloody water flowed forth, saw a child with Chen Baonian's square face pause for an instant in her hands before flying nimbly up into the sky above Maple Village, leaving only a wisp of green smoke behind.

After her miscarriage the little woman Huanzi buried herself in my family's straw bed and wept for three days and three nights. She didn't eat and she didn't drink, and she lost her previous appearance. My grandmother Jiang brought Huanzi her pickled cabbage soup as before, then stood by the bed and scrutinized the wretched city woman. As Huanzi's dried-up glance fell on that pickled cabbage soup, she started to think back on what had happened to her. She seemed to sense an unusual smell coming from that dark black broth; she felt the baby in her womb had been gradually aborted by drowning in pickled cabbage soup. It was as though she had suddenly awakened from a dream.

"Big Sister, what do you put in the pickled cabbage soup?"

"Salt. Pregnant women need to eat a lot of salt."

"Big Sister, what did you put in the pickled cabbage soup to get rid of my child?"

"Don't talk nonsense. I know you went into town to buy meat and fell and lost the baby."

Huanzi climbed down off the straw bed, latched tightly onto Grandmother Jiang's hand, and looked up into Grandmother Jiang's totally impassive face. Huanzi shook Grandmother Jiang and screamed, "Just falling down wouldn't make me lose a baby three months along; what did you actually feed me why did you want to harm my child why?"

My grandmother Jiang finally exploded with anger; she pushed Huanzi down on the bed, sprawled on top of her, and grabbed her by the hair. "You city bitch you little whore what right do you have coming into my house and having a little bastard for Chen Baonian?" Grandmother Jiang's dark gray eyes were half-full of tears and half-full of flames of hatred. While she was fighting with Huanzi, she told her little by little, "I couldn't let you have a child. . . . I gave birth to seven children and they all grew up just to die. . . . They'd been better off dying in their mother's belly. . . . I put something dirty in the pickled cabbage soup, but I won't tell you what sort of dirty thing it was. . . . You don't know how much I hate both of you. . . ."

I really should avoid describing this kind of a scene. I feel uncomfortable depicting Grandmother Jiang's character in this manner, but in the face of my 1934 family history I have no other choice.

I miss Huanzi's unborn baby; if he or she had been born in my Maple Village ancestral home, my clan would have had another member, my father and I would have had something more to long for; and the eternally dissolute Chen family bloodstream would have produced a new tributary.

On that account would my family history have had a richer and more detailed story line?

As with her entrance, Huanzi's disappearance left a scar on my family that was very difficult to heal; this scar would continue to suppurate and fester indefinitely, and we would one day bear the pain of licking it smooth.

When Huanzi left the house, she kidnapped my father out of his cradle. She disappeared from Maple Village, taking the Chen family baby with her; obviously she took my father away as a form of compensation for her own loss. Perhaps women are all like that: When they lose something, they compensate with something else. No one saw that city woman steal the Chen baby away; do you think Huanzi relied on the strength of her maternal love to grow a pair of wings?

My grandmother Jiang pursued Huanzi and my father that entire winter. Her footprints extended all the way to the banks of the Long River before they finally came to a halt. It was the first time she'd ever seen the Long River. In the winter of 1934 the water of the Long River roared down with a rush like one of the nine rivers of the primordial flood. The turbid, yellow silt, which had built up in the river for a thousand years, bore down with the heavy force of iron and steel, and smashed against the walls of a country woman's heart. Grandmother Jiang walked up and down on the banks of the river, carrying in her hand the eighth pair of straw sandals she had worn out in her pursuit; her hair blew around wildly in the wind off the river; and her emotions swirled dizzily like a dried-up leaf caught in a whirlpool. She threw her eighth pair of straw sandals out into the boundless river and turned around for home. That great river constituted the furthest border of Grandmother Jiang's mental world. She was powerless to cross over.

I need you to pay careful attention to Grandmother Jiang's

return journey in order to understand the final resting place of her life. She walked through the long winter of 1934, walked through three hundred miles of small towns and villages, and on the road she underwent a complete transformation. The people of Maple Village remembered that it was the end of the year when Grandmother Jiang returned. The people of Horse-bridge had already hung up red paper lanterns to welcome in 1935. Grandmother Jiang walked empty-handed past those lanterns while their red shadows flitted across her face. She wore men's shoes and was dressed completely in men's cotton-padded clothing, with a belt of plaited straw tied around her waist. People who recognized her asked, "Did you catch up to the baby?"

Grandmother Jiang finally leaned against the wall, looked at them, and smiled slightly. "No, they went across the river."

"They crossed the river, and you just stopped chasing them?"

"They went into the city; I can't follow them there."

Grandmother Jiang walked back on the eve of 1935; with the trace of a smile on her face, she gradually walked out of my endless family history. Later on she stood on the northwest slope of Maple Village and gazed up at the rich landlord Chen Wenzhi's black brick building. Just then a pack of dogs ran over from many different directions and walked around, sniffing her unfamiliar odor; the winter had passed, and the dogs of Maple Village no longer recognized Grandmother Jiang. Grandmother Jiang waved the dogs away with her hand, then looked up in the direction of that black brick building, and started to shout Chen Wenzhi's name.

Chen Wenzhi was called up to the roof by Grandmother Jiang, and the two of them looked at each other from a great distance through the colors of nightfall; he saw that woman standing there on the hillside like a profuse tangle of branches and leaves shaken loose from a stalk of bamboo. Chen Wenzhi had a premonition that in 1934 this branch of bamboo would escape and be transplanted in the palm of his hand.

"I'm not pregnant. . . . Do you still want me? . . . Just send that red palanquin down to pick me up. . . ."

The metal gate of Chen Wenzhi's house creaked open while Grandmother Jiang was still calling out; Chen Wenzhi led out three robust women of uncertain status carrying a red palanquin and slowly making their way toward where Grandmother Jiang stood bathed in moonlight. The likes of that troop of sedan bearers has seldom been seen in history, but my grandmother Jiang really did ride that red palanquin into Chen Wenzhi's house.

In just this fashion I have slowly to remove Grandmother Jiang from my family history. My father told me that, right up to the present day, he never knew her given name. Many of his memories of his mother were not very accurate because in 1934 he was still a baby.

Nevertheless, our family prepared the largest pile of straw to welcome the arrival of Chen Wenzhi's woman, Grandmother Jiang. Father said she will certainly come someday.

Grandmother Jiang and the little woman Huanzi competed like the moon with the stars to raise my father; they were both the most outstanding images of motherhood ever to appear in the history of my family. Perhaps they were just two different meteorites that collided together in 1934, and the dark blue sparks from that collision were simply my father, myself, our sons, and grandsons.

The city our family lives in now was, at that time, the ultimate destination of the little woman Huanzi's escape; this city is 450 miles from our old Maple Village home. From the age of seventeen or eighteen, I began to enjoy telling my city friends, "I'm an outsider."

What I have narrated here is actually a story of escapes. These escapes began, and were carried out, very early in just this manner. Now that you've waited to the end of this story, you may want to remember well the cause of my grandfather Chen Baonian's death.

SECRET REPORT ON THE DEATH OF CHEN BAONIAN

On the night of the eighteenth day of the twelfth lunar month in 1934, when Chen Baonian came out of the brothel on the south side of town, someone hiding on the roof of a nearby building poured three buckets of cold water on him. After this sneak attack Chen Baonian ran back to his shop as fast as he could; he wanted to work up a warm sweat by running that way; but when he reached the bamboo goods store, his whole body was covered with ice, and in this way he contracted an unknown illness. He died at the end of the year; just before he died, he held on tightly to his ancestral big-handled bamboo knife. Thus the ownership of the Chen's Bamboo Goods Store changed hands. The current owner is the little blind man. Word that leaked out from the brothel south of town has it that the little blind man was the one who poured those three buckets of water on Chen Baonian.

With the death of my grandfather Chen Baonian, I intend to present you a big basket of flowers in honor of my clan history. I'm going to pick up this basket of flowers and walk outside right now, walk through the streets in the dead of night, walk by, under your windows. If you all open your windows, you will see my shadow cast upon this city, fluttering in the wind.

Who can say what kind of shadow it is?

OPIUM FAMILY

The storehouse was full of rakes, hoes, ploughs, and other such agricultural implements, all stacked neatly up against the mud walls like a row of people. A smell of rusty metal came from their bodies. It was my family's storehouse: a deep, dark, unfathomable space. Grandmother's spinning wheel was still hanging there in the air, the wheel and the spokes wrapped all around in webs of gossamer. Yanyi thought of that spinning wheel as a huge spider, a spider forever looking down at the tops of people's heads. The sunlight gradually dimmed on the paper covering the window; all the farm implements and other miscellaneous items darkened, leaving only vague silhouettes. Glancing over at them, they did look just like a row of people.

It was about to grow completely dark. Yanyi's hunger attacked him again; he ran over to the door, pushed and pushed and pushed as hard as he could on the wooden door leaves. He heard two big locks clang together; Dad had locked the door fast, and it could not be pushed open.

"Let me out. I won't steal any more steamed rolls!" Yanyi shouted in a high-pitched voice. He squatted down and peered out through a crack between the door leaves. A group of long-term laborers and maids stood around in the big compound. They seemed to be very happy about something as they darted here and there like dogs sniffing the air. Yanyi wondered what they were so happy about as he slammed his fist against the door, making it rattle like crazy. He saw the colors of dusk lowering in the sky, lowering like pieces of gray steel. Yanyi was afraid of the growing darkness; as soon as it grew dark, his stomach would growl with hunger. His hunger would turn Yanyi into an angry little beast; then you could hear his shouts shake the great house of Liu in 1930. Yanyi shook the door and shouted, "Let me out. I want to eat some steamed rolls!"

Some people looked over at the storehouse. Yanyi wondered to himself, "If they hear me, why don't they unlock the door?" He could tell from the shape of their mouths they were calling him a hungry devil. "Hungry devil, hungry devil, sooner or later I'll kill all of you."

Yanyi bashed his head against the door. A maidservant walked over with a ring full of keys hanging at her waist. The reddish-purple glow of late afternoon light hit him full in the face when those two iron locks fell off; Yanyi covered his eyes and staggered slightly from the force of the light. Then he picked up a staff made from a tree branch and thrust it at the maid's stomach. (This action will be repeated again later.)

"I'll kill you," Yanyi said.

"Stop it, Eldest Young Master." The maid said as she retreated, "Hurry on in and watch your mother have a baby."

"What?"

"She's having a baby. After this, you'll be even more useless." The keys rattled noisily as the maid ran off, then she turned and smiled at Yanyi. "It's Chen Mao's seed, you know!"

Yanyi was eight that year. He stuck his staff into the muddy earth and leaned against it; his walnut shell of a body swayed back and forth with the staff. The evening light weighed heavily on his little gourd-shaped cap. "My head hurts like hell; hunger's creeping down from my head, tying up my whole body." Yanyi's ears suddenly trembled; he heard the sound of a baby crying from inside his mother's room. Yanyi thought it was a cat screeching in his mother's room.

Two men were sitting at a round amboyna-wood table drinking; one was already old, and one was still young. The old one was dressed in white silk; his face was growing redder as he drank, and the clear juice from pickled soya beans dripped from the corners of his mouth. The young one was ill at ease; the ceremonial brass trumpet hanging on his belt kept hitting the table. That was the long-term laborer Chen Mao; you could pick him out from the crowd of workers by that trumpet of his. He held his wine cup with one hand while continually rubbing his crotch with the other; this was an extremely subtle movement, rich in meaning, but often overlooked.

"It's a boy. I've named him Chencao, Liu Chencao," said Liu Laoxia.

"A boy. Congratulations Old Master."

"You want to see him?"

"I don't know." Chen Mao stood up, took a couple of steps forward and another step back; he was suddenly aware of a problem: The old landlord was smiling. It was hard to divine whether the old landlord's smile portended good or evil for him. Chen Mao turned and looked inquiringly at Liu Laoxia. "Should I go?" he asked. You could not tell if he was asking Liu Laoxia or himself.

"Dog!" Liu Laoxia bellowed out as expected. He threw his wine cup at Chen Mao faster than thunder follows lightning. Chen Mao saw a round splotch of wine like a slug crawling up his chest. His chest felt hot and sore.

"Get back here," commanded Liu Laoxia.

When Chen Mao returned to the table, Liu Laoxia slapped him across the face. Chen Mao did not dodge the blow; he just felt like that slug had crawled onto his face. His whole body was covered with gooseflesh. He watched as Liu Laoxia kicked over the table and chairs with a crashing noise. Liu Laoxia grabbed Chen Mao by the throat and said, "Chen Mao, you're a dog. Tell me you are my dog."

Chen Mao's bare feet stepped on a bowl of pickled soya beans; with his throat constricted he could barely repeat the words. "You are my dog."

"Fool! Say it again. Say it right."

Liu Laoxia tightened his grip on Chen Mao's throat. Chen Mao's handsome face was going from red to purple. He shook himself free from those powerful old dragonlike hands, panted heavily, and said, "Chen Mao is your dog."

Chen Mao went through the central room on his way out; passing by Jade Flower's room, he was assaulted by the sickening sweet smell of blood blended with the fragrance of a woman's lower body. That sort of odor made his head swim. He stood in the doorway of the big house and made a wry face in the direction of the other long-term laborers and maids. He made an obscene gesture with three fingers. The others laughed joyfully by the side of the wall. Chen Mao laughed too; he took off his wine-splattered cotton shirt, put it to his nose, and sniffed. The odor of wine had dissipated. He looked down at the brass trumpet shining brightly at his waist. He suddenly picked it up and started to play; he heard that brass trumpet emit a plaintive sound: *woo . . . woo . . . woo . . .*

Chen Mao blew his trumpet as he went into the fields to work. On that day, just as on any normal day, Chen Mao hoed weeds in the Liu family's opium fields. And after he hoed the weeds he took a nap. In the pale morning sunlight, he dreamed that a baby boy pressed down like a stone on the top of his head and smashed in the top of his skull.

The Maple Village rural area stretches for twenty-five miles, and everywhere on those twenty-five miles are the footprints of your ancestors. For several thousand years the land has been repeatedly cultivated and transformed from barren wilderness to richly abundant soil. The spectacle of your ancestors wandering around dying of starvation was not repeated in the 1930s. Early in the 1930s, half the land in Maple Village was planted with a strange crop: the opium poppy. From that time on wet rice and opium poppies were emblematic of the changing rural seasons. Outsiders moved in from all quarters, and Maple Village became your rural homeland.

You could never miss seeing the landlord Liu Laoxia's big black house. You could never miss hearing the history of the flourish and decline of that big black house; the soul of the countryside would make it impossible for you to avoid it. It's been so many years now, but people still talk repeatedly about that period of history.

Grandfathers built peasant huts on a rise on the left bank of the river; the windows faced the river, and the smokestack sticking up out of the roofs of each hut symbolized men and women creating a home. Fathers went out at dawn and returned at dusk, working all day in the wet rice and opium-poppy fields; mothers raised chickens, ducks, pigs, and goats inside the fence behind the house; and the children ate thin rice gruel with salted vegetables, and stood on the riverbank gazing over at the landlord Liu Laoxia's big black house.

Maple Villagers are skinny and nimble of build, and they all have the same satisfied and lethargic expression on their faces. Prior to 1949 about a thousand people cultivated wet rice and opium poppies for the landlord Liu Laoxia; tenant farmers rented land and paid in food grains; and Liu Laoxia's renting land to buy more became a fixed way of life. As I see it, it was a typical southern village.

Grandfathers told grandsons, "Maple Village became rich because the people there had the good rural habits of living frugally and running their homes with industry and thrift. Look at the rice stored in the houses in big piles; even if the rice has mildew or maggots, it's still food grain, and you don't want to eat it anytime you feel like it. All of us eat thin rice gruel with salted vegetables; every Maple Villager does the same. Even the landlord Liu Laoxia does the same." Grandfathers spoke with great emphasis on this point: "Liu Laoxia's family eats thin rice gruel every day, too. Haven't you seen his little brat Yanyi? He's so hungry he's a skinny yellow bag of bones, hollering and complaining all day long—just like you."

Their genealogy records that Yanyi was Liu Laoxia's fifth child. The first four were placed in the river and allowed to float downstream; they looked like fish, having neither legs nor arms. With sword-shaped tails, all they could do was float downstream on the river. Yanyi was the only child who survived in those chaotic times. The country people had a special explanation for Liu Laoxia's procreative abilities: They said when his animal spirits reached their peak, he became promiscuous; his blood ran riot and he could not produce good progeny. There was another shameful secret hidden in this explanation. Yanyi was the product of his father and mother's fornication in the open fields; at that time the Eldest Master of the Liu family, Liu Laoxia's father, had not yet died suddenly, and Jade Flower, Yanyi's mother, was *his* concubine; at that time Liu Laoxia's first wife, the cat-eyed woman, had also not yet drowned in the big iron bathtub; but Yanyi was born to Jade Flower nevertheless.

Their genealogy also records that Yanyi was an idiot. You would think he looked like a hedgehog rolling around here and there; he used a staff made from a tree branch to attack all the people nearby who were forever strangers to him. It was his habit to swallow his food while repeating his favorite words: "I'm hungry I'm going to kill you."

You could see that Yanyi had inherited the blood of the Liu family from three generations earlier. Because he often found himself in a state of near starvation, the historical grandfather of the Liu family developed an appetite so prodigious he could eat a pig all by himself. Yanyi's reversion to the ways of his great-grandfather was a rude awakening to the Liu family's servants; they felt almost afraid to take Yanyi's steamed rolls away from him. For a long time Yanyi was obsessed with a black pottery crock. That crock was about three feet high and was kept behind his mother Jade Flower's bed. There was also a red lacquer chamber pot behind the bed, and those two containers placed there side by side gave a powerful stimulus to his appetite. When Yanyi saw the lid of the crock covered with a layer of fine ash from the stove, he would open it, hide a bunch of steamed rolls under his shirtfront, and run outside; he would run all the way to Firewood Hill on the other side of the storehouse. Someone would be standing there cutting firewood. That someone was Yanyi's uncle, Liu Laoxia's younger brother, Liu Laoxin. If you saw the two of them, uncle and nephew of the Liu family, sitting there on Firewood Hill wolfing down those steamed rolls like they were starving, you would never be able to understand it.

Yanyi always left his fingerprints on the lid of the crock. Yanyi saw his father come after him with a shoe in his hand, grab him by the hair, and ask, "How many did you steal today?"

Hurriedly swallowing down his sweet saliva, Yanyi answered, "I didn't steal; I was hungry."

Then Yanyi heard a loud sound as the sole of his father's shoe repeatedly struck the top of his head. It hurt like hell. "How many did you steal today?"

"I don't know; I was hungry."

"Who else did you give them to?"

"Uncle; he was hungry, too." Yanyi covered the top of his

head with his hands and watched his father walk away, kicking piles of sticks aside all the way down Firewood Hill. His father raised his shoe and shouted back, "Hungry devils, you're all hungry devils. Sooner or later the Liu family's going to be ruined by your hungry mouths."

Two people remained seated on Firewood Hill; one was the idiot Yanyi and the other was his uncle Liu Laoxin. In the big Liu family this close relationship between uncle and nephew was a solitary and unusual one. People remember that Liu Laoxin never talked to anyone; he only talked to his firewood and his idiot nephew Yanyi. And it was only when he was sitting beside his uncle that Yanyi exhibited normal intelligence and linguistic abilities; that was the result of his uncle bringing out Yanyi's latent natural abilities. At that time Liu Laoxin was no longer young, and his face was covered with purple scars. He looked peaceful and melancholy sitting there alone on Firewood Hill talking to the idiot Yanyi. Many of these conversations between uncle and nephew can help you to enter more deeply into the Liu family's multilayered historical space.

"Your father is a thief. He's been stealing from others ever since he was a boy."

"Thieves take other people's things. Dad takes my steamed rolls, too."

"Your father killed my father and stole Jade Flower away to be your mother."

"I dropped out from under my mom's armpit."

"There isn't a decent person in your whole family; sooner or later I'm going to burn the place down; nobody will survive."

"Can you burn the whole place down?"

"I can. All it takes is hate. One torch and you'll all go up in flames."

"Burn me up too?"

"Right, you little bastard. If I don't burn you up, sooner or later they'll kill you anyway."

"If they kill me, I won't be hungry any more."

Liu Laoxin, as Liu Laoxia's younger brother, is not the main protagonist of this history. I only know in the old days he was a well-known Maple Village libertine; he went off to the unfamiliar city dreaming he'd find a way to get rich other than from the land. In the end he didn't achieve anything except to get his body covered with big syphilitic lesions. When he came home riding on a salt boat, he was completely destitute. They say in ten years all the land on the left bank of the river had been gathered into Liu Laoxia's hands like a flock of pigeons coming home to roost. Finally Liu Laoxia bought his younger brother's burial plot from him—for ten silver dollars. It was on the side of a hill facing south into the sun; Liu Laoxia leveled it off with a shovel, and thus all the land on both sides of the river was combined into one holding.

This buying and selling of land between elder and younger brother left later generations speechless in amazement; they could not judge who was in the right and who was in the wrong. Nevertheless you still ought to pay attention to these extraordinary vicissitudes of human life. The last land deal between the Liu brothers was finalized in a brothel in town. A salt boat stopping at Maple Village brought a message for Liu Laoxia: "Your younger brother Liu Laoxin has just about rotted to death; he still has a third-of-an-acre burial plot left to sell."

Liu Laoxia hurried to the brothel in the city, arriving in

time to see his younger brother lying there in a pile of garbage, his body covered with suppurating sores.

The younger brother said, "I'll give you my burial plot if you'll take me home, all right?"

The older brother took the deed and answered, "Sign it over and we'll go."

Liu Laoxia pressed his younger brother's ulcerated fingers down on the deed; signing it not in red ink, but in blood. Everything was finally accomplished when Liu Laoxia had carried his younger brother over to the river and thrown him down in that salt boat; the people of Maple Village said at that point the two streams of the Liu family bloodline had been united into one. They also said that Liu Laoxin was destroyed by his own cock, the usual vice of the Liu family, but that nothing could destroy his elder brother Liu Laoxia; you never knew when you would end up selling the tiles off your roof or the grass under your feet to him.

The idiot Yanyi remembered that his uncle from Firewood Hill, Liu Laoxin, soon disappeared.

Liu Laoxin perished in a fire the next year, and nobody high or low knew anything about it. When that fire was blazing away on Firewood Hill, Yanyi was the only witness. Yanyi had walked out of the storehouse carrying a gunnysack, his face blackened by the smoke. He had placed the gunnysack down on the stairs, looked at it, and started to wail. This was the first time the tenant farmers and maidservants had ever heard Yanyi cry. They opened the gunnysack and saw Liu Laoxia's younger brother, Liu Laoxin, burned to a crisp, his stiff body giving off a fresh aroma like firewood. His mouth had been stopped up with half a steamed roll, and his expression was very peculiar. Yanyi sobbed as he spoke. "He's hungry; I gave him half a steamed roll; why doesn't he swallow it?"

They ran to the back courtyard and saw that Firewood Hill was nearly half burned up already; nobody knew when the fire had started. The fire just started while no one was looking.

The genealogy records that Liu Laoxin died on October 5, 1933.

A carpenter made a thin-walled coffin, and four long-term laborers carried Liu Laoxin down and buried him in the big graveyard on the right bank of the river. Only the sound of white pennants fluttering in the wind was audible after the mournful funeral horns suddenly ceased, and the dead man was placed in the ground. That was a very shabby funeral, an unprecedentedly unusual occurrence in the big Liu family. Everyone in Maple Village knew the story of how Liu Laoxin was burned to death in a fire he set himself. When grandfathers told grandsons about the strange death of Liu Laoxin, their last words were always the same: "Don't mess with Liu Laoxia. If you try to set a fire, you'll be the one who gets burned up first."

The baby born at the beginning of the story will become the central protagonist when he grows up; this a self-evident truth in a clan history.

Several years later, Chencao, dressed in a black woolen uniform and carrying a deerskin suitcase, walked down in our direction from the steps of the provincial middle school. The sun cast a shimmering light like a net across his fair, handsome face. It was a spring day forty years ago, and Liu Chencao, at the peak of his refinement and ability, was saying good-bye to his school life; his heart, however, was as heavy as lead. He walked across a stretch of green lawn, passed by two female students playing tennis, and saw an old-fashioned horse cart waiting at the far end of the lawn. Someone had come from home. Chencao's pace began to slow; he searched in his pocket with his hand, and brought out a tennis ball. The tennis ball was gray; as it rolled along over the lawn, it was quickly swallowed up in the grass. The melancholy feeling that he was saying good-bye to all this with a wave of his hand pressed down on Chencao's slender shoulders; he shrugged and walked toward the horse cart. He felt something slip away from him that afternoon, just like the tennis ball. Chencao looked back repeatedly as he walked slowly along. He heard his father shout, "Chencao, what are you looking at? Let's go home."

He answered, "The ball disappeared."

His father had come to take him home. Chen Mao was at the reins of the cart. Seeing some leftover strands of straw in the cart, Chencao knew his father had come into town to sell a load of straw. He sat down on the straw holding his knees and heard his father shout, "Chen Mao, let's go." The red provincial houses gradually receded with the clop-clop of the horse's hooves. Chencao would later recall that day's return journey was pregnant with intimations of his destiny. The cart hurried along a branch road, and the journey home was greatly prolonged; his father had him feast his eyes on the busy scenes of spring all across their 250 acres of land. Everywhere the blood-red opium poppies were blooming profusely. Black-clothed tenant farmers and scarecrows stared with equally dull eyes at the horse cart. Chencao grew quite upset listening to the Bakelite wheels creaking along on the wide yellow earth road. Chen

Mao's big straw hat cast an oblong shadow on the floor of the cart. I don't know what was stuck on the Bakelite wheels making that strange creaking sound. Following the side road, the cart had to pass through the Firebull Hills. This was where, Chencao would recall later, he first met the bandit Jiang Long. In the elm forest about halfway up Firebull Ridge, a troop of horsemen rode quickly by under the trees. Chencao heard them call his name in rough, hoarse voices just like his father's. "Liu Chencao, come on up the mountain with us!"

The next day was foggy; the hilly ground was moistened by clouds of diaphanous mist, and the leaves and stems of the crops and other vegetation gave off a sweet, warm scent. It was one of Maple Village's own special moist mornings: twenty-five miles of beauty and sadness. Three generations of men living on the banks of the river all woke up together at cockcrow and walked out of the village in the direction of the opium-poppy land. The fog did not disperse for a long time, and they heard the landlord Liu Laoxia's white silk gown rustling in the breeze; Liu Laoxia and his son Chencao were standing in the Straw Pavilion.

The tenant farmers said, "The Old Master's getting on in years; Second Young Master has come back."

Chencao's feelings were confused as he stood there facing the blood-red opium fields and the tenant farmers. He shrugged his shoulders and put one hand in the pocket of his school uniform. "This is my family's opium; this is the opium plant that always remained outside of the botanical curriculum; it comes from father's land, but it can turn your face ghostly pale and make you feel as though you're floating in a nightmare." The sweet, pungent odor of opium poppies rose up from every corner of the fields; Chencao discovered that he was standing on an isolated island; he felt dizzy; the murmuring sound of the waves of opium poppies pushes you onto an isolated island where everything is far far away from you and there is only that murderous odor penetrating your lungs; at that moment Chencao felt his weak, slender body floating off of that isolated island. His face went white and he grabbed hold of his father's arm. "Dad, I'm floating away," he said.

The tenant farmers in the opium fields saw with their own eyes Chencao's first fainting spell. They told me later both how frail Second Young Master's health was and how strange was his behavior, and I knew that first fainting spell was the beginning of a tragedy; it determined the course of the Lius' family history. They told me Liu Laoxia took his son on his back and carried him past the poppy fields by the riverbank. A wondrously pleasant sound rang out from his pocket as he walked by; it was rumored to be from a ring of platinum keys. If you owned any one of those platinum keys, you could open the doors of a rice storehouse and eat your fill for the rest of your life.

You've never seen Maple Village's Straw Pavilion.

The Straw Pavilion's unique silhouette was easily visible through the white mist. The men regarded the Straw Pavilion as a symbol of masculinity. Grandfathers told grandsons, "Liu Laoxia built it when he was a young man; the wind can't blow it down and the rain can't wash it away; whenever I see it, I think of all the changes in human life." Grandfathers remembered the many amorous adventures of Liu Laoxia's youth; virtually all of them took place in the Straw Pavilion. "That bastard Liu Laoxia deflowered and ruined so many Maple

Village women! They would couple together on nights when
the moon was black and the wind was up, and they never even
tried to avoid being seen." Some people hid in the bushes and
listened to them, and afterward they said, "You know why Liu
Laoxia can't leave behind a good seed? It's all because of that
Straw Pavilion. The Straw Pavilion is a natural tiger's mouth;
it swallows everything down; you go in there, and when you
come out your body is completely drained."

Many years later the old men of Maple Village still had
fond memories of that Straw Pavilion; they told me that every
man for generation after generation of the Liu family had a
lecherous cock between his legs.

"And Chencao, too?" I asked.

They thought a moment and replied, "No, not Chencao."

Chencao was undoubtedly an anomaly in the Liu clan, and
that was inevitable.

Chencao slept right through the first few days after he
returned home; when the wind chanced to subside and the odor
from the opium poppies suddenly disappeared, Chencao felt
much more clearheaded. He walked from the front courtyard
into the back courtyard and saw a man with disheveled hair
and dirty face dressed in beat-up old clothes sitting in the
storehouse doorway, chewing on part of a stale, blackened
steamed roll.

Chencao stood there watching Yanyi chew his steamed roll.
He could never believe that Yanyi was his elder brother, but
he did know Yanyi was another solitary individual in their
family. Chencao was afraid to look at him; in Yanyi's crude,
vulgar, greedy face Chencao discerned a kind of animalistic

suffering that was shared by an entire generation of Maple Villagers, including his ancestors and relatives. But Chencao knew that animalistic suffering had nothing to do with him. When the Li bloodline reached our generation, it ruptured. Chencao thought, "He's my brother? It's all too bizarre."

When the odor of the opium poppies suddenly disappeared, the sunlight grew intense. Chencao saw Yanyi jump up off the steps like a filthy ball of flesh. He saw Yanyi, pointing his tree-branch staff like a sword, rush at him; he tried to dodge, but was not quick enough, and the staff poked him in the lower abdomen.

"Yanyi, what're you doing?"

"You're laughing at me."

"No. I wasn't even thinking about you."

"You got any steamed rolls?"

"No, I don't have any. Dad has the steamed rolls, go ask him for some."

"I'm hungry. Give me a steamed roll."

"You're not hungry, you're despicable."

"If you curse me, I'll kill you."

Chencao saw Yanyi throw down his staff and pull a knife out of his belt. Yanyi waved the knife around in the air. From the glare in his eyes, like an angry lion, you could sense a genuine desire to kill someone. Chencao kept his eyes glued to the knife as he attempted to move backward. He could not figure out how Yanyi came to have a knife. Everyone in the Liu family knew that Yanyi had wanted to kill someone since he was a child; Dad ordered everyone to keep all the knives and sharp tools in a safe place, but you could never understand why Yanyi always had a knife or an ax in his hands. A knife in Yanyi's hands always made you sense a genuine desire to kill someone.

Chencao suddenly shouted, "Who gave you that knife?" as he moved backwards.

He saw Yanyi stop a moment, look puzzled, and then point back into the storehouse. "They did!"

Over by the storehouse a group of laborers were hulling rice by pounding a pestle into a mortar. Chencao looked over in their direction, but the sunlight hurt his eyes. He did not want to see their faces clearly, anyway; "everything disgusts me." The sound of pounding rice with wooden pestles echoed from the big house; you only had to listen carefully to discern the rhythm of hatred. Chencao put his hands in his pockets and walked out of the back courtyard; he believed that various conspiracies were right then underway or were soon to be set in motion.

"They hate your family because your family controls them. If you control other people, they hate you; if you want to eliminate that hatred, you have to give them what you have; hatred can only disappear when everyone is equal." Chencao's friend in the county seat, Lu Fang, said that to him once. Lu Fang said Karl Marx's communism was based on that idea. Chencao thought, "It's impossible; if you just took a look around in Maple Village, you'd know."

Chencao shrugged his shoulders and walked toward the front courtyard; he heard the unending sound of the laborers pounding rice, and he heard Yanyi shouting from the back courtyard, "Ma, give me some steamed rolls!" Every kind of thought and "ism" was far removed from Maple Village, but Chencao was perplexed about himself. What was he all about? He walked by the central room and saw his father through the door curtain, just then opening a stack of redwood boxes; the sound of his platinum keys clanging together rang in his ears. Chencao picked his ear with his little fingernail. Then he remembered it was the end of the month; his father was alone as usual in the central room counting the money. It occurred to him that someday he would play the same role as his father; his father would one day very solemnly hand those platinum keys over to him. What would that feel like? Would he control this family, control all the people in Maple Village, just as his father did? Could he bear the weight of that mountain his father carried on his shoulders?

After his return home Chencao was seized by a feeling of weakness; he forgot how many days he'd been back; he made two tennis rackets with bamboo strips and hemp thread; when the rackets were finished, he started to make a ball; he grabbed a handful of cloth strips from the maids' sewing basket and asked them to sew them up in the shape of a ball.

The maids asked, "Second Young Master, are you going to play with rag dolls?" and he told them, "Don't talk nonsense; I want you to make a tennis ball."

When they finished sewing the ball, it was as big as a grapefruit. Chencao received the cloth ball into his hands with a gloomy smile, mentally assuring himself that it would be all right as long as it could bounce. He carried his homemade tennis rackets and ball into the back courtyard where there was a threshing floor. He saw the April sun beating down on the hard clay ground, and his shadow looking like a bird that had lost its way. There was no one in the back courtyard except the idiot Yanyi sitting on the storehouse steps. Chencao walked over to Yanyi and held a tennis racket out in front of his face. He thought all he could do was hold the racket in front of Yanyi's face. "Yanyi, let's play tennis."

He watched Yanyi throw down his steamed roll and grab

hold of the tennis racket; he was happy that Yanyi showed an interest in playing tennis. Yanyi looked intently at the cloth ball he held in his hand. Chencao ran back a few yards, took a few practice swings in the air, then with a *puck* the hemp threads hit the cloth ball and sent it flying.

"Yanyi, watch the ball."

Yanyi stared wide-eyed at the ball. He threw down the racket, and his short, fat body leapt into action, bounding quickly over to catch the ball. The ball bounced off the storehouse wall and down onto the ground; Yanyi shrieked, "Argh, argh!" as he pounced on it. Chencao could not understand what he was trying to do.

"Yanyi, hit the ball with the racket, don't pick it up with your hands."

"Steamed roll, give me this steamed roll.

"That's not a steamed roll! You can't eat it!"

Chencao saw Yanyi put the ball in his mouth while he was yelling at him. Yanyi had taken his tennis ball for a steamed roll. "How could Yanyi think a tennis ball was a steamed roll?" he thought. Unable to bite into the cloth ball, Yanyi took it out of his mouth and looked it over carefully. He cursed angrily and threw the ball out over the compound wall. Chencao saw the ball describe a white-hot arc in the air and then suddenly disappear.

You will never be able to play tennis in a Maple Village family, never, never, never. Chencao squatted down and covered his face with his hands; the threshing floor had become a stretch of white cloth in the sunlight, and the white cloth was spattered here and there with dry straw and opium-poppy leaves. There was no wind, but once again he smelled the strange and all-pervasive odor of opium poppies. Chencao easily broke his tennis racket in half; the other one was under Yanyi's feet; he walked over to pick it up and saw Yanyi was stepping on it with his rubber shoes; he patted Yanyi's feet and said, "Move over a little, let me break it." But Yanyi did not move. Chencao heard him mumble, "I'll kill you." He felt something heavy coming down toward his head, then he saw the knife in Yanyi's hand aimed right at his head. "Idiot!" It was the first time Chencao had called Yanyi an idiot; he held on to Yanyi's arm with all his might, but he felt extremely weak; he kicked Yanyi in the groin, and felt his kick was also extremely weak, but Yanyi screamed and fell to the ground. The knife fell to the ground, and Yanyi rolled around, shouting incoherently, "I'll kill you, I'll kill you." Chencao remembered that he stood there, stunned, in front of the flashing knife blade for a moment of extremely long duration, then he picked up the knife and stabbed Yanyi five times in the face. He heard himself count off the stabs from one to five. He finished off the fifth stab as Yanyi's dark black blood squirted out into the sunlight.

Long after the incident had passed, Chencao was still trying to recall how many days he had been home when it happened, but he simply could not remember. He only remembered a bunch of long-term laborers and female servants crowding into the back courtyard, and then his father and mother running over. They saw Yanyi lying dead in front of the storehouse. "Yanyi didn't kill me, I killed him." Chencao stood there motionless holding that other tennis racket tightly in his hand. He looked down, bewildered, at Yanyi's bloody skull, and he gagged. He could not vomit. At his feet was a pool of dark black blood. Then he started to sob. "I wanted to play tennis with him. How could I kill him?" Chencao remembered his father put his arms around him and said, "Chencao, don't be afraid Yanyi's going to kill you; you've killed him; it was fate." Chencao said, "No; I don't know what happened; how could I kill him?" He remembered his father held him so tight he couldn't breathe; the entire household, inside and out, was thrown into confusion; with still no wind he smelled the sweet fragrance of the opium poppies in the fields; he felt that concentrated odor penetrate his utterly weak body.

The day they buried Yanyi, Chencao lay in bed in his room; he stayed in bed until after dark. His father had locked the door from the outside. Gradually the moon rose, and he heard the wind come up outside his window. The sound of the wind buffeting Maple Village was full of melancholy and terror. Chencao pulled the covers up over his head, but still could not shut out the sound of the night wind. He was waiting for something to appear out of the wind; he actually saw Yanyi's indistinct shape standing on the storehouse steps, chewing on a steamed roll and shouting at him, "I'll kill you! I'll kill you!"

Yanyi slept in his coffin. The old people of Maple Village told me Yanyi's coffin was piled full of snowy white steamed rolls; that was a real funeral sacrifice, they said; the idiot Yanyi should close his eyes in satisfaction, he'll never run out of steamed rolls again.

The cat-eyed woman is no longer among the living; she drowned one day while bathing in the big iron bathtub. She was holding the baby girl Liu Suzi in her arms, but Liu Suzi was not afraid of water, it was as though she was reborn out of the water—that offspring of the cat-eyed woman and Liu Laoxia; she had skin as pure white and icy cold as spring snow; her beauty astounded everyone around, and she was praised far and wide in the countryside.

Everyone remembered that when Liu Suzi was eighteen years old she was carried out of Maple Village in a red wedding palanquin. But three days later she came back and never again went to live in her husband's home. We see her living all year in a side room of the second courtyard, holding a yellow cat on her lap and taking a nap. She was a woman who liked to sleep, and she was a woman who loved cats as much as her own life. On many mornings and evenings a secret observer could see Liu Suzi asleep on an old bamboo mat with that yellow cat, hiding in the curve of her hip, keeping watch. The secret observer would also discover Liu Suzi's strange habit: All year round, she never slept on a bed, but only on that bamboo mat.

Liu Suzi only returned to her husband's home for three days every year; the red palanquin would leave on New Year's Eve and return home on the third day of the New Year. As the years went by, Liu Suzi's age became an enigma. Her eyes grew gradually blue like a cat's, but the snowy luster of her skin was increasingly cold, and her every smile was an exact replica of her deceased mother. There was a rumor, impossible to verify, that said that years after her marriage Liu Suzi scrupulously maintained her purity and was still an intact virgin; they said the hunchback proprietor of the piece goods store in the county seat was not a real man. What was the true story? You would have to ask Liu Laoxia, but Liu Laoxia would not tell you.

Liu Suzi would never cut that long brunette braid of hers; she just sat on the bamboo mat, and as soon as she saw her father come in, she would hold that yellow cat in her hands and say, "Don't bother me—a hundred and fifty acres." Only father and daughter understood the implications of that 150 acres. Liu Laoxia had received a 150 acres for marrying his daughter off to the hunchback. Liu Laoxia said, "My dear daughter, if you don't want to leave, then just live at home, but a hundred and fifty acres is not to our shame but our glory; Dad didn't raise you for nothing."

Liu Suzi just laughed, wound her long braid around on top of her head, and said, "Father, that hundred and fifty acres will be flooded with water and blasted by thunder; that hundred and fifty acres will slip through your hands; you just wait, that will be fate, too."

Several decades later, in the Maple Village area, I saw a photograph of Liu Suzi. The edges were scorched. I saw the former beauty of Maple Village dressed in a black and white checkered cheongsam sitting on a bamboo mat holding a yellow cat; her forehead wore the bland expression of one who has completely understood the human world, while the look in her eyes and her smile held a slight aura of death. The photograph was the work of an anonymous rural photographer; simple yet wise, it allowed you directly to experience the true image of Liu Suzi.

One day Liu Suzi's yellow cat died on the bamboo mat. Sound asleep, Liu Suzi heard the cat crying out; she thought she had rolled over on it; when she pushed it to one side the cat was quiet, so she assumed it was not hurt. When Liu Suzi woke up, she found the cat dead; it had been poisoned.

Liu Suzi wept with great sadness; with her hair still uncombed, she rushed into her father's room carrying the dead cat; she looked all around the room as she sobbed. "Jade Flower?"

"What are you looking for her for? You want to start another fight."

"She poisoned my cat."

"How do you know she poisoned your cat?"

"I know. Even if I were sound asleep, I would still know."

"Don't start a fuss; Dad'll bring another one home for you."

Liu Suzi sat in the courtyard holding the dead cat and waiting for Jade Flower, but Jade Flower was hiding and did not dare come out. Jade Flower sat on the chamber pot behind her bed; she was weeping, too. Later on, the long-term laborers revealed that Jade Flower had mixed powdered opium pith in some fish soup and fed it to the cat; they saw her do it. The long-term laborers said Liu Laoxia could dominate any number of Maple Villagers, but he could not control the two women in his own house—Liu Suzi and Jade Flower.

That night Liu Suzi buried the dead cat in front of Jade Flower's room.

The next day, however, the dead cat was dug up and returned to Liu Suzi's bamboo mat.

You can recognize at a glance the hatred between two women. That sort of hatred is small-minded, trivial, and ineradicable. Everyone high and low knew they would spit at each other every time they met. Liu Laoxia stamped his feet and shouted as he whipped Jade Flower's bare back with his leather belt: "See if you spit at her again! See if you spit again!"

Jade Flower shrieked back at him: "What do you want me to do? As soon as she sees me, she calls me a slut!"

In the Liu clan, women were just women; if they were not carried in a man's pocket, they were hung around a man's neck. People in Maple Village told me Jade Flower was a slut; they also said Jade Flower really had a pitiful life: she was kicked back and forth like a rubber ball between the men of the Liu family.

The image of Jade Flower's femininity puzzles me. It is almost the central image of this period of history. All the men in this story swarm in like locusts lining up around Jade Flower, and one end of every line descends to or from her body.

Once I tried to draw a character chart based on this period of history, and I was amazed at the striking resemblance of this chart to the female sex organs.

Liu Laoxin————Eldest Master Liu————Liu Laoxia

Jade Flower

Chen Mao

Liu Chencao

Some Maple Villagers told me Jade Flower was originally a child prostitute in the city; the year the younger son, Liu Laoxin, passed through Maple Village holding her hand, Jade Flower was still a heavily made-up, lively, playful little girl. That year, his father, the Eldest Master, was celebrating his sixtieth birthday, and Liu Laoxin simply could not scrape together enough money to buy him a proper gift, so he simply presented Jade Flower to his father as a special present. They say that Jade Flower actually grew into womanhood in Maple Village; as soon as she became a grown woman, the cat-eyed woman drowned in the bathtub.

Someone was driving a mule around the millstone in the courtyard. Even before first light you could hear the loud, grinding sound of the millstone. The person driving the mule suddenly shouted, "Get up, you fucking lazy mule!" Chencao was already accustomed to all sorts of unpleasant sounds coming from the house and courtyard, but the person driving the mule was an unusual case, and his body began once again to itch all over. This was a strange affliction. Whenever he heard that person's voice, he started to itch all over. Chencao got out of bed, opened the window, and saw a man with his shirt off sweating profusely in the morning air. "That's Chen Mao; that's the long-term laborer who has a special position in our house; Dad says Chen Mao is a bad sort, but Dad always keeps him here at home to stir up trouble," thought Chencao. "That's Dad's strange affliction."

"Chen Mao, take that mule away," shouted Chencao.

"I can't; he's a lazy mule, and I can't move him."

"What is it you grind up every day with that stone?"

"Flour. You don't understand, Young Master. In order to eat your family's rice, I have to do your family's work."

"Don't bother grinding flour, just keep the rice and eat it."

"There's too much rice, your family's granaries can't hold any more."

Chencao closed the window. He could still sense that fellow looking at him through the window paper. There was a folk song about him:

Chen Ermao, king of the night crawlers;
Visited three ladies last night, and
Tonight he'll jump your wife's fence.

Chencao knew he was a famous rural seducer. He was not offended by his fence-jumping, window-opening philandering, but he was disgusted by the confused and obsessed look in Chen Mao's eyes when he stared at him.

Chencao recalled that Chen Mao's gaze had already followed him for many years. When he was little, he remembered, every time he went into the back courtyard he would see Chen Mao sitting there under a pear tree. There were five pear trees in the back courtyard when he was little. Dad told the children, "Don't be greedy; the pears are not for us to eat; in the fall the long-term laborers will pick them and take them to market; we'll get five sacks of grain for them." Chencao remembered Chen Mao was given the job of guarding the pear trees. Chen Mao and a dog would sit together under the pear trees. "He liked to rub both sides of my face with the palms of his hands; it felt just like sandpaper," thought Chencao.

"Little wolf cub, little mutt," Chen Mao would say, with the stench of manure coming out of his mouth.

Chencao's strange itch was almost unbearable.

Chen Mao would say, "You want to eat a pear?"

"Yes."

"If you just call me something, I'll climb right up and pick one for you."

"What should I call you?"

"Father."

"No. You're not my father; you're my family's hired hand."

Chencao saw Chen Mao's brown eyes glaze over.

Thought Chencao, "His hands, reeking of manure, nearly crushed my face in."

"You don't know what *father* means; I'm your father."

Agile as a monkey, Chen Mao climbed up the pear tree and threw seven pears down in Chencao's direction. Chencao recalled that he bit into one of the pears first, but it was raw and puckery; then he gathered up the seven pears and ran to his father's room. He really did want to eat those pears, but for some unknown reason he ran to his father's room, gave all the pears to his father, and raced off shouting as he ran, "Dad, Chen Mao gave me seven pears!"

Chencao remembered the little incident that took place that night. That night Chen Mao knelt at Dad's feet. The seven already-blackened pears were laid out on the floor like seven little skulls. Chen Mao's back, sharp as a slab of stone, glistened with sweat. So many beads of sweat—those particularly large, shiny beads of sweat that came out on the workmen's backs.

Dad said, "Chencao, come over here and ride on this dog's back."

Chencao said, "Dog? Where's the dog?"

Dad pointed at Chen Mao. "He's a dog; get up and ride on his back."

Chencao looked dully at the pears on the floor.

Dad said, "Get on and ride him, Son!"

Chencao got up on Chen Mao's back, and the flesh between his legs trembled slightly. He cried out, "Dad, I'm itching all over."

Dad said, "Chencao, make him bark; make him crawl."

Chencao patted Chen Mao and said, "Bark, boy; crawl, boy."

Chen Mao crawled toward the door with me on his back, but he didn't bark.

Dad yelled at him, "Chen Ermao, you're a dog, why don't you bark?"

Chen Mao knelt motionless by the side of the door, the beads of sweat on his back burning Chencao so badly his whole body itched.

Chencao yelled, "Dad, I'm itching all over."

Dad yelled, "Chen Ermao, if you don't bark, I won't let you eat!"

Chen Mao's bald head drooped all the way down until it struck the floor with a heavy thud. I heard him bark, "Ruff, ruff, ruff," just like a real dog.

Right after that, Chencao was lowered to the floor. Chen Mao straightened up and stood in the doorway covering his eyes with his hands. He made a rasping sound like he was being strangled as he said, "Fuck you; I quit; I'm not going to be your family dog any more." He raised his head, and Chencao saw that his face continued to look both handsome and stupid even when he was furious. He staggered backward, looked out at the sky, turned to Chencao, and said, "It's really dark out; I'm leaving."

What Chencao found so puzzling was that since Chen Mao really had gone away, why did he come back? He was strong, he had women, he could always keep his belly full; what did he want to come back for? So many times Chencao had heard the sound of Chen Mao's brass trumpet disappear only to reappear later; then he'd see Chen Mao leaning against the gate to the main compound, shamelessly scratching his stomach. "Landlord, I'm back."

As the early-morning sound of grinding grain filled the air,

Chencao was suddenly startled by a strange picture: On the other side of the window paper, he saw the figure of Chen Mao driving the mule turn into the silhouette of a dog. He rapped on the window sill with his fingers, and thought maybe it was that silhouette of a dog that made his strange itch so unbearable. Chencao opened the window to look once again at Chen Mao; the sun had risen, the grindstone had a slightly reddish hue, and he discovered that Chen Mao's tired expression looked just like a dog under the hot sun.

There wasn't a man in Maple Village whose sexual history was richer or more varied and fascinating than Chen Mao's. When Chen Mao walked through the village, everyone admired two things; one was his brass trumpet, and the other was his hidden organ.

The men of Maple Village always believed that Chen Mao's golden spear could never be bent, and the women gossiping on their porches always had one everlasting topic of conversation: Chen Mao climbed into Jade Flower's bedroom window again last night.

Chen Mao climbed into Jade Flower's bedroom window again last night. In the dark of night his heart tossed like a boat on the water. He saw his true image in the light reflecting off the mirror. He reached out tentatively and rested his hands on Jade Flower's bed; they looked like two recently plucked chicken wings lying there; in the silence, he felt himself repeatedly hard and excited, then repeatedly soft and shriveled. He squatted on the wooden bed, his mouth filled with a flavor at once sweet and foul; Jade Flower was curled up like a white snake spitting out a pink snake's tongue; she held on to his ears so hard they were about to fall off.

"I'm coming up."

"Dog."

Chen Mao pushed the woman's white abdomen away and rose to his knees; he felt like he was going to vomit. He spat repeatedly on the floor, but his stomach was empty and he could not spit anything up. Jade Flower suddenly laughed out loud, raised her leg, and kicked him over onto the floor. "Get out, you big stud dog."

The floor was even colder. Chen Mao saw that Jade Flower had already pulled the covers up; then she took a steamed roll out from under her pillow and started to eat it. It was like that every time: Chen Mao watched Jade Flower eat the steamed roll and heard his own stomach growling.

"Give me half a roll," he said.

"Here you go." Jade Flower broke off half the steamed roll and tossed it down at him. "Now get out."

Chewing on the steamed roll, Chen Mao wrapped his pants around his waist and jumped out the window with a heart full of sadness and anger. As he made his way barefoot toward the servants' quarters, he heard a guard walk by outside the compound walls, the sound of bamboo clappers near and far by turns. Under the night dew a pile of fodder gave off an odor of tears and complaint. Chen Mao reflected that all of his days stacked up together amounted to nothing more than a pile of fodder; some of it he squandered on women's bodies, and some of it he wasted in the Liu family's fields; this was life, too, and he had to go on living this way.

· · ·

After the ripe opium poppies, both flowers and leaves, had been hauled inside the big Liu family compound, Maple Village's heroin workshop began production. If you travel all over the south today, you'll never see such a unique rural workshop; from the drying process through the grinding of the powder, we were surrounded on all sides by a tense and bustling harvest atmosphere. Maple Village's opium had to be dried in the sun for eighteen days by the tenant farmers, and baked eighteen days in a slow fire by the workers; after that, it was sifted to make a fine ash-white powder and loaded onto a salt boat. You know, the salt boat will take Maple Village's opium to many far away unknown places.

They had almost arrived to pick up the opium. Chencao wrote in his diary:

The salt boat comes here every year, and I'm just about to see that boat for the first time. Who knows when the history of opium growing began in Maple Village? You were not even born then. Dad said, "We have to thank your crazy uncle for this road to profit. At that time the land on the east side of the river belonged to him. One day I saw an attractive scarlet flower growing on your uncle's land. I said to him, "Laoxin, you better stick to growing vegetables; what are you doing growing flowers?" Laoxin said, "Those aren't flowers, those are the best damned vegetables of all; eat them and you won't want to eat any other vegetables." "What the hell is it then?" "Opium. Opium is what you get from the flowers." I said, "What on earth did you plant opium for?" Laoxin said, "To smoke it myself. City people don't eat vegetables; they only eat this." Listen to me Chencao." His eyes brightening, Dad said, "when I walked into that field of opium poppies and felt those big follicles, I heard those damned flowers singing to me; it's true; I heard them singing, and I was captivated."

The distinction between intelligence and stupidity was right there beside that field of opium poppies—can you hear the opium poppies sing? My crazy uncle's only expertise was in keeping his mouth and his cock happy, and so he died young. My father's intelligence consisted of being able to hear the opium poppies sing. Father just naturally recognized what was gold and what was dirt, otherwise how could our ancestors' forty acres expand to include all of Maple Village? This was father's accomplishment of half a lifetime.

You cannot clearly explain a person's congenital fear of some species of plant. During the opium-poppy harvest season, Chencao kept his window tightly closed and sat in front of his diary writing away feverishly. His father knocked on his window every day. "Chencao, get out here!" His father spoke to him as he knocked on the window. "Don't hide from the opium poppies; don't think you're afraid of the poppies."

"I'm afraid of getting dizzy," Chencao said to his father's shadow on the window.

His father knocked all the more forcefully on the window. "If you come out, you won't feel dizzy; you'll see you're already used to the poppies."

Chencao opened his door and stood in the doorway; he smelled the fragrance of the opium poppies pervading the main compound; the sound of big knives cutting off the stems, blossoms, and leaves could be heard from the back courtyard. Chencao wiped his forehead and smiled. "I'm not dizzy; I'm really not dizzy." He did not know at what precise instant this momentous change had taken place. He thought to himself, "Maybe it's a good thing that I'm not dizzy."

His father walked out of the workshop with a handful of opium powder, and held it out in the sunlight to check the quality; his facial expression was as serious and stern as if he were cradling a sacred fire in his hands. Chencao thought, "Perhaps the powder Dad has in his hands really is the sacred fire we all depend on for life. It nurtured Maple Village after a century of hunger, and it nurtured me, but I'm still confused about it."

"They'll be here soon to pick up the opium," said one Maple Villager to another.

The landlord Liu Laoxia stood in the doorway of the opium workshop of forty years ago; the scene behind him was dark. Forty years ago Liu Laoxia did not know he had become the biggest opium-poppy grower in the south. As the master of the land, he skillfully concerned himself with efficient growing and harvesting; he did not know that the opium he held in his hands burned madly out of control in the world beyond Maple Village, blackening nearly half the country. That was beyond his concern. When the Maple Villagers of several decades later learned that their old home was once an opium kingdom with a reputation known far and wide, everything was already gone forever; those boundless fields of opium poppies had already disappeared like a dream, and you could search up and down the fields on both sides of the river without finding a trace;

some people say this is only the history of the land, that it has little connection with human beings.

Grandfathers told grandsons, "Liu Laoxia planted his first acre of opium poppies at the age of thirty-seven; that summer he harvested ten pounds of opium powder. (The idiot Yanyi was also born that year.) Liu Laoxia set out with a bundle of thick bamboo tubes strapped on his back. People on the road were all curious about those bamboo tubes; Liu Laoxia shouted all the way at the people who crowded around to gawk at him on the road; he rapped on the bamboo tubes and said, 'Get back, get back, don't let these bamboo tubes blow your fucking eyes out!' Liu Laoxia went into the city alone to try his luck, didn't even take a servant with him. He traveled north by train and by boat, carrying those thick bamboo tubes on his back, and when people asked him what he had in those tubes that smelled so sweet, he told them it was grain; grain always smells sweet. Later on he really felt he was carrying grain on his back."

Grandfathers told grandsons, "When Liu Laoxia finally entered the city, his shoes were completely worn out; he was barefoot and people stared at him just like they do at us. Those city men looked like women, and the city women looked like seductive demons; they all had light creamy skin like Jade Flower, and the odor of their perfumed bodies hit him as they walked by. But nobody wasted two good glances on that bastard Liu Laoxia. Liu Laoxia thought to himself, 'I'm the one who keeps you pack of bitches and hounds alive with my rice, but you don't even recognize me.' He pushed his way wildly into a department-store crowd; he had not felt like eating since he left Maple Village, and now his empty stomach gave him gas; he started farting for all he was worth right there in that crowd." Grandfathers patted grandsons on the head and laughed out loud. "Liu Laoxia farts, too! Later on Liu Laoxia went to sleep in the doorway of a house; he was sleeping comfortably when he suddenly felt his bamboo tubes moving under his head; he opened his eyes to see an old beggar pulling at his precious bamboo tubes. The old beggar said, 'Give me a couple bamboo tubes to put some leftover food in.' Liu Laoxia jumped up and slapped him across the face.

"After that, when he was walking down a quiet out-of-the-way alley, someone told him that brothels would all buy heroin. He went down a winding alley until he saw a big house with one red and one green lantern hanging out in front. He just walked right in and put his bamboo tubes on the floor; the light in the front room dimly illuminated the figures of several despicable men and women sprawled about in various postures. Liu Laoxia clapped his hands and announced, 'I'm here to deliver the white powder.' He watched those no-good men and women stand up straight and swarm around, poking their sallow faces at him. Liu Laoxia said, 'Fuck you, you lazy bastards; I've brought you all this good stuff, but what the fuck are you looking at me so idiotically for?' He cut open one of his bamboo tubes, took out a handful of opium powder, and let it pour through his fingers. He heard one of them yell, 'Opium, opium!' and they all pounced on those bamboo tubes, pushing Liu Laoxia to the side. He stamped his feet and shouted, 'Not so fast, give me the money.' Nobody paid any attention to him; those wretched men and women emptied that bamboo tube like pigs fighting over their food. Liu Laoxia stamped his feet and shouted again, 'Give me the money, give me the money?'

He shouted himself hoarse, but they all ran away; in a flash they ran away to God knows where. Liu Laoxia said later he did not chase after that money. He said, 'They really were just like pigs; they ran up when I threw the slops down in the trough, and when the trough was empty, they all ran off to wallow in the mud.' "

It was mostly due to hero worship that all the grandfathers took great delight in talking about Liu Laoxia's trip into the city, at the age of thirty-seven. But their grandsons suspected the Liu family's opium began and ended in corruption. The opium collectors came once a year to Maple Village; the salt boat transported both opium and rice down the river. After this went on for some time, the Maple Villagers considered the two plants equal in status. Grandfathers pointed to the rice on the left bank and the opium fields on the right bank and told their grandsons, "There's food growing on both banks, and we depend on that food to go on living."

After Chencao had been home half a year, his family was raided by the bandit Jiang Long. The sound of horses' hooves rang out in the middle of the night. The sound of horses racing about rang out on all sides of the Liu family compound. In the servants' quarters the female servants screamed in alarm, "Jiang Long's coming!"

Chencao threw on his clothes and ran into the courtyard; he saw lights and shadows moving about wildly both inside and outside the compound walls; only his father's room was pitch black and undisturbed. Chencao ran over and knocked on his window. "Dad, wake up; the bandit Jiang Long is coming."

In the room his father coughed and said, "Don't panic; he

can't get through the gate; tell the men to toss a couple of sacks of rice over the wall, and then they'll leave."

Chencao stood in the hallway calling Chen Mao and the rest of the long-term laborers, but no one answered. The people in the servants' quarters were flitting here and there like headless flies, and something was kicked over with a terrible crash. As Chencao was running toward the front courtyard, he heard the two big pinewood gates creaking open.

"Who's opening the gates?"

By the time Chencao cried out, it was already too late; the sound of horses' hooves exploded into the compound, and nine horses rushed in in a straight line; the flames in the horsemen's big lanterns flickered momentarily and then brightened up again.

Chencao saw Jiang Long's bandits for the first time. They rode in carrying rifles, their heads were covered with black cloth, and they wore red hemp sandals. Chencao was surprised by their fierce martial appearance; he thrust his hands deep into his pockets and asked the one who was riding a white horse, "Are you Jiang Long?"

He heard the one on the white horse laugh out loud, then he pulled the black cloth off his head to reveal a young slender face with an impressively heroic expression.

"Jiang Tiangong!" Chencao shouted.

Jiang Long was none other than Jiang Tiangong, a fellow student from his private-school days; he never would have imagined it. Chencao lowered his eyes to the ground; standing there, facing that white horse and its rider, he recalled the many times when Jiang Tiangong had carried him to the private school on his back, for which service he had rewarded him each time with half a steamed roll.

When Chencao's father came out, he had not yet put his belt on. He did not seem to be alarmed; as he put on his belt he asked, "What did you come in for? Isn't it enough if I throw some rice over the wall?"

"Somebody opened the gate for us, so naturally we wanted to come in and pay our respects to the Liu family."

"How much rice do you want anyway?"

"Ten bags will be fine."

"This was a famine year, and we didn't have any harvest; how about eight bags?"

"Nothing doing. Ten bags and not a bag less, and we want to take someone with us."

"You want to take someone? Who do you want?"

"Your son, Liu Chencao."

"Don't joke like that; I'll give you ten bags of rice."

"We want the rice, and we want the person, too. I want to take a rich man's son into the mountains; I want to make him kill somebody! Make him rob, and pillage, and set fires!"

His father was stunned into immobility; Chencao saw his father's face darken in the lantern light; his father's lips trembled, but he stood there as straight and unbending as a tree trunk. Chencao remembered that time on the way home when they passed Firebull Ridge and he heard someone call out his name; he thought it very strange, and he walked over in front of the white horse, pulled at the reins, and asked, "Jiang Tiangong, you still remember the past?"

"I'll remember all my life. Otherwise we wouldn't visit the Liu family."

"But I gave you steamed rolls to eat."

"I shit out those steamed rolls long ago, but I can't shit out my hatred." Jiang Long snapped his whip loudly in the air. "Liu Chencao, you don't get it, do you?"

"And if I don't want to follow you into the mountains?"

"We'll burn out the whole compound and kill your entire family."

Chencao heard his father let out a long sigh and then step over and put his arms around the white horse's legs. His knees gradually buckled until he assumed a kneeling position on the ground.

Chencao covered his eyes and heard his father say, "I'll give you the whole storehouse; take all the rice you want."

"We've eaten enough rice. I want somebody from your family; if you won't give me your son, then give me your daughter."

"What?"

"Your daughter, Liu Suzi. I want to sleep with your daughter; three days and three nights, then I'll let her come down off the mountain when I'm finished."

Chencao remembered he tried to pick up the stone roller used for husking rice, but when he bent over to do so he could not budge it. His father pulled his soft weak arms back and spoke to him softly. "Don't move, Son, this is your father's business." He saw that tears were already streaming down his father's face as he walked haltingly back toward the back courtyard; he turned his head around after taking a few steps and said, "Three days and three nights; you'll keep your word?"

The nine horses crashed open another gate and raced toward the back courtyard, their wild impatient hooves shattering the night in this big compound. When the nine horses returned, one carried on it a woman rudely awakened from a peaceful sleep. Chencao remembered how Elder Sister really resembled a cat tucked under Jiang Long's arm, with her hair trailing wildly behind and her deep blue eyes flashing in the dark; her white silk nightgown was torn in many places from her struggle to free herself. His elder sister was nervously twisting her long braid, and her face was white as paper. Chencao heard her yell, "Dad, save me!" But his father stood there dryly with his eyes closed as though asleep. Chencao saw his elder sister's long braid suddenly trail down from the horse and drag along the ground like a tree branch. She stretched out her hand toward him and yelled, "Chencao, save me!"

When Chencao reached out for his elder sister's hand, he saw a burst of red flame spurt out of the muzzle of Jiang Long's rifle; his right arm fell limply to his side with a feeling like something had bitten him.

"It's broken," Chencao thought, "my right arm's broken; it all seems like a nightmare."

It was about midnight when Jiang Long and his bandits swept out of the Liu family compound like a tornado. The long-term laborers and the female servants stood at the foot of the wall watching the father and son of the Liu family. Chencao sat down on a big wicker basket savoring the feeling of having his entire body drenched in blood; his mind was a complete blank at first, but then he suddenly had a vision of Yanyi's blood-soaked face. At some uncertain time before, blood had also oozed out all over Yanyi's body. Chencao felt very cold; he pushed his way through the stupefied servants and went to put on some clothes. He heard his father finally begin to cry out loud in the darkness; his father raised his two fists and beat on both sides of his own head.

"Go buy rifles; go buy a hundred rifles."

Chencao put on his padded cotton jacket, but it did not warm him; he bit his lip and walked back out into the courtyard. Everybody had gone in, and his father was standing there alone in the moonlight; he held out his open hand as though expecting to receive something. He spoke to Chencao. "Are we going to be ruined?"

Chencao took his father's outstretched arm and saw that all he had in his hand was a single opium-poppy leaf. Chencao shook his head and said, "I don't know, Dad, I really didn't know Jiang Tiangong would come here."

On the third day the Liu household gathered at the entrance to the village waiting for the return of Liu Suzi. Chencao was there holding a Mauser pistol. The crowd said that Liu Laoxia had traded ten bushels of rice for that pistol; the pistol was very expensive, but when you have a gun, you need not fear bandits.

On that third day a single white horse trotted down out of the hills; Liu Suzi was lying over the horse's back like a soundly sleeping cat. You could not see her face; all you could see was that famous long braid hanging down like a dried-up willow branch shaking in the wind. The crowd noticed that the young woman's white silk nightgown had been exchanged for a pair of men's pants; someone said they were Jiang Long's pants.

When Liu Suzi came home after her abduction, she sat in the big iron tub taking a bath, crying and washing herself, washing herself for three days and three nights. The two maidservants tending the fire under the iron tub discovered that the young woman sitting in the water looked exactly like her dead mother; her eyes were such a deep green they made you shiver.

"Chencao, come over here; come with me."

His father took Chencao's arm, and they walked through an unforgettable moment in the Liu family history. As they walked out of the big compound, a bell was ringing somewhere far away from Maple Village. Chencao remembered that day was his father's seventieth birthday, and he was twenty years old. They walked through an unforgettable moment in the Liu family history toward the Liu family's ancestral temple. The ancestors' platinum keys clinking together weakly in front of them sounded just like his father's pulse. That was an extremely weak sound, and it announced the end of something. The people of Maple Village, jumping up out of the shade of the thatched huts where they were taking their midday naps, resembled a flock of chickens bounding out to gawk at this father and son of the Liu family. Chencao stared straight ahead and did not look at the tenant farmers on either side; he despised those stupid muddy yellow faces; he wondered to himself, "Why do these people stand here all year like a flock of feeding chickens staring at our hands? Why do they swarm all around us like horseflies we can't even drive away?" He lowered his head and walked down the long village lane. Maple Village was very narrow, just like a thin black scar growing on the earth's skin; and after a short walk he came to the end of it. He felt like he had walked down an extremely long road when the sunlight suddenly turned gray as the shadow of the ancestral temple's flying eaves, with their ancient tiles, loomed up over his head. The Liu family's ancestral temple sat there like a coiling dragon or a crouching tiger, and the moist musty odor of antiquity spread all around him as Chencao looked down at the tips of his toes and brought his feet to a halt.

"Chencao, come with me."

His father's voice kept calling out in front of him; every single breath of air was calling to him in the same manner as his father flitted into the ancestral temple like a spirit, his white shirt trailing bright sparks behind him. Eight candles were burning on the spirit altar, and incense smoke filled the air. He watched his father kneel down in front of the ancestors' spirit tablets with his body tightly contracted like a stone stele. This was our ancestral temple; this was where our ancestors concealed themselves; they gave us our lives and they control our thoughts from the netherworld. Chencao knelt beside his father with his arms wrapped tightly around his own body; he heard the creaking sound of approaching calamity descending upon his head. Trembling with cold fear, he ran his hand over the ground all around the ancestors; the ground was icy cold; then he reached over and felt his father's hand; it, too, was icy cold. He saw what appeared to be a halo around the platinum keys on the ancestral altar; those platinum keys emitted the odors of all sorts of plants, both wild and domesticated. "They're soon going to fall into your hands," thought Chencao.

"Chencao, swear an oath to the ancestors."

"I swear it."

"You are about to receive the Liu family's land and property; you are going to use these keys to open the great gates of the land. You are going to use these keys to open the storehouses of gold and silver. Swear that the estate of the Liu family will grow richer and more prosperous in your generation."

"I swear it."

At that the platinum keys fell into Chencao's hands like a shooting star falling out of the sky. He marveled at how heavy those keys were; he could hardly lift them. "Chencao," he thought, "where are your ancestors? Who really gave me this ring of platinum keys?" History and human life became chaotically confused in the darkness where Chencao could vaguely make out a crowd of vegetable-green faces gnawing on black steamed buns; he could see his crazy uncle burning up in the crackling fire; and, most clearly, he could see Yanyi's blurry blood-smeared head as though it were placed in a celadon plate up on the ancestral altar. "I'm cold." Chencao once more hunched his shoulders together as they walked out of the ancestral temple. A breeze blew quickly over their way. He heard his father say, "Straighten up your shoulders." "But I'm cold," he thought. His father walked emptily behind him; separated from the platinum keys, he had become unbearably old.

Chencao would remember that long dark noon when Maple Village was slightly startled out of its lonely solitude; the dogs set to barking, and the pigs and goats ran wildly around beside the ditch. The tenant farmers stood in the fields and beside their houses staring at him; he did not know what they were staring at. Then he heard a woman herding goats call out to him, "Master."

"Master," Chencao mumbled to himself, then stared angrily at the woman herding the goats. "Who are you shouting at?"

That noon grandfathers and grandsons stood by the side of the river, and grandfathers said to grandsons, "Don't expect their family's going to change any; people are just like crops: Whoever plants them, reaps them, and they reap whatever they sow. You don't know Chencao, so don't expect any better days to descend on you from heaven." Grandfathers said, "The sun's high in the sky, let's go on into the fields." And just like that you see 1948 sweep in like a meteor, and you see the history of a landlord family undergo certain changes.

. . .

I discovered that the history of the Liu family of Maple Village underwent many changes in 1948; the rise and fall of nations and great unpredictable changes in human affairs sometimes happen in the blink of an eye. You say Liu Chencao is kind of a mixed character in this period of history, and you can also say that Liu Chencao was the last landlord of the 1940s. You hear those ancient platinum keys rattling in his leather pants pockets and gradually falling toward the ground; that is a mysterious sound and difficult to comprehend. Those platinum keys are just about to fall to the ground. Maple Village shook itself once in its thousand years of silence, and thus a new ripple coursed across the surface of the dead pool of history.

That was 1948, the brief era of Liu Chencao; grandfathers have a deep impression of that peculiar period. They said, "Liu Chencao let all of us till the land." He drove the long-term laborers and the maidservants out of the house, and rented the rice-paddy lands to migrants from outside; many people from north and south crossed the river and rented five acres of land from Chencao. They said, "That's how the outsiders on the right bank of the river came to live there." People remembered Liu Chencao's ashen face as he gave his land away to others; he said, "I don't want so much land, but you do want it; if you want it, take it; I only want half the autumn harvest, so everyone gets his share. You understand what I'm saying?"

Some people kneeled down in front of Liu Chencao and asked, "Young Master, do you really mean it?"

Liu Chencao yelled at them, "Get up! Don't kneel in front of me!"

He said, "I hate all of you just as much as I hate myself!"

The people of Maple Village never really understood the Liu Chencao era. The grandfathers' evaluations of him were invariably vague and confused, calling him, for example, a young benefactor, a strange character, or one with an evil face and a good heart. But grandsons told their grandfathers, "What did Liu Chencao give you? He didn't give you land, he gave you a curse; he's got you tied up with no chance of escape until your blood and sweat are exhausted and you die of old age working in the fields. You should hate him; why is it to this day you still can't forget 1948?"

That year the opium collectors did not come.

The salt boat did not come, but the people were still waiting and watching by the riverside.

The opium-poppy fields dried up after the harvest, the ditches and dry ruts looking like zebra stripes cut into the earth. The open fields were incomparably dry and lifeless in the wind that swept down from the four directions and shook my Maple Village like a thousand giant hands. When you walked out of your black mud hut and down to the riverside, you would see the usual colors of autumn on both sides of the river, but the wind really would shake you from all sides like a thousand giant hands; the wind was trying to throw you into the river, where you would drift back like a fallen leaf following the direction of the current. The autumn wind that year was terribly fierce; you only had to walk to the riverbank and you would see the pages of that period of history torn off by the wind; that was an even greater pile of fallen leaves drifting back, following the direction of the river.

The south had been liberated for a long time, but Maple Village did not know it.

People remember that Chen Mao was the first one to bring news of liberation across the bridge at Horsebridge.

Chen Mao, the former long-term laborer who had been driven out of the Liu household, was waving a yellow cap; from far off you could see a five-cornered red star on the cap flashing in the light. That was a material symbol of the history of 1949 pressing down on you. Chen Mao ran up into the depths of the history of 1949, his bare feet passing through the village lane and bearing down on the big Liu family compound. He shouted as he came, "Hurry over to Horsebridge, hurry over to Horsebridge, hurry over to Horsebridge—the Communist party's coming to make the revolution!"

Chen Mao put the yellow cap with the five-cornered red star on his head and stormed into the Liu family compound. Puzzled, he stood there in the courtyard for a moment; then he saw Jade Flower shouting at a flock of chickens to eat their grain, and Liu Suzi sitting on the porch in the sun with a cat on her lap. The two women's faces were expressionless. Jade Flower shouted at him, "Stupid fool, what are you yelling about? Come on back and go to work."

Chen Mao fingered the cap on his head and laughed, "I'm never coming back again; I'm following the Communist party!"

As Chen Mao ran out of the big compound in the direction of the village, he heard Jade Flower follow him to the gate and shout, "Stupid fool, come back and go to work."

Chen Mao made a face in her direction and said, "You slut, I'm never going to work for any of you again."

The sound of the wind swept across the black earth as Chen

Mao took his brass trumpet off of his belt; the sound of the brass trumpet rose up into the highest heaven, and he heard the roar of the great earth trembling as lava burst forth. He ran on wildly and felt as though he were soaring into the air like a big golden-headed barn fly. Some tenant farmers he met along the road ran blindly along with him and asked, "Chen Ermao, what's happening?"

"Hurry to Horsebridge; the Communist party is coming to make the revolution!"

Chen Mao blew his trumpet as he ran along, and more and more people joined him; they looked like an army of ostriches running hungrily along after him. They ran through the barren rice and opium fields following the riverbank until, at last, they caught sight of the Straw Pavilion; then the hungry flock came to a sudden stop.

The Straw Pavilion rose up in front of them like a sacrificial altar, and incense smoke drifted all around their heads. Through the smoke they saw two men dressed in white tending the red incense burners. Somebody said this was the ninth day of the ninth lunar month, the Double Ninth Festival, a sacred ceremony of sacrifice to the earth that the Liu family had carried on for a hundred years. But nobody understood why they had met there in front of the sacred fire.

The hungry army spread out and stood around on the ground staring intently at the father and son of the Liu family. Father and son both wore blank expressions as they walked out of the Straw Pavilion in total silence. Liu Laoxia was already very old, but he still stared down at their weak little souls like a giant beast. This was the first time they had seen Liu Laoxia in 1949. They heard Liu Laoxia cough and spit on the ground; then they heard him spit out a familiar syllable: "Dog!"

"What are you up to?"

"We're going to Horsebridge; the Communist party is coming to make the revolution!" Chen Mao rose on tiptoes above the crowd.

"Dog. What did he say?" Liu Laoxia asked Chencao.

"He said revolution," Chencao answered.

"We're never going to sell our lives to you again," Chen Mao said.

"Liu Sanwang, Liu Xizi, tie Chen Mao up," Liu Laoxia ordered.

They just stood there gawking; those blank dull faces that made up a hungry army.

"Tie him up; tie him up, and I'll give each of you a sack of rice."

"A sack of rice? You're not trying to fool us?"

"No, I'm not fooling, you hungry devils!"

"A sack of rice—I'll tie him up!" The hungry army jumped up and went into action; Chen Mao turned around and tried to run, but it was already too late. The tenant farmers closed in and grabbed Chen Mao from all sides. "A sack of rice!" they shouted out, as they lifted him up above their heads. "There's nothing to tie him with!" someone shouted. "Pull his belt off!" another answered, and thus Chen Mao was hoisted high in the air and had his belt stripped off. Chen Mao tried to cover his embarrassment, but both his hands were quickly tied up. "Let me go, Liu Laoxia!" he shouted angrily, but no one listened. "Pull off Chen Ermao's pants!" A happy band of tenant farmers laughed uproariously as they carried Chen Mao into the Straw Pavilion and right up in front of the Liu family father and son.

Chencao moved back. He saw Chen Mao's exposed genitals

bobbing up and down above the heads of the crowd; Chen Mao's black pants were torn completely off and thrown up into the air to be blown about by the wind. Chencao felt nauseous and his whole body itched strangely; the sudden onset of that peculiar itching made him wrap his arms tightly around his body and wish that he could simply die. What was going on? When he bent over and spit on the floor, he saw countless bare feet trample down the sacred fire, and the joss sticks, broken in half, lying on the ground. Chencao picked up one half of a joss stick, but it still burned his hand, and he threw it down; then, scrunching up his face and neck, he yelled, "Stop all this; get the hell out of here all of you!"

But his voice was drowned out by a raging tide of joyous shouting.

The tenant farmers asked, "Old Master, where should we tie up Chen Ermao?"

His father said, "Hang him up; hang him up on the roof beam."

Chencao watched Chen Mao's body lifted up above the heads of the crowd; he watched it rise quickly to the roof beam of the Straw Pavilion. Chen Mao's mouth fell open, and he looked like a dead bird swinging back and forth from the roof beam. Somebody hung his brass trumpet around his neck, and the trumpet accompanied its master swinging back and forth in the wind. Chencao thought Chen Mao looked very funny, but he could not laugh; rather, his strange itching doubled in intensity. He thought, "Some kind of organic connection exists between this man and myself. Whenever I see him, I have a strange unbearable itching, and premonitions of disaster fill my mind."

Chencao pulled out his revolver, raised it up, and took

careful aim; hanging there in the air, under the gunsights, Chen Mao's genitals looked bigger and more powerful.

"Dog," Chencao thought, "he really is a dog; it makes me sick."

Chencao wondered to himself, "How many times have you aimed at Chen Mao? Do you want to kill him? Why are you so painfully weak in front of him? Maybe," Chencao went on thinking, "it's because you are afraid of him. It's always like that when you are afraid of someone."

Chencao lowered his hand holding the revolver; he discovered the tenant farmers were staring wide-eyed at that hand. He brushed his face with the gun barrel and looked at how small and pale his image appeared when reflected on the body of the gun; the exhaustion and disgust in his heart were reflected onto the burnished blue of the gun barrel. "I can't kill anybody except that idiot Yanyi. I might as well save these bullets for my final day."

His father gave an order regarding Chen Mao: "Let him hang there, nobody touch him."

As Chencao helped his father down off the Straw Pavilion, his back felt like it was crawling with hot insects. He looked around suddenly and discovered Chen Mao's eyes following them with a dark red glare the color of opium poppies. As they stared at each other, Chen Mao opened his mouth, laughed, and pissed right in their direction. Chencao noticed that Chen Mao's piss also described a deep red arc, and he wondered if the fellow was a man or a dog; once again, in the air before him, he saw the fantastic image of a creature with the body of a dog and the face of a man.

.   .   .

Bound hand and foot, Chen Mao swung there naked in the Straw Pavilion for an unforgettable day and night. During the night he managed to work his brass trumpet into his mouth, and we heard the loud mournful sound of his trumpet reverberating out from the Straw Pavilion and spreading out all over Maple Village. That was deep in the autumn of 1949; what we heard was actually the pages of history being turned with unusual rapidity.

The next day Lu Fang's work team arrived in Maple Village from the township of Horsebridge. From the bank of the river they saw a naked man hanging in the Straw Pavilion, playing a brass trumpet; it was an extremely peculiar sight. Lu Fang, the work team commander, told me, "When we cut Chen Mao down from the roof beam, we almost wept." Chen Mao's lips were greatly swollen, and his body was crawling with little black gnats. Lu Fang took a pair of pants out of his bag and gave them to Chen Mao to wear, but Chen Mao did not take them; the first thing he did was greedily grab some dried camp food out of another man's hand. He chewed on it as he said, "I'll eat some dried bread first, then I'll put those pants on."

Lu Fang also said that from the outline of Chen Mao's face he could instantly make out the features of his old schoolmate Liu Chencao; Chencao really did resemble Chen Mao. And everybody thought that was quite strange, too.

Lu Fang said, "Maple Village was one hell of a place; when you first arrived there it was like falling into a labyrinth." Lu Fang compared the task of his 1949 work team to dredging a sunken ship up from the bottom of the ocean; you could see the ship lying there on the bottom, but you had no way to bring it up; it was like it was growing there. And besides, all of the inhabitants of Maple Village acted just like fish, seaweed, or submerged rocks, preventing you from diving down deeply; you were caught in treacherous, complex, and ever-changing currents—you didn't know how you were going to drag that ship up.

Lu Fang remembered the old landlord sitting in his gateway in the autumn of 1949, gazing off toward the south. Every day he waited for the opium collectors to arrive, waited for the salt boat to come and anchor off his riverside dock.

"We've been liberated. The opium collectors aren't coming any more," Lu Fang told him.

The old landlord remained silent. Lu Fang stepped through the Liu family's gate and saw the main courtyard was covered with bamboo baskets of many different sizes; they were full of white and brown opium-blossom powder drying in the sun; this was the first time he had ever seen the blossoms of that mysterious plant; the odor of the opium poppies made him nervous; he clutched his holster and looked away into the big compound; he felt the sunlight in there had undergone a profound transformation; some people were standing in the dark corners of their rooms repairing agricultural implements or making shoe soles; their expressions were dull and stupid; Lu Fang knew that was the immemorial and unchanging expression of Maple Village.

Walking into the central courtyard, Lu Fang saw the two Liu family women. The only rays of sunlight fell on the plump white flesh of Jade Flower's arms; her arms, decked out with six gold and silver bracelets, were crossed in front of her chest, and her bosom was extraordinarily high and full. Jade Flower leaned out of the window, nodded, and smiled at Lu Fang. "Come on in, Commander."

At the same time, Liu Suzi was feeding her cat; he did not know why she was wearing men's clothes, but Lu Fang required only one glance to make out her true sex. Lu Fang could not stop himself from smiling at Liu Suzi. His leggings came loose, and when he squatted down to tie them up, he saw Liu Suzi break an old porcelain bowl on the ground and run off toward the eastern side room. When she paused in the doorway and looked back at him, her cat's eyes suddenly grew terrified and angry. After all these years Lu Fang still cannot forget Liu Suzi's eyes: "She really did look like a cat!"

When Lu Fang walked by the darkened storehouse, he heard a cough. Through a gap in the window curtain he saw a man sitting bolt upright on a big crock. He could not see his face clearly, so he shined his flashlight into the room. The flashlight illuminated a familiar pale face; the man looked very drowsy, but he had something in his mouth.

"Who's there?" the man asked.

Lu Fang pushed open the wooden double doors. In just that fashion he reencountered the old schoolmate he had not seen for a long time, and in just that fashion Lu Fang met all of the Liu family members living in the compound. He said, "All of China's landlord families could basically be comprehended at a glance. You only had to look at them to see how things stood; in most cases our work teams were enough to take control of them."

Chencao sat on the big crock in the storehouse. That was also the place where the idiot Yanyi used to sit and eat his steamed buns. If you had ever experienced eating opium, you would have understood what Chencao was doing. Liu Chencao was eating opium. You will discover that this little detail does not accord with Chencao's temperament; you will recall Chencao's dizziness in the opium poppy fields when he first arrived home from school. But now he was sitting there on the crock, and he, Liu Chencao, was actually eating opium.

He heard the sound of rain all over Maple Village. He was walking in the rain. Out of the boundless rain and mist a long road stretched toward the north. There was a many-storied red brick building on the sandy slope of the northern hills. He saw that he had been transformed into a snail crawling along in the rain. He saw a tennis ball rolling down the roof of the red brick building; the ball fell from the building and bounced away on the rain-soaked ground. The snail was actually crawling toward that tennis ball. By the time the snail reached the grass, the tennis ball had long since disappeared. He heard the sound of rain all over Maple Village. The shell on the snail's back was terribly heavy; he lay down in a shallow pool of water and went to sleep, but many people were running wildly along that road; they were running wildly up behind him; the snail heard the frenzied sound of their running feet; he wanted to hide, but he could not move his shell. He saw his shallow pool of water trampled underfoot as beautiful drops of water splashed up into the air. He heard the loud reverberations of a crisp clear crackling sound as the snail's shell was squashed into the ground.

In the courtyard somebody knocked over a bamboo basket. Chencao walked out of the storehouse with the sweet aroma of opium powder still on his breath. He stood on the steps holding his head and feeling extremely exhausted after living through that rainstorm. His father was cursing somebody as he scooped the opium powder off the ground and back into the bamboo basket. At that point, those opium poppies seemed to be shining brightly in his direction like the winter sun. Chencao stood there trying to recall how his feelings toward them had mysteriously changed. He vaguely remembered that a long time ago he was disgusted by those flowers, but when did all that change? Chencao could not remember; he felt extremely tired; his head drooped involuntarily, and he leaned against the wall; but his eyes were still half open, and he watched his father mixing the opium powder up and down in the bamboo basket.

"Never mind drying it out; the opium collectors aren't coming," Chencao told him.

"The poppies will rot, and you'll have worked a whole year for nothing."

Chencao licked his lips continually as he spoke. "We'll eat it ourselves, Dad, it's a wonderful feeling; just try some and you'll understand."

Chencao heard himself speaking and saw his father throw down the opium blossoms and look over apprehensively at him.

"Chencao, you've been eating opium?"

His father suddenly cried out, grabbing and shaking him.

Chencao felt as light as the ash of a single burned-up blade of grass; his frail spirit was exhausted. "Dad, I want to sleep," he said, but his father pushed his tightly closed mouth apart with his fingers and smelled the still-lingering odor of opium.

"Chencao, you've been eating opium?"

His father slapped him hard across the face as he said this. It did not hurt. He still wanted to sleep and to await the reappearance of the visions he had seen in the rain.

He leaned his head on his father's shoulder and said, "Dad, I saw that tennis ball; that tennis ball fell off the roof and disappeared."

Five years later, Lu Fang recalled that Chencao's appearance was no longer handsome, no longer melancholic; his skin was waxy and sallow, his back was bent like a shrimp, and from a distance he looked just as aged and pale as his landlord father. Chencao always tried to avoid Lu Fang, but Lu Fang could always find him sitting in the dark in the storehouse. Chencao walked a few times around the big crock and then jumped inside the crock and lay down; he coiled up in the crock like a snake, and lay there motionless except for his constant sneezing. Chencao did not recognize him, and Lu Fang wondered if he had not already lost his memory; but he guessed Chencao was only pretending, and for a moment he did not know what to say. Then, because he did not want their first conversation to be too stiff or commonplace, he considered very carefully what its content ought to be.

"Chencao, it's the weekend, let's go play tennis."

"What about the lawn; where's the lawn."

"We can play in your family courtyard."

"We don't have a ball; the ball fell off the roof and disappeared."

"I brought a ball."

"I've already forgotten how to play tennis."

"Chencao, do you know how much land your family owns?"

"I don't know; it seems to me all of the land in Maple Village belongs to my family."

"Do you know how much wealth and property your family owns?"

"No, I don't know."

"Don't pretend ignorance; you're carrying your family's platinum keys."

"I honestly don't know; those are all my father's things; I've never even opened them before."

"Chencao, do you understand what I've come here to do?"

"I don't understand, and I don't want to understand; whatever you want to do, go ahead and do it."

"We want to practice land reform; we want to distribute your family's land and property to the poor."

"I don't care, but my dad won't agree."

Lu Fang watched Chencao stand up in the big crock, his eyes glazed over and unfocused. Chencao raised his head and looked at a spinning wheel hanging from the roof; after some time he sneezed.

Lu Fang suddenly heard Chencao softly call his name. "Lu Fang, help me out."

He reached over and took hold of Chencao's cold clammy hand.

Lu Fang later remembered how their old friendship had been rekindled when their arms were entwined. In the middle of the dark shadows of spider webs that filled the storehouse, the two of them saw, at the same time, a big light green stretch of lawn bathed in countless golden specks of early-evening sunlight; they swung their rackets and hit the ball square, and that tennis ball flew and bounced across the lawn court.

Lu Fang said, "Chencao, let's go play tennis."

Chencao's whole body convulsed momentarily, his eyes flashed brightly for an instant, and then grew dull once more.

He raised his hand and rubbed his eyes; his body gave off the odor of dried opium poppies. "That tennis ball fell off the roof and disappeared." Chencao sighed.

Lu Fang quickly pushed Chencao's soft limp arm away and said, "So it fell off and disappeared; if it disappeared, there's nothing I can do about it."

I hear the loud clear sound of a brass trumpet ring out over a village at dawn; it was during the last days of 1949, just before the storm. The sound of the trumpet was calling all of the land and people of Maple Village, calling all of the confined spirits to rise up on the wind.

The storm was coming. Everyone was going to be dragged out of his ancient abode and gathered together on the high ground of a new history.

"Follow me, my rural comrades! Follow me, and bring down the rich landlord Liu Laoxia!"

I see Chen Mao running through Maple Village shouting. An antique brass trumpet is fastened to his waist. (Later on, such a brass trumpet became a symbol of revolution in Maple Village; all of the men in the peasant association had a brass trumpet hanging from their waist.) Lu Fang said he remembered that Chen Mao was the most highly conscious peasant revolutionary he encountered after he began his rural work: "His will to emancipate himself was extraordinarily strong; it was just like dried straw—all you had to do was put a single spark to it, and it would burst into flame. He was an extremely rare agricultural cadre; too bad he made a mistake."

Lu Fang said, "The conditions of existence of the southern peasant were like a pool of stagnant water; great bitterness and harsh suffering was not enough to give rise to the will for emancipation; he didn't even care if you expropriated his labor; his was an ingrained indolence. The tenant farmers and long-term laborers of Maple Village all regarded themselves as agricultural implements—and the owner of those implements was the landlord Liu Laoxia. When Lu Fang's work team questioned the peasants about their poverty and suffering; all they heard from them were Liu Laoxia's great achievements. They said, "In a thousand years Maple Village produced one Liu Laoxia; he can stamp out gold ingots with his bare hands."

Lu Fang said, "Only one kind of peasant could make the revolution against the rich landlord Liu Laoxia: He had to possess absolutely nothing of his own; his labor and all of his spiritual resources had to have been completely expropriated; somebody like Chen Mao, for example; he stood out in the image of an all-around revolutionary, and you had to trust him."

That year Chen Mao naturally became the chairman of the Maple Village Peasant Association. He received a .38 rifle from the work team. Marching proudly around Maple Village with his brass trumpet hanging from his belt and his rifle on his shoulder, for a brief moment Chen Mao really became the man of the hour. When the rural children saw Chen Mao coming, they hid behind the haystacks and sang a different folk song:

Chen Ermao, he's changed his style,
Marching to east and west all the while
With his brass trumpet and his brand new gun,
He's got the rich old landlord on the run.

Chen Mao walked up to the gate of the Liu family compound and stopped suddenly, took his brass trumpet off his belt, and blew a long drawn-out blast. He did not even understand why he did it. Perhaps he was warning the whole landlord family, "I'm here; it's me, and I'm here." He kicked open the gate and shouted, "Here I am," but the courtyard was as still as death; a few chickens were scratching around the moss on the ground looking for grain, and the doors to all the side rooms were closed. Chen Mao picked up his trumpet again and blew another blast; then he kicked a chicken, sent it flying, and called out, "Is everybody dead in here?"

A window of the east side room opened. Chen Mao saw Liu Suzi appear sleepy-eyed in the window; she had black rings around her eyes, but her face was as pale as paper, and there was another cat perched on her thin frail shoulder. Chen Mao saw his rifle reflected in Liu Suzi's light green completely unmoving pupils. Once more she was frightened to death by a gun.

Chen Mao glanced in her direction; he always discerned an expression of fright on that cold, clear jade-white face of hers.

"Don't be afraid." Chen Mao walked over holding the rifle by its shoulder strap. "I'm certainly not like that bandit Jiang Long; I'm not going to do anything to you."

Liu Suzi remained speechless, but the cat meowed softly. Chen Mao bent forward to lean against the windowsill and took a close look at that woman who kept her door closed and refused to come outside; he saw the scratch of a cat's paw in the shape of a plum blossom clearly visible where her snow-white neck was exposed above the collar of her cheongsam. The cat meowed again. Liu Suzi trembled suddenly and slammed the window closed; the wooden shutter hit Chen Mao with great force full in the face.

"Get out of here right now; don't look at me like that."

Chen Mao rubbed his face with one hand and pushed in on the shutter with the other.

"Don't close the window; I didn't come to sleep with you."

"I'd sleep with a dog, but I would never sleep with you."

"Women say terrible things, but no woman ever dared to talk to me like that; Jiang Long must have driven you crazy."

"What are you doing here? Jade Flower's not home, and it's not dark yet, so what are you doing here, anyway?"

"I'm not looking for that slut. I'm on revolutionary business, looking for your father and your younger brother."

"I don't care about that. I just don't like to look at a dog; it makes me sick."

"Some day you'll know whether I'm a dog or a man; now just tell me where they went."

"They've gone to burn incense at the big temple in the hills."

"Burn incense?" Chen Mao laughed and pushed the shutter open slightly with the rifle barrel. "Your family's karma is all used up and no one can save you; I'm your bodhisattva now, understand?"

"If you're a bodhisattva, you better go to the outhouse and collect your offerings."

"You little whore, you know what you can offer me; you're the best kind of offering for me."

"You dog; you're a shameless dog." Liu Suzi finally managed to close the window completely on Chen Mao, and he stood there, puzzled, outside the window. He wondered how she got that plum-blossom cat scratch on her neck. It was like a little sun shining on him; making him hot and bothered, it stirred up his lust.

"You little whore; I'll fuck you yet." Sweat broke out on his forehead; the woman's little sun really made him unbearably hot. Chen Mao wondered to himself, "What's going on here? What is my connection to this family anyway?" He could not penetrate the mystery; and since he could not figure it out, all he could do was play his brass trumpet.

Chen Mao sat in the doorway blowing his trumpet. The darkening light of evening gradually seeped into the desolate courtyard while the leaves of the scholar tree faded and fell in rotting heaps on the moss-covered ground; he heard a mule braying in the millhouse; it was his old partner from his days as a laborer. Chen Mao suddenly wanted to rub down that old mule; he got up and walked to the mill house where he saw the mule, reduced to a mere bag of bones, half kneeling in front of an empty feeding trough. If it stayed with that family, the poor old mule would starve. Chen Mao poured all the feed stacked in the corner into the trough and watched the mule greedily chomping it down. As he brushed the mule's dirty dried-up skin from top to bottom, he fondly recalled, in a confused way, the more than half a lifetime he had spent as a laborer.

After he did not know how much time had passed, Chen Mao thought he heard footsteps behind him; he turned around quickly and saw three members of the Liu family standing in the courtyard; their faces were covered with incense dust, and each of them was carrying a single opium plant. Chen Mao hoisted his rifle, cocked the bolt, squinted, and watched the landlord family through half-closed eyes; he thought they appeared mighty strange, holding those opium plants and looking like they were about to go on a trip.

"What are you doing with those plants?"

"Going up the mountain to beg the spirits to protect the opium. The Mountain Spirit said the opium collectors are coming soon." The old landlord's face was devoid of expression; his gaze, completely ignoring Chen Mao and his rifle, looked sadly lifeless. Chen Mao watched the landlord's family walk by single file in front of his gunsights; Jade Flower was last in line; her gold bracelets jangled as she reached out her hand, tilted his rifle barrel up in the air, and, without the least trace of fear, pinched him hard in the crotch. Chen Mao jumped back a step, but he was too late to avoid her hand, and his balls hurt like hell. After calling her a filthy little slut, he suddenly remembered the mission the work team had sent him there to perform; he ran over, barred their way again with his rifle, and bellowed out at the top of his voice, "Stand still, the meeting is tomorrow!"

The landlord family stared suspiciously at Chen Mao, and he stared back at them.

"What did you say?" The old landlord shook his head. "I don't understand you."

"You don't understand? The meeting is tomorrow!" said Chen Mao. "You understand 'have a meeting,' don't you?!"

"What meeting?"

"A struggle meeting, to struggle against you and your landlord family."

"What for? What do you mean struggle?"

"We're taking you to the Straw Pavilion! Then we'll tie you up and struggle against you just like that time you had me tied up."

"Whose imperial order is this, that lets a dog attack a man?"

"The peasant association's. The work team's. Comrade Lu Fang said Maple Village can only be liberated after you have been overthrown through struggle."

Chen Mao saw the opium plant fall from the old landlord's hand onto the ground, and he thought to himself, "Heaven has also fallen to earth, so why can't a dog attack a man? With geomancy and transmigration, what else is there that cannot be changed?"

Chen Mao spit on the ground in front of the old landlord, then walked away. He was so happy he decided to blow his trumpet, and he did so as he walked out of the Liu family compound; the trumpet sounded to him like frightening explosions of thunder, thunder that would blast to bits the Liu family's hundred years of glory.

No one knew why the three members of the Liu family went up into the Firebull Hills. Chencao knew that it had to be something he must always keep secret. His father was taking his wife and son into the mountains to look for the bandit Jiang Long. Chencao thought his father was getting senile; how could the Liu family go into the mountains looking for a bandit like Jiang Long? He asked his father, "What are you up to, anyway?"

"I'm going to give them some money and ask them to come down off the mountain," his father answered.

Chencao said, "But he ruined Elder Sister, and there's nothing so dirty they won't do it; you can't go begging to them."

His father said, "I remember the wrong done to your sister, but that's not the same sort of thing; no matter how bad Jiang

Long is, he never wanted my land; I can't let anybody take away my land."

Chencao stamped his feet and asked, "What do you want Jiang Long to do if he does come down off the mountain?"

He saw a dark blue flame blaze up in his father's eyes as his father ground his jaw together and spoke through his teeth in a voice like a sob:

"Kill them. Kill Lu Fang. Kill that dog Chen Mao. Nobody—*nobody*—is going to take my land away from me."

As Chencao walked up the mountain with his father and mother, he recalled that time on the road coming home from the county seat when he had seen Jiang Long and his troop of horsemen ride quickly down from Firebull Ridge. There was a sound that still reverberated in the forests like the growth rings of the trees. "Liu Chencao, come on up the mountain with us!" Chencao still thought it strange: Who's idea was it to call his name like that?

"Who wanted me to go up into the mountains? Could it have been me myself?" Ruminating this way, Chencao felt he was walking along trapped inside some sort of mysterious cage; he was powerless to walk out of the cage, and was so confused he did not know how to make it back.

Following a secret guide, the three walked along searching for Jiang Long's tracks. Somewhere in the depths of the Firebull Hills they smelled the stench of blood floating on the mountain air, and they walked in the direction of that ever-increasing stench; on the back side of the hill they saw three dead horses and several pairs of red hemp sandals. There was dried purple blood caked all over the cliff and the brown withered grass. The secret guide said he had heard gunshots on Firebull Ridge; he guessed that Jiang Long and his bandits were heading south.

Chencao discovered a round crystalline object in the tall grass that he took to be a little ball; when he walked over and picked it up, it instantly stuck to his palm like a magnet to metal; he turned his hand over to examine it closely and suddenly let out a high-pitched scream. "An eye, somebody's eye!"

He tried to throw it down, but no matter what he did he could not shake it off his hand; he could not understand what in hell was going on; why had he picked up a human eye?!

Chencao stood there frozen as if in a dream, his hand stickily clinging to that human eye. When his father and mother reached him, they could not pry his hand open; Chencao clung tightly to that human eye exactly as he had held on tightly to that tennis ball. He saw his father kneel in despair beside the body of a dead horse.

"The mountain wind is blowing this way; now the mountain wind is going to blow us off the face of the earth," thought Chencao. This is what it feels like to sink into the depths of despair.

Chencao heard his father speaking to that dead horse. "He's dead; there's nothing left to hope for."

Chencao felt the Firebull Hills were just like a huge cage; on a desolate and deserted mountaintop one experiences the emptiness that follows the ascent. "We're looking for the bandit Jiang Long, but Jiang Long's gone." Chencao could never forget the grief-filled self-deprecating smile on his father's face as he looked toward the south. His father never smiled; as soon as his father smiled, calamity had already descended upon them. That day it seemed as if they were sleepwalking on Firebull Ridge, with his father carrying an opium plant and looking for Jiang Long! Chencao thought, "Father really is senile; you can hear a sound in the mountains, but you cannot see the person who made it; it's only a trap."

Chencao was completely exhausted walking along behind his father and mother. Thinking back, he recalled clinging all that time to that human eye. He thought, "Maybe that tennis ball rolled all the way up here, and when that tennis ball disappeared this human eyeball appeared in its place; this is a trap, too, and I'm stuck and can't get out; I have to hold on to this human eyeball."

Maple Village grandfathers told their grandsons, "Passing on a family line is not the same as sowing fields and harvesting grain. Even if you work like hell, you won't necessarily get a good harvest. Just look at landlord Liu Laoxia: He planted flowers and got bushes, planted melons and got weeds, and who knows why? A strong bloodline can't last forever. Just look at landlord Liu Laoxia: When the pure, strong unmixed bloodline, passed on for generations, reached Chencao, it got mixed up and diluted; and when it got mixed up and diluted, it declined; that's just the way heredity works."

I realize that the Maple Village peasants' ideas represent a kind of primitive anthropocentric thought. But you can't expect the people of Maple Village to come up with any more sophisticated explanation of the historical changes in the Liu family's fortunes.

Work team commander Lu Fang told me, when during the struggle meeting against Liu Laoxia, they asked the landlord if he had anything to confess, his answer made even his work team comrades laugh in spite of their position; Liu Laoxia said, "I've betrayed my ancestors; I never fucking produced a decent son. I also blame myself for being too compassionate and lenient; I should have killed that dog son of a bitch a long time ago."

Lu Fang knew right away that the "dog son of a bitch" Liu Laoxia referred to was Chen Mao, the chairman of the peasant association.

In the spring of 1950 three thousand residents of Maple Village participated in a struggle meeting against the landlord Liu Laoxia. That meeting is still fresh in their minds to this day. Liu Laoxia stood in the middle of the Straw Pavilion, and his former tenant families and long-term laborers sat all around in the opium fields. Lu Fang said the atmosphere at the time was just like market day in Horsebridge: Children cried and adults shouted; many of the male peasants secretly chewed on opium leaves; and the whole place was so permeated by the pungent odor of dried opium that the work team could hardly stand to carry on. Lu Fang said, "The people of Maple Village were naturally so undisciplined there was no way you could change them." When he had peasant association chairman Chen Mao shoot three rounds into the air, things finally grew quiet around the Straw Pavilion.

"Liu Laoxia, put your head down!" Lu Fang commanded.

The old landlord refused to bow his head; rather, he raised his head and kept his eyes focused on the black-headed crowd of people pressing in around him. His expression was obstinate and unbending, and his eagle eyes blazed with a fierce light as his terrifying gaze continued to sweep over the people of Maple Village. The people noticed that, far from weeping, Liu Laoxia's face appeared to be smiling.

"Liu Laoxia, stop smiling!" ordered Lu Fang.

"I'm not smiling; when I want to cry I look like I'm smiling."

"Never mind, put your head down!"

"You're going to divide my land anyway; why do I have to bow my head, too?"

Lu Fang gestured to Chen Mao; he wanted him to push Liu Laoxia's head down, but Chen Mao misunderstood; he ran over and hit him in the head with the butt of his rifle. After a deep thud Liu Laoxia wobbled slightly and then stood up straight again. The old landlord's eyes still shone as he spoke one word softly: "Dog."

At that Lu Fang said, the meeting really got out of control. All those Maple Village peasants stood up; and he saw Jade Flower run out of the crowd with her gold bracelets jingling; she cried all the way as she ran over beside the old landlord; she had taken a bunch of opium leaves from one of the men, and she used them to staunch the old landlord's wound; the old landlord pushed her away and shouted, "This is none of your business; get the hell on home."

Then Jade Flower ran right over to Chen Mao and tried to take his rifle away from him. All the time she struggled with Chen Mao, she kept up a steady stream of invective. "How dare you strike the Master, you untiring sonovabitching dog prick, you goddamn indestructible dog cock."

The people of Maple Village started laughing and shouting.

Lu Fang yelled at Chen Mao, "Push her off of there!" But Chen Mao only tried to dodge Jade Flower's well-aimed blows.

Lu Fang heard the people down below hollering. "Chen Ermao, Jade Flower Liu, get together and let us see you do it . . . !"

He could not make out the rest, but he'd had all he could take when he bellowed out, "Don't mess around with her, push her off of there!"

Chen Mao's face was red and white in turns; finally he cursed Jade Flower as a "stinking slut" and kicked her right in the breasts; then he, too, told her, "This is none of your business; get the hell on home."

Lu Fang said, "That's the way the struggle meeting against Liu Laoxia was carried out; it was such a damned farce I couldn't help laughing." The weather was also strange that day: The sun was shining in the morning, and there wasn't any wind; but about noon the sky suddenly grew dark, and many of the peasants were anxiously watching the sky. Just as he was about to set fire to a pile of Liu Laoxia's land deeds and account books, the wind suddenly started to blow; the wind came down suddenly off the Firebull Hills and blew out the flame of Lu Fang's cigarette lighter. The wind suddenly blew all of those deeds and records up into the air above the heads of the crowd. At first the three thousand residents of Maple Village just held their collective breath and stared as those land deeds fluttered around in the air like butterflies, their wings making a soft warm rustling sound; then somebody in the middle of the crowd shouted at the top of his voice, "Grab 'em!"

The crowd started scrambling around wildly as the three thousand Maple village residents pushed and shoved and stretched their dark hands into the air after those deeds. Lu Fang's work team members shouted as loud as they could, "People, people, stop it; those land deeds are useless." But nobody listened to them. Lu Fang said there was nothing he could do but have another three shots fired into the air. He said, "Maple Village peasants weren't afraid of anything but the sound of a gun." After the three shots were fired, the crowd was quiet once more; but they had already stuffed all those land deeds into their shirt pockets. They held on to those pieces of paper with expressions of great satisfaction, just as though they had actually occupied the land itself.

"What else could I tell them?" asked Lu Fang. He said in the end he just let them go on home with the land deeds in their pockets.

"Chencao, come over here."

His father was calling him. Chencao walked over beside his father's bed and stared at the hand his father was stretching up toward the sky; that hand had a musty rotting odor just like the opium plants left in the fields to be drenched by the rains.

"Dad's sick."

"I know."

"Dad's sick for the first time in his life."

"I know."

"Dad can't go on, so he got sick; I'm counting on you."

"What?"

"You never understand what I say. I should have drowned you in the manure pit when you were born."

"I don't care. I didn't want to live this long in the first place."

"I should have let Jiang Long take you with him that time; being a bandit is better than being a dog; now it's our turn to be dogs."

Chencao saw that his father was still holding on tightly to that opium plant. "Might as well put it down now," he said. "The opium collectors aren't coming any more."

His father nodded, dropped his hand, and scratched at Chencao's hip.

Chencao said, "Dad, what are you looking for?"

"The gun, the gun I gave you."

"Here it is."

"Let me hear you shoot off a round."

"There are only two bullets; there won't be any left if I shoot them off."

"Then you better save them; you'll need them on the road."

Chencao walked behind the bed; his mother had already packed his things; they were there in a big bundle on the floor. His mother was sitting there on the red lacquer chamber pot, crying; she always sat on that chamber pot when she cried. Chencao felt hungry, and he turned and looked for the black pottery crock in which they stored dried provisions; the wooden lid had not been opened for a very long time; it was covered with a thick layer of dust. He reached inside with his hand, but the crock was empty; he pulled out only an old steamed roll as hard as a rock; a bite had been taken out of one side, and the crescent-shaped tooth marks had turned black. Just as Chencao was about to bite into it, he heard his mother scream, "Don't eat that, it was Yanyi's!" He examined that stale dried roll from years ago and saw Yanyi's blood-covered face carved into the side of it, but he still could not put it down. "I'm hungry." He gagged as he bit into the roll; it upset his stomach as much as bitter herbal medicine; he gagged as he ran toward the door and heard his father angrily pounding the bed and shouting behind him, "Don't eat that thing; get the hell out of here; get the hell out of here now!"

It rained and no dogs barked the night Chencao ran away; the sound of the rain drowned out the confused stumbling footfalls of Liu Chencao. The next morning a confused mass of footprints like the honeycombs of a beehive appeared before the front gate of the Liu compound. The Maple Village peasants, on their way to irrigate the rice fields, walked around those footprints shouting, "He's run away; the landlord's run away!"

"If you think about it now, we could have just let him run away; we really didn't have to hunt down a half-dead animal," Lu Fang said. "But in 1950 I was all caught up in the excitement of the day and just couldn't restrain myself. I took Chen Mao and the work team and followed Chencao's footprints all the way to Firebull Ridge; I saw him trudging slowly as you please up the side of the hill; he really was taking his sweet slow time; sure didn't look like he was trying to escape. Loaded down with five or six bags, he looked like an ancient warrior in a suit of armor carrying a lance and heading for a faraway battlefield. He heard the sound of the horses' hooves, turned around, and stood there staring at me like a wooden puppet. Chen Mao wanted to ride his horse up on the ridge and cut him off, but I held him back; I saw Chencao standing on a ledge and was afraid he'd jump off. I yelled at him, 'Don't try to run away; no matter where you run to, you'll never get away from me.' He just went on standing there motionless like a wooden puppet. Then he started to put all those bags down and toss them hurriedly over the cliff; I heard the sound of metal crashing against the rocks and guessed that he was throwing the Liu family's gold and silver into that deep ravine.

"When only one big bag remained, Chencao sat down on it at the edge of the cliff and waited for us to come up. I kicked that bag, and it was soft; then I saw some white powdery substance pour out of a tear in the bag and give off a strangely intoxicating aroma.

" 'What's this?' I asked him.

" 'Opium.'

" 'Who told you to run away?' I asked again. I watched him collapse against my leg with a trapped expression on his face as he wearily admitted, 'My father.'

" 'Where did you intend to run?'

" 'To find Jiang Long.'

" 'You want to become a bandit?'

" 'I don't know. I really don't know.'

"Trapped like that he looked as pitiful as a leaf caught in the wind, but you could not see his gun." Lu Fang said, "I didn't know he had a gun hidden in his pocket."

When those who knew the inside story discussed the history of the Liu family, they always emphasized the blood relationship between Chencao and the long-term laborer Chen Mao. They said that Chencao's birth was a turning point in the fortunes of the landlord's family, a defining moment that led to the decline and destruction of the house of Liu. "You have to learn how to see the ocean in a single drop of water." They said Chencao's birth heralded the physical decline and death of Liu Laoxia; their assertion was based on the dialectical relationships between a multitude of karmic elements that I am powerless to explain fully; all I can do is honestly and realistically describe the unfolding of events in the Liu family history.

I know that you are still interested in the former laborer turned peasant association chairman, Chen Mao. Chen Mao certainly was an unusual character. Both his arrival and his departure inevitably established a certain frame of reference for the fortunes of the landlord family. As Lu Fang said, it was only possible to carry out the land-reform revolution in Maple Village because of the presence of Chen Mao. To this day Lu Fang still fondly recalls that peasant association chairman Chen Mao with his trumpet on his belt and his rifle on his shoulder. I asked him, "Later on what happened to Chen Mao?"

Lu Fang had a pained expression on his face, as though he did not want to talk about it; then he said something as if it were a closely guarded secret. "You can change a person's fate, but you can't change what's in his blood." He went on, "Some men are destined to die because of a woman, and there's no way you can save them."

Nineteen fifty was also a turbulent year in Chen Mao's sexual history. In that year Chen Mao overcame his feelings for Jade Flower, tangled feelings that held him like a spiderweb for so many years; the people he had enchanted with his brass trumpet hoped then that his life would begin to run a more normal course. You could see that his handsome lecherous face had changed, a change that made him appear young again; his whole body radiated with the rejuvenated attractiveness of a young man. A steady stream of women came forward with offers of marriage, but Chen Mao just smiled and said nothing. When the women asked him teasingly, "Chen Ermao, did the landlord's old lady screw you to death?" Chen Mao would hoist his rifle onto his shoulder and shout them down. "Fuck off. My cock's none of your business; I know who I want!"

You can imagine who Chen Mao wanted.

Chen Mao stole into the Liu compound in the dead of night. The moon was bright and clear that night; he felt perfectly calm, and the feverish emotions of spring were almost imperceptibly buoyed along on the night air. He stood in front of Liu Suzi's window with his rifle on his shoulder and looked back to see his own familiar shadow greatly elongated on the moss-covered ground. Recalling the many nights like that when he had made his way to Jade Flower's window, his emotions were quite strange; he was neither excited nor nervous, but felt rather like he was about to fulfill some long-cherished desire. He saw Liu Suzi's cat reclining on the window sill, its turquoise eyes glowing in the moonlight.

"Fucking cat," Chen Mao mumbled as he aimed his bayonet and thrust it straight into the cat's eye; the cat moaned as dark red blood spurted out of its eye.

Chen Mao then silently used the point of the bayonet to push the window open and bounded into the east-side room. He saw Liu Suzi still sleeping soundly on a big bamboo mat; he knew she was a woman who loved to sleep.

The top half of Suzi's naked body stuck out from under her cotton quilt. This was the first time he had really seen Suzi's large full breasts; he thought the Liu women must certainly eat well to have such tantalizing tits. Chen Mao took his scarf off and placed it lightly over the woman's eyes; then he picked her up off the bed. Her soft flesh felt cool and fresh like tender young bamboo leaves. He could not understand why she still had not awakened; maybe she was dreaming. When he carried her into the courtyard, he heard the cat moan once again, and his hands trembled slightly; he had not expected a dead cat to make any noise. The woman he was abducting finally woke up and tried to struggle out of his grasp; her half-opened eyes glowed green with terror.

"Jiang Long, it's the bandit Jiang Long!"

Chen Mao held the woman tightly and ran toward the gate; he saw the light go on in Jade Flower's room, and then Jade Flower came out and chased after him. He leaned against the doorway and shouted over his shoulder, "What are you chasing us for, you bitch?"

Jade Flower said nothing as she grabbed for his rifle, but he dodged away from her and continued running; he heard her fall over something, and then finally Jade Flower shouted, "Dog, put her down, you dog!"

"If you scream again, I'll kill you," Chen Mao said as he picked up Liu Suzi again. He ran carrying that icy cold woman toward the open fields. The moonlight was clear and bright, but the night wind was moist and red as it blew past his ears; he felt the woman in his arms growing colder and colder, so cold he couldn't stand it any longer. He had to sink his own flesh into this icy cold body. Chen Mao ran like the wind, and as he ran, he heard the sound of the wind rushing by as though he were flying through the air; he knew it was no dream, but it felt more like flying than any dream he had ever had; he ran toward the Straw Pavilion; the Straw Pavilion rose straight up in front of him in the moonlight like a sacred temple calling and beckoning him to come in; he had to fly fly fly in there!

"Put me down, dog; you can't touch me!"

"I have to touch you." Chen Mao spoke through gritted teeth. "I was bound to screw you someday."

"Who are you?" The woman opened her eyes wide, but she just could not make out his face.

"Chen Mao." Chen Mao thought for a minute and answered, "I'm not Jiang Long; I let Jiang Long go first."

Chen Mao put Liu Suzi down on the floor of the Straw Pavilion and looked up to see a pair of night birds fly down from the pointed straw roof. That was an excellent place to make love. Chen Mao laughed silently to himself as he strad-dled the woman's body; her cold milk-white body glowed under the chill moonlight; he closed his eyes, and his hands slithered snakelike up and down her cold round flesh until they came to rest on her high firm breasts. He felt the woman had already gone completely limp, but his own body shivered un-controllably as if in a malarial fit; he panted for breath and felt a weakness he had never before experienced in his life. "I was bound to screw you someday."

He bit down on the woman's nipple and heard his brass trumpet roll off his hip with a loud crash.

Lu Fang said he always felt there was some mysterious connection between Chen Mao and landlord Liu's family, but he could not unravel the tangled skein of their multiple rela-tions. He asked Chen Mao, but Chen Mao could not understand it himself; he only knew that he hated the whole damned landlord family. Chen Mao said, "Either I'm a dog or they're dogs; that's all there is to it; that's all there is between me and them."

Lu Fang did not learn about Chen Mao's violence against Liu Suzi until one day when Jade Flower ran out of the front gate of the Liu compound, grabbed him, and accused Chen Mao—saying Liu Suzi was pregnant with Chen Mao's bastard. Lu Fang told her, "Don't go insulting our cadres."

But Jade Flower swore by Heaven above. "Commander, don't believe Chen Mao; he's a filthy no-good dog; he's screwed every woman in Maple Village, and now he's knocked up Liu Suzi too; go look at Liu Suzi's stomach and see for yourself; that's his little bastard!"

Lu Fang went to check with Chen Mao, and Chen Mao

admitted it openly. "Right, I screwed Liu Suzi." He asked Lu Fang, "Does revolution mean I can't screw Liu Suzi?"

Lu Fang could not answer. He thought about it for a long time and finally decided to remove Chen Mao from the chairmanship of the peasant association and take away his rifle. He remembered that when he took away his rifle, Chen Mao's face was red with anger; he held on to the rifle, and shouted, "Why can't I fuck her? I hate them all, and I can make the revolution against them!"

Lu Fang said he felt sad about it, too, but things had gotten too far out of control; he knew the work team could cut Chen Mao down from the roof beam of the Straw Pavilion, but they could not prevent him from acting like most Maple Village men. Lu Fang wanted to find a more ideal peasant association chairman in Maple Village.

It was raining at dawn that day, or maybe it wasn't rain, but only the sound of the wind blowing through the trees. Chencao recalled that he was curled up inside his own imagined sounds of rain; he saw himself transformed into a yellow jacket hiding among the opium and sucking the nectar from the blossoms; his mouth was full of fragrance, and his sleep, as always, was fitful and half-waking. After the first rooster crowed, he heard the sound of footsteps coming closer through the rain; he heard something hard knocking on his window and saw a cold white shadow behind the window paper. "Who's there?" The shadow did not answer, but Chencao had already made out that the shadow was his elder sister Suzi. She stood there silently. When Chencao was about to throw on a shirt and get out of bed, he heard her say, "Chencao, if you're really a man of the Liu family, you'll go kill Chen Mao."

"What did you say?"

"I'll go pick some opium, and you go kill Chen Mao."

By the time Chencao put on a light, his sister had disappeared from outside his window. He thought she was really strange; maybe she was walking in her sleep as she regularly did. The sound of her footsteps were lost in the rain; where was she going to pick opium? Chencao fell back into a confused sleep; after he'd lay there curled up for some time, he heard a commotion over at the east compound; somebody was weeping and wailing. Still in a daze he ran and stumbled toward the east compound, arriving to see his father kneeling beside his sister's body; she was lying face up on the ground and her white silk cheongsam shimmered coldly in the early-morning light; he could see several tooth-shaped red marks going all around her neck in the pattern of a heavy rope. The rope itself was still slightly swinging back and forth from the rafters. "She hanged herself. Why did she hang herself?" mumbled Liu Laoxia. Chencao saw his father weeping with his hands covering his face, then he said, "My dear daughter, no man was good enough for you."

"She said she was going to pick some opium," said Chencao. As he walked aimlessly around his sister's corpse, Chencao smelled the odor of rotten opium coming from her half-opened mouth; she had a peacefully relaxed expression on her face. Chencao thought, "If I could spit that odor out of my mouth, I'd be relaxed and peaceful too."

"She said she was going to pick some opium and I should go kill Chen Mao." Chencao saw his father suddenly raise his head, open his lips, and smile bitterly. Chencao thought, "A catastrophe is really coming this time."

His father stood up, hugged him tightly around the neck, and rubbed his cheeks with both hands. "She's done what she said—now what are you going to do?"

"Going to do?" Chencao stood there stiffly while his father pinched his cheeks; he remembered that Chen Mao used to pinch him the same way when he was little; it used to hurt then, but he didn't feel a thing now.

"What are you going to do?"

Chencao fingered the gun on his hip; it was still there, but it had not been fired in ages. He thought for a moment and then replied, "All right, then, I'll kill Chen Mao."

Chencao stood up straight, slapped away the hanging rope from in front of his face, and walked out of the room. His mother ran up from behind, threw her arms around him, and shouted, "Chencao, you mustn't go; whatever you do, don't go!"

His father then ran over to restrain his mother, and insisted, "Go on; come back after you kill Chen Mao."

His mother said, "How can you come back after that? You're the Liu family's last hope."

His father said, "Never mind all that, get going."

His mother shouted again, "Don't go Chencao! Kill somebody else, but you can't kill Chen Mao!"

At that his father kicked his mother to the ground and swore at her, "You little whore! You still can't forget that fucking dog!"

Chencao looked back at the three of them scuffling there and thought it made a ridiculously funny scene. He said, "Do you two want me to go or not?"

He saw his mother lying on the ground crying while his father's face grew black with anger; then his father pushed him away and said, "Go on, Chencao, go on and do it."

At that time the people of Maple Village still did not know what had happened at the Liu compound. The people in the fields saw Liu Chencao walk out of the compound with his shoulders pulled in together like he was afraid of the cold. He walked over to where several people were working together and asked all those he recognized, "Where is Chen Mao?" They all looked with curiosity at his strangely bemused expression and asked, "What do you want with Chen Mao?" Chencao said flatly, "They want me to kill him." The people just laughed; they figured Chencao had finally lost his mind, and nobody believed what he said. For the first time, somebody made a rude joke right to Chencao's face. "A son can't kill his old man." But Chencao had absolutely no reaction. He passed through group after group of people until at last he heard a long trumpet blast coming from the direction of the Straw Pavilion. He headed straight for it.

You have to believe that fate had arranged for the meeting in the Straw Pavilion that day. Chen Mao was blowing his trumpet there that morning, blowing it so annoyingly loud that everyone all over Maple Village heard its restless, troubled sound. Chen Mao caught sight of Chencao walking toward him with his shoulders pulled in together for fear of the cold; he threw down his trumpet and asked, "Young Master, what are you doing out walking so early?" He suddenly realized Chencao did not look quite right; Chencao frowned and reached down by his hip; Chen Mao saw a revolver with a strip of red cloth tied to it pointing right at him. Chen Mao thought Chencao was joking, but he knew that he never joked with anybody. He scratched his face and asked, "Chencao, what are you doing?"

"They told me to kill you."

"What did you say?"

"They told me to kill you."

"Don't listen to them. Chencao, haven't you ever heard, I'm your real father?"

"I've heard it said, but I don't believe it."

"Chencao, it's true, I am your real father; how can a son kill his father?"

"I don't believe it."

"If they want to kill me, let Liu Laoxia do it; you can't do it."

"Yes I can; I've already killed one person."

At the last minute Chen Mao started to reach for his rifle, but then he remembered it had been taken away.

"Fuck your mother!" Chen Mao swore as he threw his brass trumpet at Chencao's head. Chencao did not dodge; he stood perfectly straight and still as he cocked the trigger. One shot went off just like that. Chencao fired twice; he aimed one shot at Chen Mao's crotch and the other one between his eyes. He looked down at the smoking revolver, tossed it lightly up and down in his palm a couple of times, and threw it on the ground. A small round shiny crystalline ball was rolling on the ground; he picked it up and discovered it was Chen Mao's eyeball; it was slimy, and stuck between two of his fingers. Blood was oozing out all over the floor of the Straw Pavilion; Chencao looked around for Chen Mao's penis, but could not find it. He felt around inside Chen Mao's crotch and found it was still there, fully erect. "Couldn't even shoot it off," Chencao mumbled to himself; he thought it was very strange.

Throughout this entire process, Chencao's sense of smell was particularly acute; he smelled the everlasting odor of opium wafting across the fields, sometimes thick and pungent and sometimes so tenuous as to completely disappear. Chencao heaved a deep, long, thickly audible sigh; at last his mind was as clear and bright as the deep blue sky over his head. He thought Chen Mao's body looked just like an old opium plant that had crumpled to the ground. He thought, "I've finally spit out that rotten odor; now I can be as relaxed and peaceful as my sister."

Lu Fang said that after all this had happened, the murderer Chencao was nowhere to be seen, and nobody knew where he had run off to. They ran over to the Liu family compound and found Liu Suzi's body laid out in the courtyard; she was lying on a long bamboo mat, and her face looked like she was sleeping peacefully in the middle of the night. A bright red fresh opium poppy had been placed in her long black hair. The height of the opium-poppy season had long since passed, and nobody could understand how the landlord family managed to preserve that flower.

"Where's Liu Chencao?" Lu Fang asked.

"He's dead; he's bound to be dead," answered the old landlord.

"Why don't you go up on Firebull Ridge; Chencao went to join Jiang Long," offered Jade Flower.

Lu Fang took a posse up to Firebull Ridge to look for the murderer Chencao. They found Chencao's black school uniform and Chen Mao's brass trumpet in a cave in the hills, and the sight of those two things lying together seemed extraordinarily incongruous; but they didn't find a trace of anybody and didn't know where Chencao had run off to.

It was after dark when Lu Fang and his men came back into Maple Village, and from a long way off they heard the noise from a great commotion in the village. Men and women were running wildly through the village lanes, pulling their children behind them. Then they saw the fire. Fire was raging up from the Straw Pavilion, reaching up into the sky like a giant torch. Lu Fang urged his horse forward and witnessed one of the most frightening scenes in the history of Maple Village.

The first thing he saw was that Chen Mao's dead body had been dragged out of the village police office and strung up once again from the roof beam of the Straw Pavilion; Chen Mao's dead body, tied and bound, was burning there in the air, already curled up and black as charcoal; and the Straw Pavilion was burning and crackling so loud you would expect it to collapse, but it remained standing nevertheless. Approaching closer, he discovered three more corpses lying there intertwined on the floor—Liu Laoxia, Jade Flower, and Liu Suzi; they had not yet caught fire; it was amazing that these four people were ultimately united together in death.

"Liu Laoxia . . . Liu Laoxia . . . Liu Laoxia . . ."

Lu Fang heard some of the people in the crowd yelling out the old landlord's name. You would never have imagined Liu Laoxia's bizarre desire before he died. Lu Fang said, "He wouldn't even let a dead man go." He had Chen Mao's corpse strung up in the Straw Pavilion to serve as a funerary sacrifice as he himself was about to die. Lu Fang said from that point on he forgave the dead Chen Mao his many mistakes and began to hate that self-immolating landlord Liu Laoxia with a passion, to hate that whole generation of an already destroyed and extinct landlord class.

.   .   .

In the winter of 1950 work team commander Lu Fang carried out the order to "suppress" the landlord's son Liu Chencao, and with that the last member of the Liu family of Maple Village was eradicated.

Lu Fang walked into the Liu family storehouse where Chencao was being held and saw the arrested and bound escapee sitting inside a big crock. Lu Fang recalled that the first time he came to Maple Village and met Chencao he was also sitting in that crock. The sound of something being torn up once again echoed through the dark empty storehouse: You could hear one more history book falling to the ground after the pages had all been turned. Lu Fang walked over, knocked on the side of the crock, and said, "Liu Chencao, climb up out of there."

Chencao looked like he was sleeping. Lu Fang bent down and peered into the crock, where he saw Chencao chewing on something with his eyes closed.

"What are you eating?"

"Opium," replied Chencao, as if in a dream.

Lu Fang wondered how Chencao could get hold of opium when he was tied up. When he pulled Chencao up out of the crock, he discovered it was an opium crock, and it was full of opium powder that had been stored there for years. Lu Fang picked Chencao up; since he had been captured and brought back home, his body was as light as a baby's. Chencao hooked his arm around Lu Fang's shoulders and said softly, "Please put me back in the crock."

Lu Fang hesitated a moment, then dropped him back into the crock. Chencao closed his eyes and waited. As Lu Fang cocked his gun, he heard Chencao's last words: "I will be reborn."

Thus Lu Fang executed Liu Chencao as he sat in an opium crock. He said that when the shot went off he felt like the opium exploded inside the crock. "That was really the most powerful organic odor in the world; it sprang on you like a crazed animal clinging to your head, your hands, your whole body, and there was no way you could escape it."

Right down to this day Lu Fang says he can still smell the odor of opium on his person; no matter how much he washes, it will never wash off.

The author pens a last remark in the Liu clan's genealogical record: On December 26, 1950, the biggest landlord family in Maple Village was destroyed by a shot from the gun of work team commander Lu Fang.

FOR THE BEST IN PAPERBACKS, LOOK FOR THE

In every corner of the world, on every subject under the sun, Penguin represents quality and variety—the very best in publishing today.

For complete information about books available from Penguin—including Puffins, Penguin Classics, and Arkana—and how to order them, write to us at the appropriate address below. Please note that for copyright reasons the selection of books varies from country to country.

In the United Kingdom: Please write to *Dept. JC, Penguin Books Ltd, FREEPOST, West Drayton, Middlesex UB7 0BR.*

If you have any difficulty in obtaining a title, please send your order with the correct money, plus ten percent for postage and packaging, to *P.O. Box No. 11, West Drayton, Middlesex UB7 0BR*

In the United States: Please write to *Consumer Sales, Penguin USA, P.O. Box 999, Dept. 17109, Bergenfield, New Jersey 07621-0120.* VISA and MasterCard holders call 1-800-253-6476 to order all Penguin titles

In Canada: Please write to *Penguin Books Canada Ltd, 10 Alcorn Avenue, Suite 300, Toronto, Ontario M4V 3B2*

In Australia: Please write to *Penguin Books Australia Ltd, P.O. Box 257, Ringwood, Victoria 3134*

In New Zealand: Please write to *Penguin Books (NZ) Ltd, Private Bag 102902, North Shore Mail Centre, Auckland 10*

In India: Please write to *Penguin Books India Pvt Ltd, 706 Eros Apartments, 56 Nehru Place, New Delhi 110 019*

In the Netherlands: Please write to *Penguin Books Netherlands bv, Postbus 3507, NL-1001 AH Amsterdam*

In Germany: Please write to *Penguin Books Deutschland GmbH, Metzlerstrasse 26, 60594 Frankfurt am Main*

In Spain: Please write to *Penguin Books S.A., Bravo Murillo 19, 1° B, 28015 Madrid*

In Italy: Please write to *Penguin Italia s.r.l., Via Felice Casati 20, I-20124 Milano*

In France: Please write to *Penguin France S.A., 17 rue Lejeune, F-31000 Toulouse*

In Japan: Please write to *Penguin Books Japan, Ishikiribashi Building, 2-5-4, Suido, Bunkyo-ku, Tokyo 112*

In Greece: Please write to *Penguin Hellas Ltd, Dimocritou 3, GR-106 71 Athens*

In South Africa: Please write to *Longman Penguin Southern Africa (Pty) Ltd, Private Bag X08, Bertsham 2013*